Out by Ten

Anne E. Thompson

The Cobweb Press

Cover Photograph: M. Todd
Editor: J. Todd

Published by The Cobweb Press
www.thecobwebpress.com
thecobwebpress@gmail.com

For Bob Beffins

Part One

Chapter One

I didn't begin to feel safe until I reached Norwich. As the train heaved towards the platform, with a great screeching of wheels and complaining of brakes, it was as if I had been holding my breath and finally, with a sigh, allowed myself to think that perhaps I had managed to escape after all.

Passengers began to struggle into coats, preparing for the cold of a spring morning. While the train slowed, a conveyor-belt of painted faces peering in, I joined the general shuffling of the masses and edged towards the doors. People were staring at suitcases stored near the exit, ensuring no one stole them, mothers were gathering a plethora of plastic toys and sweeping sweet wrappers over the edge of the grey tables so they fell like confetti to the carpet below, children slung school bags over their shoulders, men in crumpled suits with tired faces were clutching briefcases and over-night bags. We inched forwards, any bond formed during the journey through smiles or the fleeting meeting of eyes was now dissolved; we moved individually, each person isolated from the other passengers, until finally, with a giant step down from the carriage, we were free.

I moved cautiously, looking for security cameras. I chose two boys, one with chaotic hair and a blue coat, his friend wearing a beanie and carrying a backpack, and stayed as close to their backs as I could. Anyone watching would have thought we were together, student friends returning to Norfolk, off to find a taxi together. The ticket barriers all gaped open, passengers filtering through like a line of ants entering their nest. I shoved my redundant ticket into a back pocket and walked in the footsteps of my unsuspecting buddies as we left the canopied platform, past the Starbucks and the single policeman staring aimlessly into space. It was the end of the morning commuting time, and a few people in business suits were still hurrying to work. There was a child wearing pink bunny ears chewing a breakfast donut, spilling crumbs as she ate. A man, walking while he read a text almost walked into two girls as they emerged from *M&S* carrying their tiny bag of food. Everyone was in their own isolated capsule, and I felt invisible as we headed towards the Victorian red brick wall of the main concourse. As we neared the ticket office, I peeled off, said a silent farewell to my pretend friends, and stood in line at the automatic ticket machine.

I knew the timetable by heart—weeks of planning and surreptitious trips to the library to use the computer ensured I was prepared, and when it was my turn, I bought a single ticket to Sheringham. A man was standing behind me, and although I knew he was probably simply waiting his turn, he made me nervous, and I tried to cover the screen, to hide where I was going, in case he remembered later and repeated the information. I heard him sigh when I pulled out money—I knew he was impatient, surprised that I wasn't using a card, which was surely what the machine was designed to receive. But I couldn't risk using cards, couldn't risk being traced, so I ignored him, and smoothed out the crumpled notes as best I could, and fed them laboriously into the slit designed for paper money. The machine whirred. Coins clinked into the bottom section, followed by the orange ticket and matching receipt. I pushed back the plastic flap and retrieved my things, clutching them in my hand as I moved away. I glanced up at the departures board, checking the times splashed in orange letters matched the information in my head.

The public toilets had the same damp chemical stale air as all other public toilets in England. The same middle-aged women were washing their hands while checking their hair in the mirror, the ubiquitous harried mother was trying to stop her three-year-old touching every surface, and handle, and wall; while a teenager smeared eye-liner around the rim of her eyes. I crossed the wet floor, edged past the yellow plastic "cleaning in progress" warning placard, and locked myself into a cubicle. Which is when I actually, for a moment, properly relaxed.

People assume that being a prisoner is all about locks—being locked into a space by someone else and not being allowed to leave. But actually, the reverse is as heavy a burden. Unless you are free, the ability to lock yourself *into* a place is also denied. The prisoner is unable to lock a door, to shut out the world, to enclose themselves into a space that is truly private. They are always on view, watched, analysed—whether they are aware of it or not. I leant back against the door and closed my eyes, savouring the precious moment of being unobserved, hidden from the world. No one knew where I was, no one was watching. I was truly, wonderfully, alone. But only for a few minutes.

When I emerged, walking straight to the row of damp sinks, there was a woman with two daughters standing by the driers. They were Chinese—or some similar ethnicity—and while they shook drips from their hands and spoke in their sign-song chatter, I noticed how similar the two girls were. Separated by a couple of years, one was taller, but that was the only difference I could discern; they seemed identical. Both were laughing, their dark eyes dancing beneath thick fringes of black hair, wide lips drawn back to show their small straight teeth. They were pretty, with their slim bodies and smooth skin, and as they giggled and chatted, they drew the attention of the other women using the washroom. Two identical dolls. I wondered what it would be like, to grow up with someone so similar in appearance as to be almost interchangeable, to potentially, when the height differential lessened, have a physical substitute at hand. I smiled briefly, exploring in my mind the wonderful freedom of being able to ask another person to take my place, to never be missed, because someone else was fulfilling my obligation. It would, I felt, be the most wondrous thing ever.

But then, as the pair moved away from the purring drier and turned towards the exit, both swishing long black plaits down their slim-shouldered backs, I realised that to have a substitute, they must first be willing. To have someone take my place in life, would involve giving up their own, and that, I knew, would be an impossible ask. No one, I thought, would willingly give up their own happiness simply to fulfil the dreams of another. The girls left, and I moved to take their place, holding my hands under the warm flow of air until they were dry.

I kept an eye on the time, moving back to the platforms when my train was due to leave. I chose a seat near the front, thinking that when we reached Sheringham, I could be out and away before most other people had alighted, and that a ticket inspector, if there was one, would be watching the masses as they stepped from the train, and would barely focus on the first few passengers to hand him their tickets.

I found a seat near a window, and moved my bag next to me, closing my eyes so that people would think I was asleep and would choose somewhere else to sit. The train was rumbling in the way that only diesel trains are able, that gradual warming-up hum, the sound of an over-stretched engine which is trying to find the gears. I opened my eyes when the train jolted into motion, and looked around the carriage.

The train was fairly empty, the only person who could see me was an elderly lady, who sat in the seats opposite me, across the aisle. She had a fat shopping bag, with groceries spilling from the top, and a small brown handbag which she moved from her knee to the empty seat next to her. She smiled at me when I glanced towards her, and opened her mouth as if to speak, so I turned quickly back to the window, and watched as the city was replaced by fields and bushes and lines of trees that rushed past in an endless line of green and brown.

"Excuse me."

I looked across the aisle. The elderly woman had removed her coat and headscarf, and was leaning towards me, waiting. I nodded, sighing inwardly. Old ladies seem to enjoy talking to young women; I tried to appear discouraging.

"I wonder if you would be very kind and watch my things for me," she was saying, her face creased into a smile, her eyes trusting. "I need to use the ladies' room, and I was wondering if you could watch my bags while I'm gone? So no one touches them?"

I stared at her, took in her blue-grey hair, the kind eyes behind the wire-rimmed glasses. We were strangers, two people who happened to choose the same carriage to sit in, but apparently, that was the only criteria necessary for her to trust me. Or perhaps it was because I was female, and there was some unwritten code which meant that she could trust me, someone who shared her gender, that I as a woman would ensure her bags were safe. Maybe in her era, young people were more honest.

I opened my mouth, not sure how to respond, wanting to warn her, to protect her from the dangers of trusting strangers; then closed it and nodded.

"Thank you so much dear. I shan't be long."

I watched as she stood, she waited a moment to find her balance as the train swayed, then walked towards the doors at the end of the carriage. They clicked shut behind her departing back.

I looked across the aisle. There was her coat: brown, not new, neatly folded, topped by the square of her red headscarf. On the seat next to them was her handbag—*her handbag*—presumably containing her purse, possibly her house key, probably stuffed with old receipts, and a tissue and a pen, maybe even a phone. I thought for a long moment about that phone, savouring the possibility of it, the ease of owning it, making anonymous calls, connecting to the internet. My mind wandered back through the handbag, pausing for a moment on the purse, imagining the coins and notes, each in their designated place, counted after each purchase. And a credit card, which may well give contactless payment which if I was careful, if I used it sparingly, would last for a few groceries. I toyed with the idea, ran possibilities around my head, considered the morality of perhaps taking just some of the money, thinking that need probably justified deed, and my need was certainly greater than hers; my poverty was lurking just around the corner, my next few meals were far from certain. Plus, I thought, I was already a thief, I couldn't deny the label, there was no way to pretend that I was anything else. And I was no Robin Hood figure, the only person to benefit from my illegal acts was myself, there was no justification, therefore this tiny, almost offered-on-a-platter act, was just a tiny part of the whole, barely significant.

But then I pulled back my thoughts, reigned in the tantalising exploration of possibilities, and reminded myself of who I was, who I hoped to become. No, I might indeed be a thief, I might take those things I had no right to, but I wasn't a *petty* criminal. I had not yet stooped low enough to steal from elderly ladies on trains. I would not let circumstance mould me into a creature I would loathe.

I turned back to the window, watching trees like hunchbacked old men guarding the road, and muddy fields full of pigs with slices of upturned barrels to sleep in, and roads that raced beside us before curling away into towns and villages and places we could never reach, glimpses of rivers and boats and occasional docks, all blurring into an indiscernible haze. I strained forwards, trying to see the roads, wondering which were the ones that we had driven along, a lifetime ago. But it was too hard to see them, they all looked the same. My eyes closed, and I slept.

Chapter Two

I was the first to leave the train when we arrived in Sheringham, and there was no ticket collector, so my fears were unfounded. I walked from the station and paused for a moment next to the road. It was quiet still, the morning not yet properly awake, and only a few tourists meandered half-heartedly through the town, staring blankly at racks of postcards they would never send, the closed signs on coffee shops, the buckets and spades from another era.

I was anxious to get to Blakeney, to discover whether my planned accommodation was possible, but I was hungry, and the supermarket in Sheringham would be cheaper than the tiny shop in Blakeney. I crossed the street and walked to Tesco, surprised by how full the car park was, and the number of people struggling with laden trolleys. It reminded me of shopping at Christmas time, when everyone was focussed on finding supplies; there was a palpable excitement in the air.

The shop remained as I remembered it, there was something comforting about taking a wire basket and walking along the aisles, seeing familiar brands. Supermarkets are safe places, set apart from the stress of the real world, providing milk and bread and cleaning products while politicians argue, and wars rage, and people lose jobs, and fall in love, and die.

I walked around, my eyes touching products that I recognised, my mood settling as I absorbed the wonderful *ordinary-ness* of the place. I passed the fruit section, with the underripe bananas, and the slightly dry oranges and the apples in their plastic bags looking hard and sweaty. I lingered over a red grapefruit, remembering to smell it, to test that it was fresh, to squeeze it to test for ripeness; before I remembered that I did not especially like grapefruits, red or otherwise, and I no longer needed to eat them.

It was delicious, this feeling of freedom, of being able to choose my own food, and with the abrupt realisation came a renewed feeling of excitement, as if it really was Christmas, and I was a child again. I began to search the shelves for food which I had not eaten for years, food which I actually enjoyed eating. My basket became cluttered with strawberry yogurt, and bagels, and grapes, until, wonder of wonders, I found a Twix. There was a shelf of newspapers, and I selected one, glancing at the headlines about a virus, eager to catch up with what was happening in the news but unwilling to linger any longer, keen to finish my journey. Some shelves were empty, and I guessed they were waiting for a delivery to arrive, perhaps the supply chain to these out of the way holiday towns was less rigorous out of season.

I came to a stand of make-up, and stopped. Make-up. The chance to enhance my appearance, to outline my eyes, cover my blotchy nose, lengthen my lashes. I couldn't move, simply stood there, looking at the choices, feeling guilty. For so many years now, my face had remained naked. It felt wrong even to be looking at something that had been considered worse than frivolous, almost sinful; it had caused so many lectures, such long explanations about how cheap, how brazen, it made a woman look. Could I afford to buy some? I decided not yet. One step into normality at a time.

I stood for a moment longer, feeling the weight of my basket, considering the sense of buying the items I had selected. *If* my accommodation was sorted, and I gained access to the cottage, then buying food was sensible. However, should my hopes be unjustified, should systems have changed in the last five years, the key be unobtainable, the door locked against me, then to carry so much excess baggage was foolish. I stared into the basket, weighing prudence with hope. Hope won. I walked to the queue of people waiting to pay—not the self-service tills because they only accepted card payment—and calculated the bill. My money was beginning to disappear, and I realised that after today, which I was considering to be a celebration, I would need to be more frugal. I glanced at the person in front of me in the queue—a man balancing several packs of toilet rolls on top of an overly full trolley—and resigned myself to a long wait. I noticed again that the shop was surprisingly busy for a Monday morning and there was a tension in people's faces, a certain hardness and unexpected concentration.

When it was eventually my turn, the cashier passed my groceries across her scanner, and I delved into my purse for the money, giving notes so that I could receive coins in my change. My notes were rolled together in a fat sausage, and I peeled one off, glad that high-value notes are less remarkable in a supermarket, that it would be broken down into change that could be more easily spent. I wasn't sure what the bus fare would be, but I hoped I could pay it exactly.

As I left the shop, I pulled out the Twix. For a moment I simply stared at it, absorbing the sight of the wrapper, enjoying the feel of it in my hand. A memory flooded back, of lying on my bed as a child, listening to the wonderful rustle as my sister opened a Twix, knowing that my own bar was waiting under my bed, savouring the sound of her eating, smiling in anticipation. The mere sound of the wrapper made my mouth water, and I lowered my bags to the ground, tore the paper, pushed the first bar up, and took a long leisurely bite. The chocolate and toffee and biscuit dissolved into sweet perfection, I was ten years old again, and nothing else mattered. I stood there, in everyone's way and not caring, and ate the whole delicious bar.

Then I lifted my bags and walked back to the station in search of the bus.

There were three other people waiting at the bus-stop, and I avoided eye-contact and therefore conversation, until the bus arrived. A lady with a small white dog waved an arm across the road, and the bus glided into the layby and the doors hissed open. We filed on board, and I asked for the *Blakeney Church Stop*, threw two pounds into the plastic tray, and found a seat towards the middle.

The bus jolted its way along the Cromer Road, passing through villages—offering the occasional glimpse of the sea

—full of early-morning shoppers returning home and elderly people who all seemed to know each other. Some of the villages had bends that the bus could barely navigate, and it swung wildly to one side before almost skimming the fronts of shops as it turned the corner. I recognised the towns, remembering the names: Weybourne, Salthouse, Cley. I stared into the shops I had been unable to visit, the pubs that had welcomed other visitors for hundreds of years, the tea-shops that had been forbidden.

It was five years since I had last been here, and many things seemed unchanged. But as I sat, looking for the green, and the windmill, and the shop that sold paintings, I wondered what *had* changed. We had stayed in a cottage, and although I knew the address, and could find my way to the door, I was unsure whether I would be able to get in. Five years ago, the key had been left ready for visitors. Five years ago, when we had arrived, we found the key, safely hidden under one of the flowerpots, to the right of the long slate step. Five years ago, when we left, we returned the key under the flowerpot, to the right of the long slate step. But today, five years later, would security have improved? Would the owner now meet people who hired the cottage, and hand them the key in person? Or would the delicatessen further down the road now hold the key, ready for when visitors—legitimate visitors—arrived? Did the delicatessen still exist?

As we neared my stop, I could feel the Twix heavy in my stomach, and I felt slightly sick as I considered what I would do if the key was not there. I had done my research, looked online, and I knew that the cottage had been occupied last week, and the visitors would have left today, they would be out by ten. I knew the next two weeks were free. School's half-term had ended two weeks ago, people would have returned to education and work, and normal lives; holiday cottages would be cleaned and checked and left empty until the occasional out-of-season guest, or the next wave of visitors descended at the beginning of the Easter break. A stranger, if noticed in town, would be unremarkable, a continuation of the Spring-Break guests.

I glanced at the time. It was still early, if I was lucky, if I was managing to arrive in the sweet spot between the paying guests leaving, and the hired cleaners arriving, if the key was left in the same place that it was left five years ago, then I would have a place to stay. But there were a lot of variables within this plan, too many things beyond my control, and I had no backup. If the key was not there, if the cleaners had already arrived, if there was no way inside, then I was destitute, with nowhere to stay. Nowhere to hide. My freedom, hard won and desperately gained, would have lasted less than a day.

I could see the church now, a beacon on my left, and I reached up and rang the bell for the bus to stop. We swept past the church, and for a second I thought perhaps the stop had disappeared, and that I was to be whisked to the next town, when the driver suddenly lurched sideways, and we came to a stand at the bus-stop. I rose from the seat, glad to see I was the only passenger leaving, and jumped down onto the grass. The bus was already moving away.

I could see Blakeney Church, back the way we had come, and I began to walk towards it, hearing Timothy's voice in my head, his lectures about the tower being used as a lighthouse in days gone by, his insistence that we should visit, his fury when the door was locked. I assumed the door would still be locked today, though there was a poster advertising a service for Mothering Sunday, welcoming visitors.

When I was almost level with the church, I stopped and stood at the kerb, waiting while cars sped towards Cromer or Hunstanton, the corners of the road making the crossing treacherous. A gap appeared, and I ran over, towards the High Street, my bags bumping against my legs.

The cottage was the fourth one, and as I walked towards it I could see the pots, standing proud—the shrubbery replaced during the five years, but both pots still in place, the wide slate step separating them. There was no car parked outside. I peered through the net curtains—there was no movement detectable within. I stood on the slate step, feeling the sun on the back of my head. I pressed the doorbell. There was a shrill ringing that echoed through the house, but no answering footsteps, no slamming doors, no sign of life.

I turned and scanned the road. Cars were sweeping across the end of the road. A van was reversing near the corner, workmen were placing a ladder on scaffolding that caged a cottage further down the street. No one returned my stare, no one was watching.

I placed my bags on the slate step, and moved to one side; another glance down the road, up the road, at the window. Still no one. Using both hands, I eased the plant pot on the right to one side, tilting it slightly, and stared at the floor beneath.

Chapter Three

As I tilted the flowerpot, careful to support the weight, I peered down at the damp patch on the ground underneath. There was a key. It was attached to a small yellow fob. Something in my stomach fluttered with relief.

I leant down, retrieved the key, replaced the plant. Another glance down the road, up the road, then picking up my bags, I put the key into the lock and opened the front door. I was in.

I stood in the tiny hall, my back hard against the front door, and allowed myself one huge breath and the smallest of smiles. Another step accomplished. Before me, rising sharply, were the stairs, bookshelves against the wall, the painted skirting-board battered and peeling where excited feet had kicked against it on their way down.

I pushed myself forwards, away from the door, and set about the next part of my plan. On both sides were doors with wooden round knobs, and I took the one on the right, turning the handle, pushing open the door, striding ahead. I walked over the carpet, barely glancing at the fireplace, the dried flower arrangement, the cushions scattered in the window seat. I crossed the room, ducked under the low plinth that led to the kitchen, and went straight to the door. There, as I had remembered, as I had hoped, was the key-rack, with all the spare keys helpfully waiting.

I selected the spare key for the front door, and struggled to open the keyring. It was too stiff for my fingers, splitting a nail and refusing to open. I glanced at the time, knowing that at any moment I might hear the front door crash open, the bump and clatter of the cleaner arriving. I pulled out a kitchen drawer, searched through the knives, found one with a blade thin enough to push through the tight-clenched rings that held the key, forced them apart, then yanked the key, round and round, until at last it was free. I delved into my bag, found the key— Timothy's key, let us not forget—and reversed the procedure, attaching his front door key to the little ring which was clearly marked *"Spare Key for Front Door"* plus a little heart, as if to encourage visitors to use it. I hung the substitute back on the hook and surveyed my work: it was indiscernible, no one, glancing casually (which was what I assumed the cleaner would do) would guess that the key had been replaced.

I retraced my steps to the front door, turning to check as I walked, looking for footprints, or specks of dirt—anything which would betray my presence. I closed the sitting room door behind me, and prepared to leave, then stopped.

I had no way of knowing when the cleaner was likely to visit. I could assume that a cleaner *would* visit, that someone would check the fridge had been left turned on, that the bins were empty, that there was nothing that could damage the property; and that visit would have to be soon, within a couple of days. However, it might be today, it might be in two day's time. I had no way of knowing, and nor would I know, when I returned, whether this visit, this checking of property, had actually taken place. Whilst I would need to be constantly vigilant, there could be some relaxing of caution after the property had been checked, it was unlikely they would return again within a week. I glanced out of the window, the street was still quiet. I returned to the kitchen.

All I required was something that would show me a person had entered the cottage, checked the basics, and left again. I went to the sink and opened the cupboard below. Lemon scents and chemical smells rose to greet me. I found a bottle of bleach, resting at the back, and pulled it out. Bleach was dangerous, not to be left unattended in a cottage designed for a family. I placed it in the centre of the kitchen floor, and draped a dishcloth over it for good measure. I could think of no logical reason why departing guests might have left a bottle of bleach on the kitchen floor, but it was not so totally out of place that the cleaner would be alarmed. They would simply sigh at the eccentricities of people who hired cottages, of which I was sure they had witnessed many, and then replace it safely back under the sink; hence leaving a beacon for me, a clear sign of their visit.

I looked for a moment at the cloth-draped plastic bottle, nodded, and left.

The street was clear as I eased the front door shut behind me, and returned the front door key to its resting place beneath the shrub to the right of the wide slate step. I turned and headed away from the main road, towards the sea.

The sea does not, in reality, wash as far in land as Blakeney, not today. Timothy told me—even now I cannot ignore what he taught me—he told me that once it did, once the little town was an important port, a resting place for merchant ships from Europe. All that remains today is a tidal river and a quay and a thousand sailing boats stranded on the mud at low tide. I walked down to the quay and then turned right, towards the duck pond and a seat.

The morning was sunny. A wind coming towards the land pushed my hair away from my face, made my skirt dance around my legs; but it wasn't cold. I could sit on the little bench next to the duck pond, and any observers would consider this a normal activity, nothing noteworthy. I could eat some of my food, have a celebratory breakfast, while I decided what my next step should be. I didn't plan to return to the cottage until later, after dark—it seemed unlikely a cleaner would arrive after dusk, so even if my bleach still sat on the kitchen floor, I could shelter there for the night.

I delved into my bag for a sandwich and the newspaper. The wind snatched at the paper, tugging at the pages while I clutched it, folding it so the main story showed, holding it steady while I chewed my lunch. I looked first for any mention of my own name, fearing a photograph or description, asking for the reader's help in tracing me. But there was nothing, a quick scan of each page showed it was all wonderfully impersonal. I turned back to the front page and began to read in earnest. The lead article was unsettling. There was a virus, originating in China but spreading through the rest of the world with roughly 300 cases in the UK. Was I the only person in the world who didn't know about this? I stared at nothing, remembering again that feeling of tension I had noticed in the supermarket, my mind replaying images of trolleys full of cleaning fluids and toilet rolls. Was this real? I squinted my eyes, tried to decide whether this virus was something to worry about or simply media hype. I decided I was unlikely to be affected, though perhaps I should buy some more toilet rolls as people stock-piling seemed to be an issue. I could try to find out more another time, it wasn't urgent. Then I folded the newspaper and watched the ducks in front of me.

The pond had a mix of birds. It was an enclosed space, tall fences protecting the wildlife from foxes and children, the freshwater pond surrounded by tiny wooden hutches, and ramps and reeds. The water was teeming with life. There were ducks, several varieties, their colours bright, a range of sizes. I assumed they had been placed there by whoever owned the pond, and as I saw none fly, guessed that their wings had been clipped; they were trapped within the enclosure. It occurred to me that they were deemed to be safe, the owner had tried to provide a safe place, protected from foxes, full food-bowls, designated places to lay their eggs and raise their young. And yet, they had no choices, they couldn't choose to fly away, to live as free wild birds, they were captive. They had no way to protect their young from smaller predators, and were defenceless when seagulls swooped down to eat the ducklings, when rats came to steal their food or eggs or hatchlings; so their purpose in life—to raise young—was thwarted. In its place they had a meaningless existence which served no purpose but to look nice for when visitors arrived, and wanted to eat their lunch and look at the pond. ..

I sighed. The newspaper article had unsettled me, and I was over-thinking things. This was a pretty spot for eating my lunch, and unlike the ducks, I was now free. I should be enjoying my freedom and ensuring I stayed free, not worrying about ducks. I took a breath and reached into my bag for an apple. It was crisp and sour and perfect.

Chapter Four

I returned to the cottage after dark. As I walked up the High Street, away from the sea, light and laughter and the heavy scent of beer spilled from the pub, beckoning. I avoided looking, and headed up towards the cottage, welcoming the darkness as I left the busier areas, keeping to the shadows. When I was level with the cottage I stopped for a moment, and looked.

Either side of the cottage, lights blazed in windows, the blue flicker of television betrayed the occupants' activity. But the cottage, *my cottage,* was mercifully dark, the windows black. I crossed the road, pulled the key from my pocket and entered.

Moving soundlessly, I edged open the door to the sitting room, peering through the gloom for signs of life, but nothing looked disturbed, so I eased into the room and walked on light feet towards the kitchen. There was no sign of the bleach, and the cloth—supposing it was the same one —lay folded next to the sink. I smiled, and felt the tension seep from my muscles. The cleaner had arrived, done her duty and left. I was alone.

First on the agenda was a cursory check of the other rooms, just in case by some tiny piece of bad luck, the cottage was showing as unoccupied on the website but the owners were planning to use it themselves. I couldn't afford assumptions, not if I was to stay free. I moved through the second lounge area, peering into the darkness for signs of life.

Returning to the square hallway, I began to climb the stairs, keeping my feet on the edge of the treads, anxious to avoid creaks. The landing was bare, with four doors wide open, immodestly showing their insides. I pushed my head into each one, scanned the shadows, sniffed the air, all the time my ears straining to hear a footstep, a breath, a warning of life. I smelt a whiff of cleaning products, heard nothing but sounds of traffic leaking from the windows, the occasional yellow light pushing into the rooms. Inside, all was quiet.

There was the child's room, with bunkbeds pushed hard against a wall; the double bedroom was opposite the bathroom, and I saw the contour of folded bed linen, and drawn-back curtains, and a puddle of moonlight on the floor. The twin room held bare-mattressed beds, empty surfaces, and the door to an en suite bathroom. I stepped into the room far enough to push the bathroom door open, and scanned the bare shelves, the dry shower, the towel-rack empty of towels, the still-wrapped new soap by the sink.

The best room, I knew, was higher, a floor reserved for the master of the house. The door designed to conceal the stairway was propped open, and I accepted the invitation and advanced towards the third storey. The stairs were polished wood and I grasped the handrail as I ascended, staring upwards, senses alert. As soon as my head had cleared the floor level, I paused, looked around, felt relief at the apparent emptiness. Again, the bed was unmade, the floor was empty of suitcases; all was impersonal, a room holding its breath until the next jolly holiday-makers filled it with life and muddles and scattered belongings.

I realised the hand holding my bag was aching, and I switched hands, stretching the fingers and wiping the sweatiness on my skirt. I was alone in the house, it was mine—at least for now.

I returned to the twin room and sat on the bed nearest to the door. I considered that this was the best room for me to sleep in. If the front door opened, I would hear it, and have at least a few minutes before I was discovered, whereas the downstairs rooms would offer mere seconds before an intruder barged into my space. The master bedroom was too far away from the front door, and I knew it had no cupboards large enough to hide me, should that become necessary.

I decided it was safer to wash in the early morning light. The owner might still arrive, having travelled after work, entering the cottage in the small hours, turning on lights and turning me out of my shelter. If the sound of the opening door woke me, I could grab my bag, and either hide until the exit was clear, or slip down and out of the front door while they bustled through the lower rooms. However, if I was washing, I would be deaf to intruders, vulnerable to discovery. I felt that soon after dawn, when all civilised people would be still asleep, was my safest time, the hours least likely for an arrival.

I went to the tall cupboard in the corner, and found, just the same as five years earlier, piles of spare bed linen. A snowy duvet and lumpy pillow would suffice, and I spread them onto the bed, slipped off my shoes, and crawled into their comforting warmth. I pulled the cover up to my chin, feeling my cold hands against my cheek, and for a moment, they are not my hands, they are the hands of Timothy.

***

Timothy has good hands, long slender fingers speckled with short tufts of fair hair. During the day they are adorned, with a loose gold watch on his right wrist, and an even looser silver chain on his left wrist. I gave him the silver chain, bought from a jewellers in Bond Street, soon after he proposed to me.

The first time I visit this cottage, in a bubble of excited anticipation, is our honeymoon. I watch Timothy's hands as he carries the cases up the second flight of stairs, feel their strength as he holds my wrist, leads me around the house, showing me each room in turn. The master bedroom, up in the eaves of the house, has its own bathroom, complete with free-standing tub in the centre of the room. The door from bedroom to bathroom doesn't close properly, the wood misshapen over time, but this suits us, in our longing for constant contact, our desire to be as physically close as possible at all times and I bathe unashamedly, allowing him to stare at my nakedness, enjoying his gaze. We are in love, the world is rosy and perfect, nothing matters but our love and our longing and the promise of our entwined lives stretching out before us.

It is the second day, and I want to phone my mum, to tell her where we are, that I am okay.

"But you're with me now," Timothy, my husband, says. "If you phone your parents, it will look as if you miss them, as if you want to talk to them, not me. Couples on honeymoon live in seclusion, they don't contact other people—that would look odd. *Are* you missing them? Aren't I enough for you?"

I look at his head, tilted on one side as he waits for my answer, a smile playing around the corners of his mouth. I reach up to kiss his mouth, and shake my head, laughing. I don't need anyone else, he is my everything.

We spend the whole week in seclusion, even browsing shops would be an intrusion.

"Don't waste time looking at stuff you can't afford to buy," Timothy tells me, grabbing my hand and leading me away from the window stuffed with pottery and paintings. "Let's just walk together. I'll buy some treats at the shop, we don't want to be invaded by waiters in coffee shops, we can make our own fun at the cottage."

I laugh as I am led away, and I know that he is as besotted with me as I am with him, and that he doesn't want to share me with anyone else. It makes me feel warm inside, and I realise that I have never felt like this before, never been truly loved and desired and protected. We walk along the raised footpaths, and through the salt marshes, and we stare at seals from the side of a boat, always together, avoiding other people, complete in our world.

But Timothy wasn't here now, I was alone. I rolled onto my side, and when the tears rolled across my face and tickled my nose, I realised that I was crying.

Chapter Five

I woke early, and stared from the window just as dawn was beginning to paint light along the horizon, shadows of buildings beginning to be discernible, some street lights still glowing yellow, others blank. It was delicious, that sense of being safe, unseen, alone in my world. I knew it was too early for anyone to arrive at the house, even if the owner or a last minute visitor planned to come, no one would set off in the middle of the night to arrive at dawn. This was my time. I could relax, revel in my freedom, at least until 7am. I would be more alert after that, tune my ears to outside sounds, be ready to hide if necessary, but the hours before then belonged to me.

After a quick morning shower—with no towel, as I hadn't thought to buy one and only sheets were stored at the house—I sat in front of the television and tried to learn more about the situation I had read about in the newspaper.

First, I learned about the virus—Covid-19 as it was called. I sat on the little blue sofa, tea mug in one hand, television buttons in the other, flicking through as many news channels as I could find. I watched for over an hour, hunched towards the television set, which I had angled so the light wouldn't be seen from outside, the volume set low so I would hear the first sounds of anyone arriving at the house.

I gleaned the virus had started in China, jumping from animals to humans at a meat market, and was now spreading throughout the world. Some of the information didn't seem to make sense. I heard that in most people, the virus caused mild symptoms, sometimes barely noticeable; in elderly and ill people, the virus went from a temperature and mild cough to a dangerous respiratory problem. Many people were hospitalised, some had died. And yet, I couldn't tally the apparent numbers with the information they were giving. I heard that flights to and from China had stopped several days ago. I listened to a reporter, a middle-aged woman with a sensible haircut:

"Despite the apparent mildness of symptoms in most people, we now have a situation where a whole country is being quarantined. This was not implemented for either SARS or Ebola, and is unprecedented in our times."

I watched the reporter, her face serious, her voice undulating to convey tension. Was she exaggerating, or was the world was going into meltdown?

The disease had spread to Europe. Each case was being isolated, the patient going into enforced quarantine, contacts told to self-isolate in their own homes, and yesterday, Italy had instigated a whole-country lockdown. I watched, open-mouthed, as scenes from a deserted Italy flicked across the screen. Shops deemed non-essential had been closed, public gatherings banned, schools suspended. I watched white-suited officials, resembling spacemen in their 'hazardous materials' suits—visors distorting their faces, turning them into something not quite human as they administered health care to anxious patients. It felt surreal, as if I had jumped into the middle of a science-fiction novel, and even as I sat on the blue sofa, and sipped lukewarm tea, I felt disorientated.

Was Italy, an apparently sophisticated society, overreacting? Were such measures necessary? I couldn't shake the dream-like feeling about it, what I was watching on the screen did not seem real.

When I had absorbed as much information as possible, and the reporters seemed to be on their third loop of the facts, I switched off. The house was silent. I sat, and considered. I thought about the tension I had seen in people's faces at the supermarket, the empty shelves, the over-loaded trolleys, and it began to make sense. I realised that I needed to formulate a plan that would work in the current changing world situation. It was annoying, because I had a plan, well thought-through, beautiful in its simplicity. But that was before, that would only have worked in the world that I knew, and the new world, the one I was watching unfold before me on the television, was very different. I felt annoyed with myself, my absorption in my own world for the last few weeks had blocked out everything larger. It seemed as if, in a surprisingly short time, the world had changed, from the one I knew to one that resembled the early chapters of a novel.

My initial plan had been to stay in Blakeney for a while, perhaps earn some money at the local pub, become established as a resident. I could then move on, either legally paying my way, or possibly travelling to another cottage we had rented previously, and hope the key was still left in the same place. But I preferred the legal option. After several years, the chances of finding the key had been slim, and although I had risked everything through desperation, I had assumed that once free, I would have time and resources to refine my plans. But the unfolding news was unsettling, and I was uncertain of the implications. I decided I needed more information, which entailed access to the internet. I would have to buy a phone.

The nearest big town—somewhere I could probably buy a phone without being noticed—was Cromer. It was on the same bus route from Sheringham. I tidied the house, returning bedding to the cupboard, checking for signs that I had visited. I decided to store my few belongings, including my bags of food, under some garden furniture in a small side room. It was cool in there, and less likely to be explored by a visiting cleaner or owner, as the weather was still too cold to sit outside. I realised that if anyone moved into the house in my absence, I would probably be unable to retrieve my belongings, but I couldn't face taking them all the way to Cromer and back. I would have to risk it.

I edged open the front door, checking the road was clear. No one seemed to be around, only the builders working on the house down the road, shouting instructions and abuse at each other, their vans hooting in warning as they reversed. I left the house, and walked to the bus stop.

Cromer was a bigger town than Sheringham, and even out of season the town was busy. I left the bus at the stop before the supermarket, I'm not really sure why, but at the time it felt sensible to be careful, just in case I was noticed and someone was asked about me later. As I walked up from the Runton Road, towards Morrisons, I noticed a couple leaving a house. It was still early, the couple were probably obeying the unvarying *"out by ten"* rule that seemed constant in all holiday homes. The road was lined with red brick Victorian houses, and the couple were loading suitcases into a car, and as I approached, I saw the woman go back to the house, shut the door, and slide the key under the mat. She returned to the car, and I watched as they drove away. I smiled to myself, thinking that people were very careless about another person's security.

I bought a phone—the cheapest I could find—and stocked up on supplies. The aisle of cleaning materials was almost empty, and all paper products had long-since been bought. I hoped it wouldn't be a problem, I had four rolls of toilet paper, plus one that had already been in the Blakeney house—it would have to be enough. There was also a shortage of tinned food, and absolutely no pasta or rice. People were preparing. Perhaps I should too.

As I left the supermarket, feeling the weight of heavy shopping bags, I passed the same house that the couple had been leaving. A car drew up, a chubby middle-aged woman driving. I saw her pull on rubber gloves and a face-mask, and heave a bag of cleaning products and a vacuum cleaner from her boot. I was interested that she had donned protective clothing *before* entering the house. It struck an alarm inside, I heeded the warning. Life was changing. I glanced into the woman's car as I passed. It had sweet wrappers on the floor, and an old cardigan slung onto the back seat. I didn't think the value of anything looked very expensive, the car itself was a cheap model—I decided she was the cleaner, not the owner of the house. I filed the information away. It might prove useful.

I shared the bus ride back to Blakeney with a gaggle of teenaged girls, who looked as if they might be bunking off school. As I sat, staring at their snagged tights and improbable shoes, I heard their intense voices, and I remembered being that age, and the glorious excitement of new situations. It was only a few short years ago—and a whole lifetime. I immersed my thoughts in the sound of their whispers, looked at their carefully arranged hair, their casual closeness as they touched an arm, a knee rested against a thigh, feet slid near each other; they didn't bother with personal space, the flicked hair of one girl brushed the cheek of another, their perfume spilled towards me with their whispered giggles. I remembered the intoxication of friendships, the undiluted energy; I remembered when I first saw Timothy. . .

***

I am sixteen, my school bag is bouncing on my shoulder, I glide into the classroom and slump into the chair next to Carol. I am looking for Nigel, searching the room for his blond hair whilst pretending to look for my homework book. Perhaps I should be worrying about my father, and his recently diagnosed cancer, but I'm not, I am absorbed by Nigel, hunting for his gangly legs stretching out from his desk, and the slant of his shoulder when he reaches for his bag. Carol digs me in the ribs and jerks her head forwards. I look up. I see Timothy.

He is standing at the front, his stance casual, his eyes watchful. I notice his eyes first, set below straight brows, a deep, dark brown that seems to glow; even from my seat at the back I can tell he is noticing, watching us, in control. He wears a faded jacket, with patches on the elbows, and a white shirt, with the tie knotted to a perfect neat nobble, giving his appearance a tidy, meticulous look. His hair is brown. He has good hair, thick and wavy, cut to just above his ears but not so short that he looks like my dad. He doesn't look like *anyone's* dad, though I suppose, given his age, he might be. He smiles, I forget all about Nigel, forget he exists, forget that he has until now been the focus of every maths lesson I have attended this year.

Timothy is speaking. I notice his voice is deep, and posh, and it makes my stomach tingle. He is telling us his name is *Timothy Oakfield* and I want to write it in my book, and scribble variations of it. *Mr. Oakfield.* I realise that maths lessons will never be dull again. He is telling us that he's our new teacher, that he's pleased to meet us, let's begin with an evaluation of what we have studied so far with Mr. Corbin. Mr. Corbin has had to leave, we don't need to know why; I don't *want* to know why, I don't care. All is absorbed by the deep, posh, voice, and the brown, almost black eyes, and the apparent youth of our new mathematics teacher. He is asking for someone to raise their hand, someone who can give him a quick synopsis of work already covered by the unfortunate Mr. Corbin. Not me, I can't breathe, let alone speak. I feel Carol stir beside me, she is raising her hand, introducing herself, telling him, Mr. Timothy Oakfield, that we have covered up to page 52 in the text book, and we all completed the questions at the back for homework. He smiles at her. I hate her.

He speaks, telling us about simplified equations, and exponential data, and I am barely listening. His words wash over me as I feel the tingle his voice stimulates, and I imagine how he would look in casual clothes, and wonder if he is married. He issues instructions, and everyone turns to a page in their text books, and I have to stop hating Carol long enough to ask her what the page number is. She slides a piece of paper towards me:

"Dreamy, huh?"

Dreamy is not a word I have ever used before, but it fits, I nod. I glance up.

Mr. Timothy Oakfield is walking round the classroom, peering at books. He pauses by John Simpkins and points at something. John Simpkins looks up, his face is very red, he hunches his shoulders and begins to frantically rub at his exercise book with an eraser. I wonder what he has written.

I glance across to my friend Charlie, she is frowning. I'm not sure if this is because she always finds maths difficult, or because her hair has recently been plaited again and I know that it pulls at her scalp and hurts. Her hair is a constant source of trouble for her, teachers repeatedly tell her it's untidy and she should cut it. But it grows fast and surrounds her face with frizz, and there is nothing she can do but endure small tight plaits that hurt. Her mother shaves her head and wears a wig, I wonder if Charlie will when she's older, if she will hide her hair in shame and try to look more 'white.' I hope not, I think her hair suits her face, and should be allowed to grow naturally. I wonder if my father will wear a wig too, when he loses more of his hair to the poison of chemotherapy, but this is too horrible to think about, so I spin my thoughts back to Charlie, and I wish she would look up so I can grimace to her in sympathy.

Mr. Timothy Oakfield is on the prowl again, I stare down at my book. We are all quiet, I don't think this class has ever been silent before, there is something about him, an irresistible authority that has cast a spell on us. I try to see if he is wearing a wedding ring. He sees me raise my head, and approaches. I can feel my heart pounding behind my worn-out-doesn't-fit-properly bra, the blood has rushed to flood my face and neck, *so* not-cool. I feel him approach. I have written nothing. I glance sideways, Carol's book is neatly numbered 1 to 12, I begin to write the numbers in a long line down the margin, as if preparing my page for the answers that will surely follow; I haven't even read the questions yet. He is here, I have only written up to number 7, and there are no words. He is leaning down, I can smell aftershave, he places a hand on my desk, it is his left hand, it is naked. I glance up, and drown in brown eyes.

"Are you okay? Do you understand what you need to do?"

I nod, my face a furnace. I do not have the first idea what I am supposed to be writing. He moves away. I breathe again, force myself to read the questions. They make no sense, words bouncing on a white page. I sneak a look at Carol's book. I hate her, but I need her. I begin to copy her answers.

Chapter Six

I arrived back at the Blakeney house a little before midday. I approached with caution, but all was as I had left it, and after a cursory walk through each room, I relaxed, added my food to the fridge, retrieved my bags from the side room, and washed my hands. There were lots of warnings in the media about washing hands, saying that this was the best way to stop the spread of the virus.

I ate some lunch while setting up my phone. I had bought the same brand as my previous one, the one I had not dared to bring in case it could be traced. I had wondered, during my months of planning an escape, whether it was possible to add a new sim card to an old phone, and if this would make the phone untraceable. But my knowledge was entirely based on films about spies and criminals, and they always destroyed the whole phone, not just the sim, so I didn't know. There was no one I could ask.

**

I spent two weeks living in the Blakeney house. I left only at night, walking down to the little quay, staring at the silhouetted sailing boats, walking past the little duck pond, listening to the rats scurry, the ducks dive through the water when they heard me approach, the wild birds taking flight and leaving the enclosure, the owned ducks trapped by their clipped wings, taking to the water in a futile attempt to avoid danger. If I saw anyone else, I crossed the road and stayed in the shadows, but I only saw other people twice, and both times they were lurching unsteadily on their way home from the pub, so I think it unlikely they would have remembered me afterwards anyway. Gradually, I grew less nervous walking at night, I stopped fingering the penknife in my pocket so regularly, I became at peace with the scream of foxes and the hoots of owls, and in turn the night accepted me as one of its own, sheltering me from prying eyes.

I ate uncooked food sparingly, and washed my dress and underwear by hand because I didn't want to cause a spike in the use of electricity that might alert the owner and instigate an audit of the house. My only luxuries were tepid showers and hot drinks, and I only allowed the kettle to be boiled twice a day. I spent my days reading news reports, and watching strangers pass the house while I stood invisible behind the net curtains. Watching people was my only social contact, and I gave names to my unsuspecting neighbours: Mr Needs-to-Lose-Weight, and Mrs Can't-Park-Straight. I watched the edges of their lives, as they rushed to unknown appointments, or stooped to clean up after their dogs, or greeted friends in the street while I strained to hear snatches of words through the glass of my hiding place.

I studied the news and the internet, and plotted the spread of the virus and the response of the nations. I watched Spain follow Italy with a lockdown, confining people to their homes, cancelling schools and churches and clubs. Three days later, France followed. Each evening I stared at the numbers, charts plotting the spread of the virus. The death rates seemed unreal, 300 deaths in one night, over a thousand a few days later. I searched the internet for relevant comparisons, learning that tens of thousands usually died of flu each year. I tried to imagine the situation if those numbers were compacted into three weeks rather than several months, decided that it was the strain on the health service rather than the ferocity of the virus that was worrying governments.

I needed to make my own plan.

A lockdown in England began to look inevitable. In some ways, this made my situation easier—there were not likely to be any unexpected bookings of the holiday home, and the owner and cleaner were also unlikely to do random trips. However, I was not sure that Blakeney was a very sensible place for me to stay. It was too small. If there was a lockdown, I thought it likely that public transport would stop. This would limit my shopping to the few small shops in the village, where I would definitely be noticed and spoken to. I might be asked to explain my presence in the area, as strangers would be unexpected during a national lockdown. Someone would know the owner of the house, I would be discovered.

I decided that Cromer would be a safer place, but it depended on whether the key I had seen being placed under the doormat was left there after the cleaner had left. I searched several websites, looking for the house, and found it listed on one specialising in Norfolk cottages. It was vacant until Easter week, but I decided that if there was a lockdown, holidays to Norfolk would be cancelled, and if not, I could return to Blakeney. It was a risk, but less risky than staying.

On Saturday, I packed my belongings into three carrier bags, and prepared to leave. My early morning shower felt sad, there was something comforting about the little house, I had been safe here, and free for the first time in years. As the tepid water ran over my body, and I slid the soap over my skin, smelling the familiar perfume, bracing as I plunged my head under the water, wishing it was warmer, I felt as if I was preparing for execution. A last shower. I dried myself on the small pink towel I had bought when I shopped for my phone. It was rough from being rinsed by hand, and I longed for the feel of a fluffy towel dried with fabric conditioner. I ate some bread and butter, swallowing uncomfortable lumps because my mouth was dry. A last meal.

I placed my bags next to the front door, and walked once more around the little house, looking for footprints, marks in the dust, forgotten debris in the plughole. I saw nothing to betray me. I pulled on my jacket, picked up my bags, feeling the plastic handles dig into my skin, and opened the door. It was still fairly early, but fully light, and I squinted, feeling my eyes water at the shock of sunlight. I stepped from my hiding place, locked the door, and walked to the bus stop.

When I arrived in Cromer, it was busy, people walking purposefully around the shops, families heading towards the beach. Even without an influx of holiday makers, the little town was well-populated, and they all seemed to be outside, enjoying the sunshine and ignoring the cold wind. I walked to the Victorian house, head high, trying to appear confident, as if I belonged.

I walked down the short path, feeling as if every house had eyes watching from behind windows. I looked around, but saw no one; I waited for the shout, someone asking who I was, what was I doing? None came. I reached the front door, and took a deep breath, before reaching for the door mat, lifting it, peering at the empty step.

Nothing except a dead leaf and some dirt mingling with sand. No key.

I turned and walked back to the road, head high, still looking as if I was meant to be there, as if all the air hadn't been swiped out of me and I was empty and alone, and frightened. My bags were heavy, the plastic handles stretched to capacity, digging into my skin. I looked up the road, in the direction of Morissons, but I couldn't carry any more. I was stumped. I began to walk, simply because I needed to do something, and I must make a plan. Even if I decided to return to Blakeney, a plan which had so many problems it barely counted as a plan, but even if I did, the bus wouldn't arrive for another half an hour. I walked on. I passed houses, and shops, and found myself in a busy one-way system with narrow pavements and traffic edging round corners, and people hurrying to buy flowers. I saw a sign advertising Mother's Day cards. It was Mothering Sunday this weekend. I had forgotten.

I continued on to the church. There would be flowers, and I wanted to smell them, to see their colours, to have something to think about other than my predicament. Plus, there would be people, and I could sit in the church, strangers were not uncommon in the pews of churches, especially when there were flower displays for Mother's Day. I could be a person again, amongst other people, without being noticeable.

The door to the church was shut, I tried the handle; it was locked. The locked door felt personal, as if I alone was being shunned, not allowed into a hallowed place, not good enough to enter, even to see the flowers. I walked to a nearby bench and folded onto it, feeling the rejection of the locked door like a slap in the face. I had not attended a church since my aunt's wedding, way back in my childhood, but I still wanted the right to attend if I wanted to. I needed to have the option to enter a church, and to be denied was an insult.

I folded my arms, and stared at the neat flower beds bordering the path, and the low wall separating the church from the high street. I wondered if perhaps I had been mistaken, if the door was simply stiff. I returned to the porch, and was about to turn the handle again, when I saw the notice, pinned to the board next to the door, one corner flapping in the wind where it had escaped the fastening, as if beckoning to me, telling me to read it:

"Due to advice from the Archbishop, and in line with sensible care for the vulnerable, all church services have been suspended due to coronavirus."

I nodded. This made sense. There were more words on the sign, explaining that the church was more than the building, and offering numbers people could contact if in need—but they didn't mean me. I felt relieved, but also unsettled. I could not recall a time when churches had suspended their services, churches were *always* open. There was a creeping insidiousness to this disease, something unstoppable, and I was unsure whether I would escape the tentacles of its reach, and what that might mean.

However, for now, I simply needed a place to wait, somewhere that I could sit and plan. I would stay in Cromer. I had decided. I would go somewhere that I could sit for a long time without comment—the beach perhaps— and I would scroll through the holiday letting websites, and find other houses that were vacant this week. Later, much later, when it was dark, I would visit each one in turn. I would look under flower pots, and doormats, and in sheds, and hope that someone, somewhere, had lax security and I might find a key. I had decided. I would try harder to stay in this town, at least for a few weeks, until I knew whether the government intended to lockdown England too. There was safety in size, and already I felt anonymous in Cromer, residents didn't expect to recognise everyone in the street. I felt the caress of the sunshine on my skin as I left the church, followed by a blast from the cold wind.

I walked towards the beach, down winding lanes full of cold wind that tried to drive me back as I passed fish shops and empty souvenir shops and a huge hotel perched on the corner of the cliff. I walked down a steep ramp, past the pier, empty of tourists, the ticket office windows boarded up, the turnstiles locked. It was even colder down by the beach, the wind unstoppable as it raced from the cold north, cutting through the sunshine. I passed the fishing boats, pulled up onto the beach, the ramp slippery with sand; there was a man walking his dog, and teenagers balanced on a metal barrier, laughing when I passed. There was a cafe, steamy windows and empty tables. I pushed open the door, a bell rang, I walked to the counter and ordered a coffee, watched the girl slop it so it puddled in the saucer, saw her not care, she was tired, it was out of season, she was marking time until she could close shop and go home. I thanked her while feeling resentful—because that is what we've been trained to do in England—and carried the cup to a seat near the window. I wondered how long I could sit there, nursing a single coffee, sheltering from the weather while I decided where to go. Was this what all homeless people feel? This stretching out of endless time, this preoccupation with being warm, finding shelter, not being disturbed.

I pulled out my phone and smiled when I saw there was signal. Then I began to search for holiday properties in Cromer, reading their details, following the links as if I was going to book one, testing to see which ones were vacant. Each one had a photograph, a description, a link to a map. I saved the details of a few that looked promising alternatives to my Blakeney house.

The girl arrived to take my cup and wipe the table. I indicated that I hadn't finished, my cup was still half-full, the cold coffee grey and unappetising, milk coagulating on the surface. I smiled, pretended to take a sip. The girl nodded, she wanted to move me on but I was still within the bounds of acceptable, so she simply wiped the table again, flicked her cloth, moved to the next table with an eloquent sigh. I realised I couldn't stay much longer, not unless I wanted to risk her actually asking me to leave. I lifted my cup, and took the smallest sip of the cold coffee, staring at the steamy windows as if absorbing the view. I could feel the girl's eyes on my back, waiting, assessing my dowdy clothes, finding me wanting. I lowered my cup, nodded my thanks, and left.

I walked down, towards the sea. The waves were grey and green and persistent, whooshing up the beach, hissing back down the sand. I chose a spot, behind a breakwater of black sodden wood that served to shelter me from the wind, and I sat on the corner of a bag, and waited.

I read the newspaper from weeks ago, knowing the articles almost by heart but needing to occupy my mind with something, and hoping to look busy should anyone be watching me. For a while I stared unseeing at the pages, feeling the wind as it crawled closer to my bones, feeling damp from the sand rise up. It was so cold. Even in my sheltered spot, the wind buffeted me, tangled my hair, buzzed in my ears. I huddled up, pulling my knees to my chest, wrapping the skirt of my dress around them like a blanket, wishing away the time.

There was a family next to me, a mother and father and two young children. The girl was about 8 years old, and after a while of throwing sand, and then having a tantrum, I heard the father and son plan to leave for something, and the volume of the girl increased, and I heard her shout and storm and rant, whilst the parents failed to placate her. The mother was the stronger parent, I heard the assertiveness in her voice, the clear control as she told the child that no, she was staying on the beach, only her brother was going with their father; they would return soon, she had to wait. I realised that this mother was stronger than my own had been, she sounded fully in charge, there was no weakness in her voice.

I watched the girl as she twisted in anger, tried to escape from her mother's restraining arms. I heard the mother speak again, forced control in her tone, as she told the child that they could make sandcastles, but no, it was too cold to paddle, perhaps later, when the men were back.

I lowered my head, not wanting to be seen watching. I could hear their voices as the wind carried them towards me, I heard the angry shout of the girl.

"I want to go too. Me too."

I realised that her vocabulary was behind her age, and her storms and tantrums were not born of selfishness or lack of discipline but rather a struggle to understand the world around her, and the frustration of being in an unexpected place at an unexpected time. Her tantrums were a way of expressing her fear, asserting her desires, they were not meant to wound. And in an instant, she ceases to be a stranger's child, shouting on the beach; she is my sister.

***

My sister is 8 years old, and she is shouting: "I want to go too. Me too!"

My mother is trying, vainly, to restrain her, to stop her grabbing hold of me, and I am walking down the stairs with caution, not wanting to be grabbed. I am dressed in my best jeans, with a new purple top that makes my breasts look bigger and make-up to enhance my eyes and mouth. I have curled the ends of my hair, and I know that I look nice, I hope that I look older—old enough anyway.

My sister is storming, screaming that it's not fair, she wants to go with me. I hope she won't have a full meltdown, and I worry that my mother might try to delay me, ask me—very apologetically but still asking—if perhaps I might delay my date? Go out a different night? But she doesn't. I keep walking, the front door is in my sights, I am calling goodbye as if I haven't noticed anything wrong, then I am through it, closing it behind me with a click. I have escaped. I smile.

I walk towards the bus stop. He will meet me there, he suggested the concert last week, after the concert at our own school, performed by our own squeaking, stuttering, honking school orchestra. We did not sit together, because that would have been noticed, but I knew he would seek me out during the interval, when overpriced glasses of warm white wine served by a dinner-lady are sold to parents. My own parents were not there, of course, they couldn't leave my sister and she would never be quiet and still enough to come, and baby-sitters were impossible because they were different, and my sister does not do different.

I had known he would find me, lean towards me as I stood out of the way in the stairwell next to the biology labs. He often gave me extra tuition in his tiny office—always with the door ajar of course because those were the rules, but his desk was behind the door, hidden from sight, we could sit very close and not be noticed. Sometimes he sat very, very, close. I didn't mind, I never pulled away. I would see him *notice* me in the school canteen, when I filed in for assembly, as I walked the corridors with friends. Not that he ever spoke, or greeted me, but I knew that he noticed, knew he was seeing me, that our times of 'private tuition' were more than academic, times when he asked about my family and friends, wanted to know about *me*. I knew that I was more than a mere pupil, I was his friend.

Now, as I hurry towards the bus, I am hoping to become more than a friend too. I know that he's a teacher, but he is very young, and I am very mature, everyone tells me so.

The concert is in the town hall, and there are hundreds of people surging towards the entrance, but I see him at once. He is walking towards me, smiling, waving the tickets. We walk in, and for the first time I feel nervous, wonder what he'll say if we see someone he knows. Everyone here is older than me, I feel like a child, I take a breath and stand up straighter. I am prettier than they are, and I am with him.

He leads me to a seat at the back. We listen to the symphony, though we can't see anything. During the second movement, in the dark of the auditorium, his hand finds my own. I feel him stroke the skin, very lightly, as if testing. I allow him to entwine my fingers with his. I glance sideways, but he is facing the front, his expression doesn't flicker.

We stay in our seats during the interval. I hope he will offer me an ice-cream, but instead he asks if I would like some wine. I don't like wine. I say yes please. He stands and walks away. I wait, it feels like a long time, I wonder if he has met a colleague, and whether he will decide to sit somewhere else. I see him approach, carrying wine in two glasses. It is cold and bitter, I sip it. There is nowhere to pour it away, I drink it all. He removes the glass, and places it with his, under the seat in front.

The lights dim, the orchestra hums in preparation for the next movement. I feel him move towards me. I don't turn, I sit very still, facing the front, holding my breath. I feel his shoulder against my own, his hand is moving, brushing my wrist, moving to my knee. I am a statue, my mouth is dry, the world dissolves into music and darkness and sensation.

The symphony finishes much too soon. We clap, and stand, and clap some more, carried by the applause of others. We turn to leave, jostled by strangers on the stairs, forced apart for a moment, joining again when we step outside. I feel light-headed and wonder if it is due to the wine. The night air is crisp. I shiver. He places an arm around my shoulder and guides me to his car. He doesn't speak, but I know that he is going to drive me home. I lean towards him, feeling the warmth of his body, the protection of his arm on my shoulder. I know that this is the first of many such meetings. I know that he is pleased with me, and I smile, knowing that I will please him more.

Chapter Seven

The sun seemed to take forever to set. I watched it melt, orange and red, dissolving on the horizon, allowing shadows to deepen and dark places to appear. Much of Cromer had street lamps, which lent an orange glow to the town and hid the stars, but they couldn't reach the shadows, and by the time I walked, stiff-limbed and cold, towards the first of the holiday cottages, it was dark enough to hide me.

The first cottage was unhelpful. A converted barn, it sat in the grounds of a guesthouse. I didn't bother to search for a key, feeling sure that it would be issued from the big house when visitors arrived. Its proximity to the main house made it unsuitable for me to force a window, as the owners were sure to check even an empty property occasionally, given its location, and I would never feel safe.

The next property on my list was a large family house, near the cliffs on the edge of the town. The website didn't include actual house numbers, but a Google map provided the position, and even in the fading light, I could match the property with the photograph provided. The house was, I guessed, a late seventies build, with an arched porch and wide picture windows. I stood for a moment in the small cul-de-sac, looking at the house. The windows were blank, no lights. There were houses on both sides, and these were well-lit, with shadows moving around and the blue flicker of televisions; a light shone from an upstairs window, throwing light carelessly into the garden, and I moved back, further into the shadows. I watched a shadow walk in front of the light, then turned back to the holiday house. I was fairly confident it was empty. It was a detached property, so although there were neighbours, they wouldn't hear me through the walls, and I would be cautious with light and sound. It was, I felt, a possible contender. I noted the number and walked back down the road, then veered off, along the cliff edge, so I could enter from the back. It had a high garden wall, overgrown with roses that scratched me when I opened the back gate. Now to gain access.

I walked around the house, keeping to the shadows, looking for signs of a burglar alarm or security lights. There were none visible. I left my bags in a bush near the gate, and slunk to the front door. There was a doormat, but no key underneath. There was a pot to one side, and a random pebble in the flower bed. Neither hid a key. My eyes skimmed the doorposts, looking for a lockbox, or a key-safe. No luck there either. I walked back round to the rear garden.

The back was less well-maintained than the front, and paint peeled from window frames. There was a kitchen window, with a door. I pressed my face against the cold glass, and peered into the murky depths. I could make out a table, kitchen appliances, a sink below the window. On the left was a picture, and what I assumed was a calendar. On the right, I could see hooks, and—good news at last—hooks hanging with keys. I measured the distance; too far for my arms to reach. If I broke a window, I would have to remove enough glass to climb inside. Next to the kitchen window was a smaller, frosted-glass square, what I assumed was a downstairs washroom. I turned, placed the back of my head back against the window and scanned the view. There were no houses overlooking the tiny window, if I managed to smash it unheard, no one would see the broken glass unless they actually came into the garden, as it was masked by a helpful shrub that had overgrown its pot and was partially covering the window. I explored further.

I overturned several rocks and pots and casually placed logs. None revealed a key; I hadn't truly expected them to, but it was silly not to look. At the end of the garden was a small shed, and I walked to it and tried the door: locked, but not bolted. I opened my penknife and slid the blade into the lock, then applied pressure, forcing the bolt back. It was stiff, and took me several attempts, but after a couple of cuts and several moments of frustration, it eventually moved. I folded my penknife, returned it to my pocket, turned the door handle. The door opened with a groan. I paused. No one seemed to hear, there were no shouts, no new lights. I eased open the door and walked into the creosoted space. It smelt of wood and creosote, spiders' webs drifted down to tickle my face. On one side were garden tools, stacked against the wall and on a low table. Flowerpots were stacked according to size, granules of dirt dusted the table top, a trowel had been left ready and was now laced with webs and dust. At the back was a long freezer. I opened the lid. A light blinked on, shocking in its intensity. I slammed the lid closed. I blinked, letting my eyes adjust again to the dark. I had glimpsed enough to know the freezer was mainly empty, the bottom half scattered with ice cubes and cold-packs for picnic bags, and half empty bags of peas and chips—probably the leftovers from departing guests, not worth them taking but too much for a frugally-minded cleaner to throw away.

To my right was a stack of garden furniture and a tool box, and I knelt down, stretched wide the concertina trays, and peered inside. It was well stocked, the tools old, some rusty, but a fair range of Stanley knives and chisels and screwdrivers—a housebreaker's dream. I removed a long thin chisel and one of the knives and left the shed, leaving the noisy door open.

The washroom window had a wooden frame, and I began to chisel around it, loosening the paintwork, removing the putty from around the glass—which I hoped to leave intact. There was a crunch, and the glass shattered, a long crack stretching across the length of the window. Not what I'd hoped, but I decided to use it, forcing the chisel into the centre, picking away at splinters of glass until a whole section came away and crashed to the ground, scattering slices of glass, tiny splinters, lethal shards. Some fell on my shoe, and I shook them off, brushed them away as best I could, went back to my work. I returned to the shed, found some gardening gloves, hoped they were strong enough, and pulled them over my hands. I used them to protect my skin while I plucked pieces of broken glass from the perimeter of the frame, scraping with the chisel, pulling with the fat-fingered gloves, removing anything that would cut me. I stepped back, and surveyed my work.

The frame was now clear of glass. It was, I judged, just big enough for me to squeeze through if I removed my coat. It was high, so I returned again to the shed, and carried a garden chair up to the house, positioned it under the window. I removed my coat, felt the wind penetrate my thin sweater as I placed my coat on a convenient bush, well clear of the glass. I stepped up, onto the chair; it wobbled, and I heard glass crunching beneath the metal legs. Using the wall to steady me, I reached up, stepped onto the back of the chair, which wobbled even more, threatening to tip, I leaned forwards, reaching for the window, pushed my head through, into the washroom. I saw I was over a toilet, a sink and mirror to the side, a door in front; behind me, I could hear the shed door, slamming shut, creaking open. I hoped the noise would be masked in other houses by the general rustle of branches and concentrated on pulling my shoulders through the gap, using my arms to heave forwards, feeling my hips scrape the window frame, my stomach bruised by the sill, my legs kicking wildly as I tried to propel myself inside. I heard a clunk as the garden chair toppled over, but I was almost in, arms reaching for the toilet, using it to pull myself forwards, trying to right myself, failing and sliding down, down, bashing onto the cistern, the seat, until I landed in a crumpled heap of bruises on the hard tiled floor. Everything hurt.

For a moment, I simply sat. My arms were scratched, and a drip of blood slid along my hand and dripped onto the tiles. My back was screaming, my sides bruised, one wrist felt sprained. I was dizzy, and frightened, and exhausted. But I was inside. My body began to respond to the innate warmth of the house, glad to be sheltered at last from that persistent wind. I could smell lemon soap, and fabric conditioner, and there was a hum from a nearby boiler.

I removed my sweater, used the sleeve to wrap around my bleeding hand, and stood. My legs shook, but I needed to keep moving, check the house and decide whether I was staying. I inched open the washroom door.

I was in a small hallway, front door ahead, stairs reaching over me. To the left were two doors, one led to the kitchen and I went there first. I checked the sink was dry, the cupboards and fridge empty of food. I then checked the second door, which took me into the lounge—a small fireplace, sofas arranged around a coffee table, dried flowers at the window. I went back to the stairs. The second step creaked when I stepped on it, the third step from the top groaned loudly; I took note. There were three bedrooms, all standing around a landing, doors open, linen folded on beds. The bathroom—just one—had an over-bath shower with a stained yellow plastic curtain, a pink sink with black rings of mould around the plug, and a tall towel rail. There was a separate toilet, with toilet paper stacked on the cistern (this had become a notable commodity in the last few days).

There were no signs of recent life, and the air smelt stale, that shut away smell of a house left empty for a few weeks. I doubted anyone had visited for a while, not even the rather tardy cleaner. It suited me perfectly.

I returned to the kitchen, still not using lights which might be seen from outside, but less cautious now, not caring about the groaning stair or the doors that clicked shut behind me. I looked along the hooks of keys, found one for the back door, another for the shed, slipped into the garden to retrieve my belongings. The wind greeted me, slapping me with cold for trying to escape. I grabbed my things, returned the chair to the shed and secured the door. Then I carried my bundle of things into the house.

I was too tired for food, too weary even for a hot drink. I bundled all my things into an empty cupboard next to the sink—they would be lost if I needed to escape in a hurry, but it was the best I could do for now. I climbed the stairs, selected the double room for its view out the back, and shook out the folded duvet. Fully clothed, I slid under the cover, smelling the dust and staleness of previous guests, too exhausted to care. At last, I was still, and gradually my bones warmed, and my head stopped buzzing, and I slept.

***

It is my wedding day. I am wearing a short white dress, which my mother made for me, and I know the hem is slightly wonky, and it worries me, even though there is no one there who will care. It is not the wedding that I dreamed about as a little girl, but I tell myself it doesn't matter, what matters is that I am marrying the man who I love.

The wedding is a compromise. I think that Timothy, *Mr. Timothy Oakfield,* would have avoided it if my father had not insisted. Although Timothy wants to be with me, and only me, forever, I think he was hoping that I would simply move into his house when I failed my AS levels so spectacularly, that he would replace my faded dream of university without any hassle, any *fuss,* as my sister likes to say.

My sister is not there. My parents say she is too young, too hard to subdue, but I know they are punishing me, showing that this is not a real wedding, not something to be happy about. They are only agreeing to it, only giving permission to their 17-year-old failure because they know there are no better options. I look up at my father. His face is grey from the chemotherapy, and I hope he won't be sick, won't spoil my day. I start to think about his illness, about how he must be feeling, and I push the thoughts away. Timothy says I must not dwell on my father's health, there is nothing I can do to change the outcome, and I must lead my own life, not live in the shadow of my parents. I am an adult now, he has made me an adult. I must not let him down. I stop looking at my father, and glance instead at my mother.

She looks nervous. She is wearing a dress but her tights are old, and I can see a snag on one leg. She keeps darting nervous little glances in my direction, and I know she is trying to ask if I am *sure,* if this is really what I want. But my mother is weak, too weak to overturn the plans my father agreed with Timothy, too weak even to ask me directly. All her energy is taken up with my sister, and keeping her safe, and avoiding situations where she might have a meltdown. There is no room for me. There hasn't been for the last nine years.

None of my friends have been invited. I don't really have friends any more, so it doesn't matter. I spend every evening with Timothy, and gradually my friends forgot me, stopped trying to entice me to their activities—their childish activities—and the texts stopped coming, and my Facebook friends dwindled, and my Twitter feed filled up with adverts and news articles and tweets from people who I don't know. But this doesn't matter. Timothy tells me I don't need anyone else, he is going to look after me now, and I don't need to go to university, because I don't need a job, he is going to provide everything I need.

The registrar is calling us forward, I am listening as her voice drones on, telling us things we don't need to hear before finally asking us those important questions. Do I take Mr. Timothy Oakfield to be my husband? Yes, of course I do, he is my whole life, the only person who really sees me, the only friend who has stayed true as I flunked my exams and dropped out of school and failed to get a decent job.

I listen to the vows, I hear myself promise to obey him, which is nothing new, I have been obeying him since that very first date over a year ago, when I was a gawky sixteen year-old and he was the wonderful handsome prince who whisked me away from my childhood and led me into the promised land of adulthood.

I feel his ring slide onto my finger, an emblem of belonging. I have no ring to give Timothy, he doesn't need one, it is traditional for only the wife to wear one. We are pronounced husband and wife, and I am aware that my mother is crying silently into a tissue and I wonder if she brought it specially, put it in her pocket so that it would be ready for when she cried, because crying is a planned thing. She shouldn't be crying, she should be happy. My father is sitting again, he has slumped onto one of the seats lining the room, and my mother is going to him. She doesn't come to congratulate me, she goes to my father, who was ill yesterday and will be ill tomorrow, whereas I am now a wife, and that is something new, and she should come to me first. But she never comes to me first, my place has always been behind my sister, because we must avoid her having a meltdown at all costs, and behind my father, because he is the head of the household.

I feel Timothy move beside me, he is taking my hand, stealing my gaze away from my parents.

"You don't need to look at them ever again," his eyes tell me. "I am the only person you ever need to look at now."

We leave. My husband, *Mr. Timothy Oakfield*, leads me, *Mrs. Timothy Oakfield*, down the wide stairs and across the car park and into his car and away. We do not say goodbye to my parents—or to the registrar, because Timothy tells me she is only doing her job, she is paid to be there, and she doesn't care whether we say goodbye or not.

We leave, and I know our bags are in the boot, and that he is taking me away, for a week, to celebrate our marriage. I wonder if he will drive to the airport, if we are going somewhere sunny for our honeymoon, or perhaps to an hotel, somewhere that I will be cosseted and fussed over. I have never stayed in an hotel. I sit back in my seat and watch the other cars as they pass, and I feel different, because I know that I am a wife now, and that Timothy properly belongs to me, as I belong to him. I am a wife; I hug the word close. I am suffused with happiness, and all is golden and perfect.

***

We are home, our honeymoon was a success, everything I ever dreamed of. We did not stay at an hotel, or eat in restaurants. This is because my husband wants to keep me all to himself, he doesn't want to share even a second of my time with waiters or receptionists. We are in our own private world, and we don't need anyone else. We return to Timothy's terraced house—our home, the house which I am fortunate enough to be allowed to share, even though I

50

have contributed nothing, because he loves me and he wants me to live in this house, his house, with him.

Chapter Eight

I woke up to the sound of the sea. For a few minutes I lay there, trying to remember where I was, why my shoulder hurt. I turned, and my back screamed with pain, and one of my ribs throbbed. I lay on my back, feeling slightly queasy.

I remembered that it was Sunday, and I was safely installed in a holiday home in Cromer, and that my first job should be to somehow repair the window I had smashed—or at least make it weather-proof, and my second job should be to buy some food. I sat up in bed, and winced. I would buy some painkillers too. I could see the sun was already up, and the sky was blue. I went to the window, careful in case someone should happen to look up. Beyond the garden I could see gorse bushes dancing in the wind, and behind them was the sea, white-capped waves rolling towards the shore. A gull was wheeling over the garden, crying as it floated on air currents, wings outstretched. Free. I reminded myself that I too was free, even if I still felt like a prisoner. Mine was an uneasy freedom, and I envied that bird.

When viewed in the daylight, the house was a pretty one. The kitchen was large, with a table and four chairs at one side. There was a fridge, and a cooker, and a creamy surface with a coffee pot and a toaster. Under the sink was a range of cleaning products, and when I searched the cupboards, I found one contained opened packets of food, which I assumed must have been left by previous residents and not wanted by the cleaner. There was half a pot of salt, and some pepper, and an opened bag of flour secured into a plastic tub, some stock cubes and a tall jar of celery salt. I wondered who used celery salt, and why they had deemed it a necessity on holiday.

The lounge had a sofa and two easy chairs, arranged around a brick fireplace. There was a low table scattered with coasters, and a jar of dried flowers on the window sill, which made me smile. Holiday rentals always seemed to have at least one vase of dusty dried flowers. A bookcase sat in the corner, stuffed with well-thumbed novels and tatty wildlife books which looked as if they had been bought from fairs and charity shops, and left by previous guests.

I walked to the supermarket mid-morning, when it was likely to be busy and I would be one of a crowd. My route took me through the main town, and I noticed that several shops were open, people buying last minute gifts for their mothers or spreading their weekly shop across the whole weekend. I smiled, thinking that shopping was the new religion in England, it was the only ritual that seemed to still exist, especially with the churches now closed.

Morissons was even busier than I had expected, and there was a queue outside. I went and spoke to the assistant standing guard by the door.

"Is the supermarket not open yet?"

She looked up, and smiled—a sort of apologetic smile. When she spoke her words sounded unnaturally bouncy, as if she had repeated them many times before, a well-learned script.

"Yes, we are open, but only for vulnerable people at this time, the over seventies and National Health workers. We are asking everyone else to observe social distancing, and to wait outside."

She glanced at the door, and smiled again, a weary smile that didn't reach her eyes.

"I think the older customers have nearly finished, we'll start to allow other people inside in a few minutes I think. We'll do *one out, one in*—to maintain safe numbers inside the shop. The end of the queue's over there." She nodded towards a woman, standing in the corner of the car park, holding the handle of a trolley and reading something on her phone.

I selected a trolley, even though I could fit everything into a basket, and pushed it to a spot a metre behind the end of the line. I could see the rest of the queue, stretching almost the entire perimeter of the car park before doubling back to the doors. A couple arrived behind me, both wearing gloves, both staring at their phones. The queue was annoying, even though I had nothing else to do today. At least the weather was dry, it would have been grim in the rain. I realised the line was not as bad as I had first thought, as the length was mostly due to the huge gaps between people, and I estimated that despite its length, I would be inside the shop within an hour. I sighed, and stared at nothing, wishing I had a book to read, or a game on my phone, or someone to chat to. It was lonely, standing with all those other people but disconnected, in my own bubble. Isolation was more than simple distance.

The woman in front of me glanced back, and smiled.

"Hello," she said. "This is all a bit surreal, isn't it?"

I nodded, wondering why she was speaking to me. There seemed to be a general jollity in the air, and I realised that several other shoppers are smiling at each other, saying hello, chatting in the aimless way that strangers do when they want to make contact but have no commonality. The woman in front was holding up several scraps of paper.

"I'm shopping for a few of my neighbours. I'm bound to get in a right muddle and end up giving them all the wrong stuff! I'm just looking at the lists now, trying to memorise them a bit. Lots of very specific items on here: *five bananas, slightly green, not too* big." She laughed, "They'll be lucky if I manage that sort of detail! They're all over seventy, so are self-isolating, and the town Facebook group asked for volunteers to help with shopping and stuff. Are you a member?"

I nodded noncommittally.

"I think it's a bit daft really," she continued, "This whole only letting over-seventies shop for the first hour. I mean, just because they're over seventy, it doesn't mean they can't be contagious, does it? They could all be in there, giving each other the virus. It'd be much better if they just stayed at home, and let their neighbours shop for them instead of risking spreading the virus. After all, it'll be them that dies, won't it?"

She lowered her voice and leaned towards me slightly, which I thought looked odd given the distance between us, but I understood she wanted to be conspiratorial, and tried to look as if I was interested.

"I've got a friend who's a medic, and she told me that they've got a list, you know, in case it gets really bad. If someone over a certain age phones the hospital, needing oxygen, they'll be turned away, told to stay at home. If they don't have enough respirators for everyone, then they'll prioritise, give them to the young and healthy, let the older people die. Because they're less likely to make it anyway, I suppose." She shook her head, as though she couldn't quite believe her own words, and I wondered why she was so keen to tell me, a stranger, such a macabre fact, and whether it was even true. I couldn't think of a response, so I simply shook my head, and looked shocked, and wondered how many people had to catch the virus before we got to that stage.

A man joined the queue wearing a white mask across the lower half of his face. No one else was wearing a mask, and I noticed several people looking sideways at him, almost scathing in their expressions, as if they thought he was overreacting, and should be taking his chances like the rest of us. I saw the mask ride up on his face, and he fiddled with it, pulling it down slightly, then trying to secure it under the ridge of his glasses. I thought that after touching the trolley handle, his hands were possibly contaminated, and that fiddling with a face-mask was probably worse than not wearing one. But all the same, I envied him, and wished that I had a mask too, to hide from both germs and people.

When I finally entered the supermarket, I was disorientated by the empty shelves. Although there was plenty of fresh fruit and vegetables, the shelves that should be stacked with tinned food were bare. Only an arrangement of red lentils sat on the shelf, near the bottom. I had never eaten red lentils, I wondered why they were rejected by all the other shoppers. I left them sitting there, and moved on to the bakery section. This too had been decimated, great white expanses of empty shelf where there should have been loaves of bread and packets of fajitas and cakes in cellophane. I picked up a couple of battered packets of rolls, and decided they would have to do. I thought I would buy cereal instead, as an easy way to fill my stomach, but those aisles too were almost empty. There were some boxes of fancy muesli, and a brightly coloured cereal full of sugar, but none of the usual staples were there. I stood still, feeling strangely light-headed, almost as if I would cry. If shopping was our religion, then this was a desecration of our holy place, an uprooting of our foundations. With so much uncertainty in my life, I felt that I *needed* the supermarket to be stable, to continue to supply all my demands and offer more than I wanted. I wasn't sure that I could cope with this barren experience, this harsh intrusion into the world I had created. The tentacles of the disease were beginning to reach me, and I didn't like it. The goalposts were constantly moving, I couldn't keep up.

I walked to the hygiene aisle. There was no hand sanitiser, and only one brand of soap. I added it to my trolley, even though I could smell the sickly perfume through the wrapper and I knew I would hate using it. The news had recommended that we should wash our hands regularly in antibacterial soap, and use hand sanitiser when out. But how was this possible when the shops had been ravished of such things already?

I paid for my groceries and left.

When I reached the comparative safety of the holiday home, using the back door as that was unseen by nosey neighbours, I dumped the bags on the kitchen floor and pulled out my phone. It was the 22nd March, my sister's birthday. I had not spoken to my sister—to anyone in my family—for several years. I held my phone on my upturned hand, weighing it as I weighed the decision: should I phone her?

Now that I was free, able to make my own choices, should I call her to wish her happy birthday, and would she be pleased or unsettled? I thought about what I would say to my mother when she answered the call, how I could possibly explain what had happened without upsetting her, and I realised that I couldn't, and that phoning was impossible and even to think about it was selfish; and then, without really knowing what I was doing, I tapped the numbers into the phone and held it to my ear. I told myself I would just listen, I simply wanted to hear a familiar voice, I wanted to belong again, even though I knew that I couldn't.

I listened to the phone ringing, heard it being answered, and prepared to end the call. But it wasn't my mother who answered, it was my sister. I heard her voice, something sloppy in her pronunciation, the words not quite properly formed.

"Hello, who is this?"

Her voice was older, she would be 14 now, a hormonal teenager. I heard a whispered conversation and recognised my mother's voice, asking who it was, trying to remove the phone from my sister. But she was as determined as I remembered, and I imagined her clinging onto the receiver as I heard her tell my mother to go away, it was her birthday, the call was for her. I smiled, wondering what she would have done if the call had been from someone else, someone not wanting to speak to her, and considered, briefly, whether I should pretend to be a sales call, someone she didn't know. But the need to belong returned, and I heard myself give my name, heard her repeat it, sounding confused, checking if she had heard correctly.

"She's gone," she said at last, as if to explain that although she recognised the name, it could not possibly be me.

"Yes," I said, "but I wanted to speak to you, on your birthday, to say happy birthday. Are you having a nice time?"

There was a catch in my throat, and I could feel tears welling. There was something wonderfully familiar about my sister, even with the slight deepening of her voice with age, I recalled the bluntness of her sentences, the unrestrained voicing of her thoughts, and I wanted to see her, to be with her again. I wanted to know what she looked like now, to find out what kind of teenager she was growing into, to discover whether she could read fluently, whether she had friends, if she was happy.

"No, I'm not. I wanted a puppy but I got another computer game and some books, and some sweets that I'm not allowed to eat yet. Harry gave me a plant. Do you know Harry?"

I shook my head, the tears falling now, blocking my throat so that I couldn't have spoken, even if my sister had paused to hear my reply, but she hadn't. The question, as all her questions had always been, was rhetorical, a means to check I was listening. She was already explaining who Harry was, a neighbour, someone who she saw when she was playing in the garden.

"And he has a wife, called Nancy. Do you know Nancy? She didn't give me a present, but mummy said perhaps it was from both of them. Mummy said that when she was putting on her coat, to go to the shops. I didn't want to go. Yesterday we went, and some people were wearing masks, and I didn't like it. I didn't like all the fuss, all this standing in queues, and I didn't like the masks, you can't see people's faces when they're wearing masks, not properly. And I think it's all a lot of fuss. We don't need masks, do we? We didn't wear masks last week, no one did. So we shouldn't wear masks this week. It's all a lot of fuss. Are you going to come back? Have you got me a present?"

I started to nod, even though she couldn't see me. I was thick with tears, smiling at the thought of my sister objecting to masks. I knew she would hate them, she had always hated anything that was different, and although she didn't really read expressions, she was very aware of faces, she wouldn't like not being able to see them. I wanted to wish her happy birthday, I wanted to say something to make her smile. But the tears were running freely, and my hand was damp, and I couldn't think of how to end the call. Then I heard my mother's voice again, asking who was calling, trying to remove the phone, and my sister shouting, saying that it was her birthday, it was her sister calling, the one who didn't live there anymore, and I took the phone from my ear, and ended the call, and sank to my knees on the hard kitchen floor, and wept. As the tears course down my cheeks, I remember another time that I cried over my family, and how that too began with a new mobile phone.

***

Timothy has been promoted, which is a cause for celebration, a rare glass of wine—which I don't dislike as much as I used to—and big smiles and gifts. The gifts are from him, he watches me open them, his dark eyes intent. The box contains two phones. They are identical. He takes one, tells me that we now can share all our data. The phones track each other, showing their positions on a map. The number is different to my old phone.

Timothy loves me, and doesn't want to share me. I am his, he tells me with a hug and a kiss; I am his wife and that is all he wants in the world. I return the gesture, truly happy. He says it is time that I started to detach myself from the demands of my family. My mother has always expected too much from me, sees me as the future carer for my sister, an unrecognised social worker. He wants to save me from that.

I start to protest, I tell him that I love my sister, that caring for her in the future is what I want to do. He silences me. I am too kind, he says, too easily manipulated by my mother into a role I should not be forced into. It is better, he says, to start breaking ties with my family now, so they start to lean on me less often, and to find other avenues of help. In the long run, this will be good for them. I shouldn't be selfish, I should detach myself now, so that in the future they will have looked elsewhere for help, will have set up support networks.

I nod. Timothy is invariably right.

For many months, I have no contact with my family. I do not give them my new number, and I never initiate contact. I do this for them, so they find other people to help them in the short term. It is good for them, and allows me to focus fully on my husband, on being a good wife. I hear no news of them from friends, because I don't need friends any more. Timothy mentioned that my friends are very immature, being so much younger than he is, and that although he feels I have matured through my contact with him, and that I am now his equal and the absolute love of his life, he finds that after I have spent time with my friends, my *immature* friends, then I revert back to type and am less his equal. It might be better, he suggests, if I stopped contacting them. He tells me that he longs for the day when I am completely his, when I truly don't need anyone else. I want nothing more than to please my husband, and I fear that he is correct, my friends do encourage a childish side of me. I stop returning calls and texts. Timothy approves.

One day it all changes. Timothy has left his phone on the counter while he uses the bathroom. A message from my mother flashes onto the screen, and I open it. My father is dying. He is in a hospital. The address and ward are in the message.

I do not reply. I mark the message as unread, and leave it for Timothy to find. He never mentions it, never informs me that my father is dying, never suggests that I should visit. This confuses me, as I am sure it is right for me to visit. Perhaps Timothy cannot cope with the thought that I will be sad, he wants to protect me from pain. This is kind and loving, but something inside of me wants to resist. I want to see my father. I make a plan.

A few days later, Timothy is at work. I turn off the tracking device in my phone. It is the first time I have ever done this. The device is temperamental, it never seems to show the position of Timothy's phone, and when I tell him this, he says it depends where the satellite is. I decide my own phone can also have this fault.

I take some of the money from the purse in the kitchen drawer. Timothy puts money there for groceries and tips, times when I can't use my credit card. He checks the credit card bill very closely, and I want this trip to be a secret. It will be the first secret I keep from my husband. I catch the bus, and go to the hospital.

The ward is easy to find, there is a woman giving directions at a reception desk, and signs hanging from the walls. I follow the signs, past photographs of pastoral scenes, my heels tapping on the shiny floor. I feel nervous, and I wonder if my mother and sister will be with my father. I want to see them with an almost physical longing, which I realise is selfish of me.

My father has shrunk. He looks very small in the hospital bed, and his flesh has been eaten by the cancer, so only the outline of his bones exists, only the core of him is left. I think that he looks like my granny, and I have never noticed that before, because the size of him always reminded me more of his father. But he has her bones, and bones and skin are all that is left. My eyes shy away from the pointy chin, the skin stretched across high cheek bones. I focus on his grey eyes, which are still bright, and his blue pyjamas, which are new.

His eyes fill with tears when he sees me, and he reaches out his arms for a hug. I hold him, he clings to me. I feel his pain. He holds me very tightly, for a long time—an unspoken sharing of sorrow. I understand everything he is not saying. He wants to talk, but his throat is too dry, I can see the words hurt him. I sit beside him, holding his hand, telling him that I am happy, I am very much in love and my life with Timothy is good. I do not tell him about the times when I long to be allowed to choose my own clothes or food, or that I yearn to see my family, or my friends, and that sometimes I feel lonely, in this cut-off world of being Timothy's wife. I only talk about the good things, our little house, the plants we are growing in the tiny garden, how much I love to bake things. My father looks at me, and I think he sees beyond the words, but he only squeezes my hand, tells me that he loves me.

I stay for as long as I can, but the time betrays me and the moments with my father are fleeting. I must leave, or dinner will be late, and Timothy will ask what I have been doing. I find that he detects my lies, it is better to avoid telling them. I kiss my father, and I smell his soap and aftershave, and feel the strangely smooth cheek next to my own, and I wonder if my heart will break as I say goodbye. I cannot stop the tears, and they spill from my eyes and flow down my cheeks before I can turn away. My father tries to comfort me, *"Don't cry my love, it'll be okay. . ."* but this is too big even for him, he has saved me throughout my life, but he cannot stop his own dying.

I walk away, the world fuzzed through tears that won't stop flowing. I walk back along the corridors, an automaton with the sole aim of getting home. I sit on the bus, and I know people are staring, but I don't care.

When I am home, I wash my face, and apply make-up, even though I know Timothy doesn't like it, and I cook supper. By the time my husband arrives home, I am composed. We never speak of my father, other than several months later, when Timothy tells me that my father died a while ago, but he has only just heard about it, as my mother didn't want us to attend the funeral. I know that he is lying, and I realise that perhaps he has lied in the past. But my overriding feeling is one of worry, and I try to guess what my mother and friends and family must have thought, when I didn't attend the funeral. And I realise that very smoothly, without causing a ripple, my husband has cut me off from anyone who might be relied upon to help me, and I have only him now.

Chapter Nine

It was Tuesday when the text arrived. At first, I thought it must be from my family, that my foolish phone call to my sister had meant that they now had my number, and they wanted, even after everything, to resume some kind of contact. So when my phone pinged, I pulled it out cautiously, not sure what it would say but filled with irrational hope. But it wasn't from my family. It was a text from the government:

"CORONAVIRUS ALERT
New rules in force now:you must stay at home.
More info & exemptions at (there was a website)
Stay at home. Protect the NHS.
Save lives"

I read it twice. There was something ironic about being told to "stay at home." Which home did they mean? Was I being given permission to stay here, in this house I was currently occupying? I was pleased my decision to leave Blakeney was vindicated, though it was weird to read a message from the government, telling me to remain at home. I felt again as if I was living in the midst of a science fiction movie, there was something very unreal about the situation. Perhaps I would wake up in a minute.

I decided that I needed to make some sort of plan—beyond my quest for freedom. I had previously thought I would find some kind of employment—one that paid cash, as I couldn't risk a bank account—perhaps bar work, or a cashier in a shop. However, I needed to consider what would happen if I caught this virus. I had read that it was mostly dangerous for the elderly, and people with underlying health problems. I did not fit into either of those categories, though even young and healthy people were at some risk, and there seemed to be a randomness about those who would end up in hospital, needing oxygen or to be on a respirator. I read that although for most people, the symptoms were very slight, sometimes unnoticed, for others they caused high temperature, difficulty breathing, complete fatigue. I could not, absolutely could not, catch this virus. There was no one to provide me with food, or to care for me, or to phone a doctor if it was necessary. Although many people were in theory 'self-isolating' I was truly alone. What more could I do to minimise the risk of catching the virus?

I decided that I would have to suspend finding a job until things were safer. I calculated that if I was careful, I could make my money last. Perhaps I could eat slightly less. I had hoped to replace some of my clothes, but that would have to wait now. I looked down at my clothes: a flowery dress, and I shuddered, remembering. . .

***

I am standing in front of the open wardrobe, looking at the clothes hanging on the back of the door. He has selected a skirt for me to wear today, with a tight sweater and low-heeled shoes. I know the shoes will rub, because they are new. My poor feet will have no rest from unstretched leather, my heels are raw. I will have to cover the red with plasters and hope they recover.

I remind myself that I am lucky my husband is so involved, most men take no interest in their wives' wardrobes. I know exactly what Timothy likes me to wear, because as soon as we were married, after we returned from our week in Blakeney, he suggested I leave my suitcase unpacked, and he showed me this wardrobe, stuffed full of the clothes which he said he would like me to wear. There are dresses, and skirts, and blouses. They are not the clothes I like wearing, there are no jeans, no tee-shirts, no baggy jumpers. Everything fits closely, and is what I consider 'old person clothing.' But this is what my husband likes.

I frown, remembering Timothy's reaction to the woman who had served us when we last shopped together. We were in the greengrocer's, buying vegetables because Timothy says they are fresher than the ones in the supermarket, and more environmentally friendly. We were standing together, waiting to be served, and I looked up from the tomatoes I was inspecting to find Timothy is inspecting the cleavage of the shop assistant. She is bent over, scooping potatoes from a large sack, and we have an excellent view past her plunging neckline, and Timothy is clearly engrossed. When it is our turn to be served, he steps forward, and gives our order, chatting while she prepares it.

"Nice weather we're having at the moment," he says, smiling his special smile, the one I recognise, with shining eyes.

The woman glances up, and smiles back. Her eyes are outlined in black, making them look huge in her smiling face, and her lips are scarlet, and she is wearing a tight tee-shirt with a daringly low neckline, and jeans that cling to her body like a second skin. I can see that Timothy is noticing her curves, touching her body with his eyes. Her eyes flicker, and I know that she is noticing too, and enjoying the attention.

"Yes, can't complain," she replies, "though we better make the most of it because it's probably the only summer we'll get this year."

Timothy nods and grins, and asks if she's planning a holiday this year. I stand there, next to the oranges, feeling like a lemon, while my husband flirts and smiles with the woman serving. When he pays, she gives him his change and a cheeky, "I've put in a couple of extra oranges, they're perfectly ripe for squeezing!" and then she looks at me, thinking I am a waiting customer, next in line.

I shake my head, and indicate that I'm with Timothy, not the next person waiting to be served.

"Oh, sorry love, I didn't realise you were together," she says, and I wonder what part of the exchange she is apologising for.

When we are outside, standing in the street, I rearrange the bags slightly and then, because I can't help myself, I say: "She was pretty wasn't she? You seemed more interested in looking at her body than buying vegetables."

Timothy scowls, and I realise at once that I should have remained quiet.

"Really? You can't cope with me chatting to some old bat in a grocery shop? Honestly, she was only a shop worker, as if I'd be interested in someone like that!"

We continue our shopping in polite coldness. I don't point out that I am *only a shop worker,* or that it was embarrassing, standing there while he openly flirted with another woman, and that if Timothy sees me smiling at another man, whatever his age or profession, then I suffer an inquisition and frosty silence afterwards.

I remember this exchange while staring at the shapeless clothes hanging in my wardrobe. They are cheap, supermarket labels fraying in the backs. I wonder why he says he likes me to wear these clothes, these middle-aged clothes, and no make-up—and yet he is attracted, very obviously, to a woman wearing lots of make-up, and modern clothes. I wonder if he would still be attracted to me if I still wore nice clothes and make-up. I wonder if I have made a mistake in acquiescing so easily to his suggestion that he should decide my clothes each day. Perhaps it is a test; I know that he enjoys setting tests for me, rewarding or punishing me depending on my result. I am weary of tests, and my head droops down, and I sigh.

***

There was a movement, and I glanced up. There, standing at the fence in the next garden, was a man; he was staring, straight through the window to where I was sitting, cross-legged, in a pool of light.There was no doubt that he had seen me, and as I stared back, he lifted his hand again and waved. Cursing my stupidity, I raised an arm to return his wave, and heaved myself to my feet. I would have to speak to him, and hope that I sounded plausible.

I opened the front door and walked towards the man, who I assumed was a neighbour as he was standing in the garden next door. What could I say? I had absolutely no reason for living in the house. I was a squatter, stealing their electricity. I had even broken their window to gain access, which I was sure was an even worse crime. While I

66

walked towards the man, thoughts spinning around my head, I glanced back, and realised the whole of the little sitting room was easily viewed during the daytime, as there were no net curtains and the window was large and single-glazed.

I swallowed, still not knowing what to say. I would let him speak first, and hope something came to me. I walked towards him, noticing dark hair that curled around his ears, and very even teeth in a wide smile. I guessed he was about ten years older than me, maybe thirty-five, possibly forty, but still attractive, even for an older bloke. When I was near enough to see his eyes, they surprised me by being very blue, a dark blue that managed to look as warm as his smile, surrounded by creases formed from years of smiling often. A good start. I smiled back.

"Hello there!" he said as I approached, which told me he did not yet suspect I was an intruder. I must try to keep it that way.

"I didn't realise anyone was staying in the house at the moment. Are you a stranded guest? I'm Jason, Jason Murray. I won't shake your hand, given the current rules. . ." He waved, and looked embarrassed, as if accustomed to making contact with people, shaking hands when introduced, hugging friends. He put his hands together, and did a sort of little bow, then straightened and laughed.

My mind began to whir, realising that to not return his introduction, to not offer my own name, would look very odd. I needed to avoid 'odd.'

"I'm Charlie," I mumbled, picking the name of my best friend from school days.

"This lockdown is all very surreal, isn't it?"

I nodded, without really answering. If I could manage to keep things simple, avoid telling lies that I would have to remember in case I was questioned again, so much the better.

"Yes, it is. Do you know the owner, Mrs. . ." My voice trailed away, leaving a gap for him to complete the name. He didn't.

"No, no, never met her. Thought it was a company actually, don't know why, suppose it might be headed up by a woman. But no, they don't ever come here I don't think. They own several properties, rent them out to holiday-makers, have a cleaning woman who comes on a Saturday, after 10 o'clock, when the people have left. That always seems to be the rule, doesn't it? *Out by 10!*" He smiled again, encouraging me to speak, then flushed, realising that perhaps his remark was tactless, implying that I should have left.

I smiled back, pleased that he didn't know the owner, was unlikely to be making any phone calls. Unless he was an exceptionally good liar, but I thought my instinct for spotting lies, honed over the last few years, would easily spot an amateur.

"So, are you stranded here? Not able to get home for the lockdown? What, do you live abroad or something?"

"It's all very weird, isn't it," I said, side-stepping the answer. "But it's a pretty place to be stranded, and at least we have the beach to walk on. As long as we keep away from other people exercising."

"Yes," he was nodding again, his brow creased. "I'm really glad we're still allowed to exercise. Some parts of Europe have had a complete lockdown I've read, they're not allowed outside for anything except to buy emergency supplies." The mention of supplies obviously made him think about the empty supermarket shelves, as he added: "How are you off for supplies? Have you got enough loo roll and things? The shops are all a bit random, aren't they? I might be able to share what I've got, if you get stuck. I was lucky, did a big shop last week, and it's only me here now, so I don't use much, it should last me for a month."

I nodded, thinking it was nice of him to ask me, a stranger, if I needed anything, wondering why someone who seemed so nice was alone. Did he not have a wife, a family?

"Are you not married then?" The words escaped before I could stop them. It was silly, I should be politely ending this conversation, not extending it, finding out about a man who happened to live next door, who seemed kind, and who was definitely attractive; someone who I would hopefully never see again. But the words were out, and I watched him colour again, and lower his head.

"I was," he paused, as if deciding whether to continue, whether to explain to this nosey stranger. Then he added, "My wife died actually, a couple of years ago. Bit of a shock at the time. . ." His voice trailed away, and he lifted a hand and pushed the curls away from his eyes, a futile gesture as the curls bounced straight back again.

"Oh, I'm so sorry. I didn't know," I stopped. Another stupid thing to have said, of *course* I wouldn't have known. There seemed to be something about this man that was making me foolish. Perhaps I had been too long without human contact, without even a normal conversation about the weather to sustain me.

He looked up at me, smiled again, and it was like the sun coming out on a cloudy day.

"No worries. I should be getting over it now, really, it's a long time ago now. But it does mean," another flash of that smile, "that I have a mountain of loo rolls should you ever be desperate!"

I shook my head and thanked him. "I think I'm okay. The only thing I can't seem to find is hand sanitiser."

"Ah well, I can't help you with that. Sanitiser sold out here weeks ago, as soon as those first reports about the virus spreading in Brighton—I think people figured if it was at one seaside town, it could be at all of them.

"But have you got soap? I think just washing your hands thoroughly with soap and water does the trick. Our lovely PM says we should sing 'Happy Birthday' through twice while we do it. Not quite sure why we're being taught how to wash our hands, I think I learnt that in primary school, but perhaps some people missed that lesson."

I smiled back, nodding, wondering if his comment about 'our lovely PM' was sarcastic, or if he was a fan. Not that it mattered, I was never going to see him again, he was simply a stranger and this was a one-off conversation. His views were unimportant.

"Hey listen Charlie, shall we plan to do something at the weekend? I think the forecast is good, it should be dry at any rate. Do you have bread?" His tone was excited, as if he'd just thought of something. I nodded, wondering where this was going.

"Let's have a barbecue! I mean, obviously we have to keep our distance, you on your side of the fence, me on mine. But if I cook the food, the virus can't survive heat, and I could pass the hot food over to you, and you can use your own bread and sauce—do you have sauce?"

I shook my head.

"Okay, well, you can either trust mine, or go and buy some. But we could manage something, couldn't we? Have a shared barbecue, bit of a natter over the fence? It would make the day less boring. I could get some cans of beer—do you drink beer?" He paused, and flushed red again. "Or am I being too pushy? Hey listen, I probably am. Ignore me, you'll be worrying about this strange man who lives next door who you've only just met who is now inviting you to share a barbecue across the fence. In fact, even saying it like that makes me realise just how weird I sound! Honestly, don't be frightened. I truly am not a weirdo— well, not one you need to worry about anyway! It was just I was feeling all sort of unsettled and lonely and hating the thought of a weekend stuck here completely isolated. Then I saw you, and realised I wasn't so isolated after all. Having someone live next door feels so much nicer than living alone next to an empty house. And I guess I sort of got carried away, and wasn't thinking straight, so bounced straight into an idea without thinking about how it must seem to you. Sorry. . ."

He stopped, as if run out of steam. But I rather liked him, this impetuous stranger with the deep blue eyes, and his manner was so friendly, so completely unthreatening, that I found myself smiling and reassuring him, and even though it was a completely stupid thing to do in the circumstances, even agreeing with him.

"No, no, I don't think it's weird at all. I think it sounds lovely. I feel unsettled too, like all the things I trusted have changed, so a barbecue, thinking about something other than this virus for a couple of hours would be lovely. Really, I think it's a great idea. I will check on my sauce supplies immediately!"

I smiled, feeling suddenly happy. Perhaps I had been starved of normal conversation for too long, perhaps it was the constant worries being circulated round and round the news reports, or perhaps I was just fed up with behaving like a recluse. I began to look forward to the weekend, and even to flirt a little.

"Besides, I think I'll be safe enough with the fence between us," I joked. "If you turn out to be a weirdo I can easily run inside and lock the door—or threaten to cough on you!"

He grinned back.

"Oh that's great! Made my day. I was feeling a bit deflated actually, the whole lockdown thing unsettled me, even though I can work from home. It's just the thought of it, you know, not seeing people, not being able to meet up at the pub or go to church, or have people round for a barbecue." He stopped, and smiled.

I was beginning to realise that I had found someone almost as desperate for human conversation as I was. I decided it couldn't hurt. We were going to be stuck in adjacent houses for at least the next three weeks, and if he was available for chatting, I was not going to complain. It was, I told myself, safe enough. I could enjoy his company, and then, when lockdown ended I could move on, find another house, get a job, start my life anew. I need never see him, this man next door, ever again.

We chatted a little longer, and then I returned to the house. I felt unsettled, but something inside was singing. I wondered what exactly I thought I was doing.

Chapter Ten

Saturday dawned bright and clear. I stretched the curtains wide, and looked outside, no longer worried about being seen by the neighbours. In their eyes I was legitimate now, at least for the time being: a stranded tourist forced to shelter in her holiday home until lockdown ended.

Of course, it was a completely different situation should the owner or cleaner happen to visit, and I was still being cautious with my belongings. My bag was at all times stowed in a cupboard in the downstairs washroom— somewhere that I could attempt to retrieve it if I arrived back from a shopping trip and found someone in the house.

After showering, I turned to my clothes. I had a whole range of three outfits to choose from, each one carefully washed by hand in soapy water after being worn. I had hoped to go online, and order more things, but not until I had a job, and that looked further away than ever now. Although I thought Cromer would have enough casual work for me to find something fairly easily, especially during the summer months, I daren't risk catching the virus. Staying secluded, avoiding people, seemed like the only safe option, which meant my wardrobe must suffice for a little longer.

I sighed, wanting to look nice for this barbecue for two, even though I knew the friendship was a temporary one. I chose a pink dress with blue flowers. It looked like something my grandmother might have worn, but it was the least creased of all my clothes. I added a blue cardigan, and looked even more like a grandmother, but it was too cold for bare arms, even in the sunshine. It hung slightly loose, I had lost weight since I left home. I went to the mirror, clutching an eye-liner and mascara tube. Forbidden fruits. I couldn't resist when I saw them in the supermarket, not when I had a reason to look nice; instead of blending into the background, I wanted to be noticed by someone. And I *did* want to be noticed, I realised. Even though I knew there was no future in the friendship, and despite giving a false name and lying about why I was there, I wanted something of the real me to be seen. When not forbidden, I wore make-up, it was part of who I was, and that tiny part of me, at least, could be genuine.

I ate a breakfast of toast and jam, selecting a small tea plate from the stack of four in the cupboard. The crockery in the house was pretty, designed with blue flowers across the creamy surface, and there were four of everything: four dinner plates, four tea plates, four cups and saucers, four mugs. Even the cutlery drawer had four of each utensil, and I wondered how inconvenient that would be, if a family of four were hiring the house, as they would be sure to need to keep washing up odd knives and teaspoons so they had enough. But for one person, who was washing and replacing everything as she went, it was perfect.

I picked up my breakfast, carrying the knife and jam pot with me to the sitting room, placing them on the coffee table while I ate. I didn't have butter, as I had decided not to risk putting things into the fridge. If I needed to leave fast, things left in the fridge would betray me. My ability to live without leaving a trace was improving.

I had bought the groceries at the supermarket, queueing outside with the well-spaced people. Another man was wearing a surgical mask—just the one person again, and people stared at him, and I could see he felt awkward. I wondered if his wife had insisted. I decided I would try to buy one myself, but there were none in the shop, and when I asked an assistant she had said there were none, and she had spent a whole evening online trying to find them, and couldn't I make one? There was lots online about making them from old bras. I didn't tell her that I no longer had any old bras, I simply finished my shopping and came back to the house.

Although I was relatively relaxed, my ears were constantly attuned to the front door. If I heard it opening, I would grab my plate, knife, jam pot and mug of black coffee, and be out of the back door in seconds. Any intruder (who in reality would be the rightful occupant) would see nothing amiss unless they actively searched for it. (Until they entered the downstairs bathroom of course, there was no hiding that broken window, patched up with masking tape and an old cardboard box.) When I wasn't in my bed, the linen was rolled up and stored in the correct cupboard. When I ate, I carried all the dirty crockery with me, washing it and replacing it in the correct places as soon as I had finished eating. I thought that my only weakness was when I showered, as for those few minutes I was deaf to anyone entering the house. But I was still waking at dawn, which I considered the least likely time for a visit. I hoped to be lucky. I had been so far.

***

I knew that Jason was in the garden, preparing, because I heard music through the kitchen window. I smiled, and went to the garden.

Jason was standing in his garden, adding charcoal to a small black barbecue. There was something thoughtful in his face as he added the briquettes to the pieces of wood placed at the bottom, and I wondered how often he barbecued, and whether it might take a long time to warm up. Timothy had been very proficient at barbecues. Timothy was very proficient at everything.

Jason looked up and grinned.

"If this doesn't work, I have a gallon of petrol stored in the shed."

I wasn't entirely sure whether he was joking, so smiled noncommittally and went to the shed in my own garden. There was a chair, and a small round table. I swept off the cobwebs and lugged the table into the garden. It was awkward, and I struggled to put it up. Jason looked over, and saw me wrestle with the catch.

"I could maybe pop round, and put that up for you?" he offered. "You could back away, keep the two metre distance, until I've done it?"

I was about to accept, when the clip snapped apart, and the table legs began to open. I pulled it upright and secured the fastening on the underside. I went to collect the chair.

When the coals were hot, Jason cooked, and I chatted, standing away from where the smoke wafted over the garden. He was good company, and he told me about his job, and his family, and that he'd lived in Norfolk his whole life but didn't move to Cromer until he was married. I watched the meat turn from pink to black, and realised that the heat was too hot, and that he should squirt some water on the coals to cool them slightly. But I said nothing. This man was not Timothy, and I discerned that perfection was less important to him. There was something terribly relaxing about watching someone completely mess up what they were doing and not care at all. Jason turned the blackened sausages, the fat hissed and spat on the flames.

He placed a round piece of wood onto the fence post, hammered a nail into the top to secure it, and then backed away.

"There! A sort of in-between table, so we can pass things without having to compromise the social distancing rules."

He placed a plate on the fence-table, and then gestured towards the meat.

"How do you like your sausages? Burnt or burnt?"

"Oh, I just love them when they have a layer of black on the outside," I laughed.

"Perfect, you will love these then," he said, and placed three, very black, sausages onto the plate.

Even washed down with the can of beer he'd provided, they were practically inedible, but it didn't matter. It didn't matter at all. As I listened to his stories, looked at his face with those deep blue eyes, I enjoyed stepping briefly from my own life into the world of everyone else; I felt human again.

We met often after that. Sometimes I would be in the house, staring at my phone, checking the latest figures for the spread of the virus, or how many people had died, I would hear noises from the adjoining garden. I would stop confirming the symptoms, turn away from the gloom of the news-feed, and go to see what Jason was doing. I watched as he trimmed a bush, inexpertly chopping randomly at branches, or knelt at a flower bed, digging up weeds; I would call hello, and he would greet me with a smile, and we would talk.

"Did you know there's a zoo in Cromer?"

I shook my head.

"There used to be a different one, years ago, when my dad was a kid, and he told us stories about hearing a tiger roaring at night, when he was trying to sleep. Apparently it was owned by the daughter of a famous clown, from a circus, which I think is quite cool!"

He finished pulling up a particularly stubborn dandelion, and tossed it onto a heap of weeds next to him, straightening up and wiping his grubby hands on the back of his jeans. He looked across the fence at me, lost in his childhood memories.

"Do you like circus clowns? I know they get a lot of bad press now, with horror stories about them and things, but I always loved clowns when I was a kid. My sister didn't though. I remember going to a circus once, as a birthday treat, and my sister told me that only babies like clowns, and we had a right old barney and my parents told us off, so we all arrived at the circus tent not speaking and glaring at each other. I guess that's just kids though, isn't it. All siblings argue. Do you have siblings?"

I bent down to a daisy at my own feet, and start to pull at the petals, letting them fall to my feet.

***

I am with my sister. She wants to share some chocolate that I have been given for my birthday, and I refuse to share. She shouts, and tells me that people should share treats. It is what she has been told. But I don't want to. This is my chocolate, a gift from my uncle, my favourite bar, and not for sharing. I turn away from her, and she tries to grab it, then begins to yell, shouting that it's not fair, people should share. She tries to pinch me, and I feel her tugging at my hair. My mother arrives.

"Can't you just give her some?" she says. "You know that Gracie doesn't understand, and she won't eat her tea later if she's upset."

I think that Gracie does understand. I think that when it comes to manipulating humans, my five-year-old sister is actually rather adept. But my mother is pleading now, her sad eyes wearing me down, and my sister is hurting me, digging her nails into my forearm. I look at the chocolate, it doesn't taste like a treat any more. I sigh, and pass the bar to my sister.

"Here," I say, "you can finish it."

***

I looked up from the flower I had picked and saw that Jason was watching me.

"Yes, I have a sister," I told him. "But we never argued much."

"Lucky you," he said, turning back to his flower bed and picking up a fork. He began to scratch at the soil, turning it over, throwing out weeds as he went.

"Maybe we should visit the zoo, when all this is over," he suggested. "If it's still open that is. I read online that they're having problems financially, that their only income is from ticket sales, and they don't have the money to feed the animals while they're shut. They've appealed to restaurants for any leftover food they might have, so they can feed the fruit to the animals. But I don't know," he stopped, and shook his head. "I think the restaurants themselves will be struggling, and I can't see a quick end to this. We're all worried about the virus, but the economy is going to be hard hit by this. I'm just not sure that smaller businesses will survive. . ."

I nodded, thinking about my own depleted finances. I wasn't entirely sure how I would survive either.

***

On one occasion, I arrived in the garden to find a gift waiting for me on the little round table. It was wrapped in wrinkled blue paper, and had *Charlie* written in marker pen across the middle. I picked it up, bemused, and saw Jason coming from his kitchen door.

"Ah, you found it," he said, walking towards me. "I thought perhaps we could try something less athletic, prove to you that I am more than a failed athlete. . . and artist. . . and cook!"

I grinned. We had enjoyed several shared activities since the burnt barbecue, and each one had been a disaster for Jason. A few days before, we had played tennis, using the fence as a net, each standing in our own garden. It had been energetic, and funny, with several dives into shrubs and precarious avoiding of flower beds. But I had won easily, Jason was no athlete. As I scored point after point, he had wailed and groaned, his eyes laughing. It interested me, this security that allowed him to fail so happily.

I turned to my gift, peeling away the paper, pleased with the treat. It was a book. My fingers traced the title, as I listened to him explain.

"You said that you like reading, and mentioned you hadn't read this one, so I ordered a couple of copies—one for you and one for me. We can read them, a few chapters each evening, and then chat about them. A sort of book club for two. You don't mind?"

I looked up, his expression was unsure, as if hoping the gesture won't be misinterpreted. It was a little early in our friendship for gifts. I knew that he had noticed my limited wardrobe, my cheap outfits, my frugal food when we 'shared' picnics across the fence. He had noticed that I spent very little money and had guessed correctly that I had none to 'waste' on a novel, so had risked buying one as a gift. It was a kind thought, and I felt tears suddenly rush to my eyes. It was a long time since I had been aware of anyone being kind to me, a long time since I had received a treat, something without obligation attached. I blinked away the tears, hoping that he hadn't noticed, and smiled across the fence.

"Thank you, that is really kind. And no, I haven't read this one, though I have seen a film of it, I think. A long time ago." I stare at the classic: *A Tale of Two Cities*. "It looks interesting," I said.

"Well, let's hope it doesn't rain, and we could meet here tomorrow afternoon, and chat about the first few chapters? Will you have time to read some by then? I've got a couple of work phone calls in the morning, but I should be able to take an hour off about two?"

I nodded.

He smiled and relaxed slightly, and I realised he had been worried about the idea, not sure how I would react. But I was genuinely pleased. We had discussed reading, and I had mentioned that I liked Dickens, it was nice that he had listened. I stroked the book, thinking how lovely it would be to become absorbed in a story, in a fantasy world, to hide for a few hours from everything that was real. Jason was talking, moving the conversation on, as though he wanted to forget about the potential awkwardness of the gift, and check that our friendship was still easy.

"Have you seen the news today? The PM has been taken into hospital. Did you know?"

I nodded, having already seen the headline.

"Yes, it makes me feel a bit, I don't know, insecure. I mean, I don't know him or anything, not even sure how much I like him, but he seemed to be leading from the front—do you know what I mean? He *seemed* to have a handle on what should happen in the UK, even if he didn't really. And we need a strong leader at the moment, even a bad one is better than nothing—not that I'm saying he's bad," I added, unsure of Jason's politics. "So it's unsettling that he's in hospital. I don't know why." I stopped.

I *did* know why, it was because my whole world was tipped upside-down and this was one more uncertainty to cope with. But I couldn't say that without having to explain what I meant, and I didn't want to lose Jason's friendship. Not yet.

"Yeah, I know what you mean," he was saying, nodding his head and looking concerned. "It's not good is it? Poor chap. I hope he doesn't die."

I nodded, a sudden pain in my chest. I knew that it was because he had mentioned dying, and death, even death of a stranger, will always remind me of my father, and the last time I saw him.

I glanced again at the book, and waved it in Jason's direction, wanting to show that I appreciated his kindness.

"Thanks for this," I said again. "It was really kind of you. I don't remember the last time that I was given a surprise gift!"

But behind my smiling face was a sharp recollection, and I realised that I did remember another gift, and it had not brought me any pleasure. . .

***

I am using the toilet and Timothy enters. I don't like this, his presence in the bathroom feels like an intrusion into privacy, and he sees my scowl and rebukes me. We are lovers, there must never be anything hidden between us, no locks on doors, no secret friendships, no conversations with others that we don't later repeat, word-for-word to each other. When we married, we became one person, and therefore I must never hide from him. We have had this conversation before. I nod.

I don't like his eyes constantly on me as I finish using the toilet, and I try to dispel the feeling of unease. It is good that he wants to be with me, that he loves me so much that he likes to watch me in the bathroom, or when I shower, likes to give advice if I am using too much shampoo, or have the temperature too warm. I tell myself I am happy under his gaze, lucky to have such attention from the man who I love. I remind myself how much I would hate it if the opposite were true, if he never noticed me.

We leave the bathroom, and Timothy shows me a package that has arrived. He unpacks the bubblewrap, and shows me square white cubes of plastic. They are cameras. He places them around the house, a few in each room. He shows me that they connect to his phone, so that when he is at work, or shopping, he can be watching me, checking that I am all right. He loves me so much that he wants to be with me all the time, and now he can be, now even when his body is elsewhere, he can see me. I smile, ignoring the lump of confusion inside, pushing away the ungrateful feeling that I don't want to be watched all the time, the selfish thought that I like privacy sometimes. He is my husband, and I am lucky to be so loved.

I try to joke about his motives, suggesting that he is like James Bond, and will burst through a window to save me! He smiles at me above the sheet of instructions, before returning to the business of how to set up the cameras, and where is the best place to have them. He asks me to walk along the hallway, and I make it into a game, walking like a model on a catwalk, hips thrust forward, swaying with each step.

When I return to the kitchen, Timothy shows me my image, stored on his phone. I watch myself walk, away from the camera, my head held high. It feels very odd to be watching myself, and I want to ask him to not turn on the cameras while I am in the house, to only use them when he's worried about security. But I say nothing. I have learnt that it is easier to say nothing, and the result is invariably the same. To disagree means constant discussion and heated debate until I acquiesce, agree that he was right all along, and I am happy with his decision.

He discusses again the app we both have on our phones, so we can see where the other person is all the time. He reminds me that I forgot to take my phone last time that I visited the supermarket. This is an indication that I don't love him properly, if I love him I will take greater care to keep my phone with me at all times, wherever I am going; in case he needs to contact me, so he can protect me. I nod, apologising again even though I said that I was sorry last week. In my heart, I know that sometimes I will leave my phone at home because I will forget it; sometimes I will leave it because I rebel at being monitored so closely. I quell these feelings, and am thankful that my husband is so attentive.

He moves the discussion on to other failings at the supermarket. I bought the wrong cereal again. I want to tell him that I like eating that cereal, it is one I have eaten since I was a child, but I know he will remind me that I am not a child now, he saved me from my immaturity, and I must eat a cereal with less sugar. He has selected *Weetabix* for us. This is the only cereal I will buy in future. I will learn to like it, like I am learning to like grapefruits and coffee and marmalade. It is good to eat foods that my husband likes, it shows we are united. He says it will be healthy, and it is important I remain healthy, for when I am pregnant. This is the first time he has mentioned having children. I remain silent.

We then discuss my internet history. We share a computer, plus Timothy has his own laptop, which he uses for work—this obviously contains confidential material, and therefore the password is denied me. Our shared computer is mine to use as I wish. He regularly checks the browsing history, and has also read an email I deleted. I do not know why the deleted email was still available for him to read, but I will try to investigate later, for now I must justify why I deleted it when we share everything, and have no secrets. Why was it necessary for my to write to my mother, telling her about our recent holiday and letting her know that we are home? This will imply that I miss her, that being married is not sufficient and I need other people. My mother might even misinterpret the email, and think it was an invitation to visit. Do I want my mother, who has never put me first, to visit? I do not. I do not want anyone to visit, I am content with my husband.

He asks why I did an internet search for dahlias. I explain that I was wondering when to plant the flowers, that I thought perhaps I might buy some for the garden. He asks why I want dahlias, who do I know that grows dahlias? Do I think his planning of the garden is inadequate in some way? I assure him the garden is perfect. The dahlias were just a whim. He indulges me, and strokes my cheek, and says I am sweet, but I don't need to worry about changing anything in the house and garden. I smile. I am lucky he is so good to me.

Chapter Eleven

At 2 o'clock, I was waiting. I had pulled the garden chair to what I estimated to be a metre away from the fence, near the little round table that Jason had made. He was late, so I continued reading while I waited. It was a sunny afternoon, though chilly, and I pulled my coat around my shoulders while I waited. I had a slight headache, and felt out-of-sorts, which I attributed to a restless night. I hoped this would be fun, discussing the book. It would, I thought, at least provide an excuse for more interaction, more time spent chatting, and that was something I found I looked forward to, a bright spot in my empty life.

Although I knew the story of *A Tale of Two Cities* from films, I had never before read the book, and it wasn't as easy as I had hoped. I wished that I hadn't boasted quite so freely about my reading taste, and that I had admitted that although I was a prolific reader, I devoured thrillers and detective stories rather than the classics. I had read *Oliver Twist* when I was still at school, but only because it was a compulsory book, not because I had chosen it. I had wanted Jason to think I was an intellectual, not a silly girl who had bombed out of school, so I had mentioned the only classical author I knew, and tried to remember something interesting to say.

When Jason arrived he was carrying a bottle of red wine and two mugs. I had read the beginning of the book last night, stumbling over unfamiliar expressions—*epoch, superlative, environed.* But I had read enough to understand the significance of earthen mugs and the red wine, and I smiled, thinking that perhaps I had understood enough to appear vaguely intelligent.

Jason lifted the mugs and grinned.

"Do you understand? Did you get as far as chapter five, when the wine cask bursts and all the poor people rush out with mugs to collect the wine? I love that bit, the descriptions of everyone scrabbling on the cobblestones, the wine flowing down the street, people grabbing anything to hand so they can drink it and it won't be wasted. You can almost *see* the scene when you read it, can't you?"

I smiled, pleased that I at least knew what he was talking about, even if I didn't quite share his enthusiasm.

Jason poured the wine into the mugs and left one on the round table for me to collect while he set up a chair and smiled at me over the fence. I smiled back and sipped the wine, hoping it wouldn't make my headache worse or my brain less sharp. I didn't need to impress Jason, but I hoped to not look completely thick. I watched him as he drank some wine, opening his copy of the book with his free hand, turning the pages, his face relaxed, his movements easy.

Suddenly, I didn't want to deceive him about my understanding of the language, I didn't want to create a role for myself where I was more intelligent, more educated, than I really was. I realised that I had been living a lie for so long, and now I was free, and I was about to embark on another relationship—albeit a brief one—that could either be founded on lies and deception, or truth. At least, as much truth as I was able to share without risking my freedom.

"Actually," I said, lowering both my mug of wine and my gaze, staring intently into the depths of the ruby liquid, "I didn't entirely understand lots of it. I mean, the bits I read. I know the story—about a woman being in love with a good man, and a bad man being in love with her, and the bad man loving her so much that he dies so that she can stay with the good man—which I think is probably the saddest and most romantic story ever written. But the words, like actually reading the book—well I got pretty stuck straight away! I understood: *'It was the best of times, it was the worst of times',* and then it pretty much lost me.

"I mean, I do want to read it and discuss it, I think it will be fun. And I did get past chapter five, so I understand this —" I raised my mug of wine, though still didn't look at him. "But to be honest, I don't even know what an *epoch* is.
. ."

I stopped. I didn't know Jason well enough to predict his response, didn't know if he would be irritated at the money he had wasted buying the books, cross that I wasn't as intelligent as he'd thought. I hoped we could continue our over-the-fence friendship, but now that he knew a little more about who I was—or rather wasn't—I couldn't be sure he would want to. My head was beginning to pound, and I was aware that I was frowning as I looked up.

Jason was not frowning. He was smiling, almost laughing.

"Oh dear, did I scare you by forcing a literary lesson on you? I'm sorry. We can chat about a different book if you'd rather, or a film, or anything really. I just like being with you."

Something inside shifted. This man was so *honest,* so completely open and unembarrassed about his feelings, about who he was. His unthreatening manner was so comforting, I found myself shaking my head, saying that no, I did want to read it and talk about it, it would be good for me; but he would need to explain some of the phrases.

"Well, *epoch* just means a period of time," he said, settling back into his chair and his role as educator. "The first bit is really just clever repeating of the same thing, showing contrasts and being a bit cynical about how people thought everything was normal. It's set during the French Revolution—you knew that?"

I nodded, pleased that he was no longer assuming knowledge. The film I had watched, curled on the sofa with a packet of fruit gums while my mother cooked dinner, had been full of death, people being executed, rich people betrayed by their servants, crowds standing to watch the deaths.

I thought about our own times, of the coffins in Italy that had been on the news, the army driving them away on trucks. I had watched the grim scenes on the television, I thought, in the same way as Dickens' characters had watched their contemporaries dying. Death today was more furtive—people betrayed by the germs that passed between people, rather than the secrets whispered behind hands, the passing of information in the ancient streets.

Jason was still talking, explaining references to things, telling me they were well-known in the age when the book was written: King George was mad, the Americans had fought for independence and the French had helped them, *Mrs Southcott* was a woman who claimed to have prophecies. These were things that would have been in the newspapers and common knowledge when the story was first published.

"I guess today, it would begin with references to the referendum, a few cynical phrases about Brexit, perhaps something about Harry and Megan leaving for America—that sort of thing."

I listened to his voice, heard the enthusiasm in it as he talked about the descriptions, the oblique references to Dickens' previous writings about spiritualism and people contacting the dead; how when it was written, it was only about a hundred years after the events in the book. It would have been like us today writing a story about the second world war—we would have grown up with stories from grandparents—it would feel distant but not so long ago as to be beyond our grasp.

"Dickens even adds cheeky references to some of his other writing, stuff that's nothing to do with the story but that his readers would recognise and smile at. I think he had fun with this story."

I liked hearing Jason's voice, watching as he drank his wine and offered me another cupful.

"Do you like red wine?" Jason asked, as I shook my head, thinking that it tasted better by the end of the cup but it was still not something I really enjoyed.

"Not much," I admitted, continuing on my quest to be honest. "I probably prefer cola to be honest."

I watched him laugh, he threw back his head and snorted, and I laughed too, then felt the pain in my head throb, and winced.

"Hey, are you alright?"

I nodded. "Just woke up with bit of a headache," I said. "But I'm fine. This is nice. I like sitting here, chatting about something other than the virus. That's all anyone on the news seems to talk about now, isn't it?"

He nodded. "And friends. When people talk online or phone, most of the conversation is about coronavirus, and what will happen, and when the lockdown will end, and how many deaths there have been. It's all a bit unsettling really, isn't it?

"It's the other governments that get me. You know, the few still left in the world who are refusing to admit the virus is anything other than a bad cold. Some countries have no social distancing at all, everyone is crowding into pubs and sports stadiums, infecting everyone else. I cannot imagine what their death tolls will be like. Ours is up to over 6,000 and. . ." He stopped and grinned. "But now I'm doing it too, aren't I? Talking about the virus again. I will stop. Now, which chapter did you read up to? Shall we agree to try and read up to. . . I don't know, how about page fifty. Is that too much do you think?"

I shook my head, wondering if I would understand anything of what I read. My head was beginning to really hurt now, it felt as if my skull was contracting, a hard pain right between my eyes.

"Actually, I'm really sorry, but I think I'd better go in now," I said, hoping that I wouldn't be sick. I could feel the red wine churning in my stomach, a bitter taste in my throat. "I'm really sorry, but my head is killing me. I think I'd better lie down."

"You look very pale," he said, peering at me with concern. "Can I do anything for you? You have pills?"

I stood up, steadied myself, and placed the mug very carefully on the round table. The world suddenly seemed overly bright, and I craved darkness, and to lie flat, and close my eyes.

"Let me have your number," said Jason, pulling out his phone. "Then I can text to make sure you're okay later."

I told him my number, struggling over the numbers, my head pounding and my shoulders hunched as if I could somehow ward off the pain. I left him, hoping that I was managing to be polite, then walked down the path, each step deliberate, forcing myself into the house, up the stairs, to the bedroom. The bedding was rolled up, hidden in the cupboard, and I couldn't summon the energy to reach up and get it. I lay on the bare mattress and longed for sleep.

***

The next day my headache was gone, but I felt wretched—everything ached. I also had a cough, a dry persistent niggle. It wasn't bad, was no more than I might have had after a cold, but all I had read online and seen in the media confirmed my fears. I had almost certainly caught Covid-19.

I tried to think about how I had caught it. Although I had been to the supermarket, I had been cautious, maintaining a strict two metre gap between myself and other customers. I had been careful to never touch my face or eyes or hair, and although I didn't have any gloves, which would have been the best way to ensure I didn't touch my face, I was pretty sure I had managed it. There was still no hand-sanitiser anywhere in the shops, but I was scrupulous about washing my hands whenever I entered the house, even if I had only been in the garden or out for a walk. I wondered if the virus could have been carried here on the few food items I bought. If someone had coughed onto the wrapper of a loaf of bread, conceivably I could have touched it, and transferred it to my food. I had never washed food packaging when I got home, considering the risk to be too tiny to be significant. Maybe I should have done.

I pulled out my phone and sent a text to Jason. It was nice to know there was someone I could tell.

> "Hi, sorry to bomb out yesterday. Slept well, headache gone, but feeling pretty rough and I HAVE A COUGH! Scary news! Probs best to isolate. Symptoms mild. Will read book. Charlie"

I debated whether to add a kiss. It was the natural way to end a text, but would it be misinterpreted? Did I mind if it *was* misinterpreted? I grinned, and added "xx."

The reply came almost immediately.

> "Tough luck. Probs not scary. You're young, only scary for old or ill. Hope you don't feel too bad. Do you need anything? Am going to supermarket, can leave stuff on step."

It was kind of him, and sort of what I had come to expect, even in the short while I had known him. At heart, Jason was a decent bloke. I hated having to deceive him, but knew it would likely end the friendship if he knew the truth.

I thought about my supplies, and my dwindling money. I could always send him a shopping list, with a promise to pay when I was better, and then skip town in a week's time. He would never find me, the amount would be too paltry to interest the police, and it would eek out my money for a bit longer.

I shook my head. Was this who I had become? I *liked* Jason, he was a nice person and had only ever been kind to me. I wouldn't become a thief—not a proper one, I told myself, even if I was in fact stealing from the house-owner simply by being here. I thought about my half loaf of bread, and my pot of jam, some pasta and the three apples in my bag. They would have to do for now. I wasn't really hungry anyway.

I spent the next five days coughing and reading, and trying to ignore the knot of hunger that settled somewhere under my ribs. Jason was a constant friend, sending me jokes, telling me about his day. In return, I sent updates on my exploration of *A Tale of Two Cities*. The two main characters looked very similar, and one saves the other in a trial simply by looking like him. It reminded me of the two little girls I had seen in the station washroom, and how I had longed for someone to switch places with me in life.

The ancient story was about wrongful arrests, and people struggling to be free, and the love of Lucie, the heroine. It was, I felt, a beautiful romance set amid the backdrop of a confused society.

On the fifth day I woke feeling much better, and wondered whether it would be safe to walk along the beach. I knew that people were meant to self-isolate for seven days after having symptoms, but I was desperate to go out, and as long as Jason didn't see me, no one would know. I wouldn't go near anyone, there wouldn't be a risk. My phone buzzed.

> "Happy Easter! It's going to be an odd one. I plan to join my church online service via Zoom. Do you want the link? It might make it feel more like Easter. Left something on doorstep. Jason x"

I hadn't even known it was Easter. All the days were identical, even before I was ill it was hard to keep track of the date. Avoiding people meant the days had nothing to define them, time had no structure other than mealtimes, nighttime, and dawn—when I got up to shower. I had become dependent on the sun and dates had become meaningless. Easter. It was Easter Sunday.

I opened the front door. A large Easter egg sat on the mat, purple foil covering the chocolate. I smiled, paused as a coughing fit interrupted me, then stooped to lift it. There was no message, but the gesture was simple and kind, and I hugged it to me, feeling happier than perhaps was merited by one chocolate egg. I carried the egg to the lounge, and picked up my phone to text a thank you, coughing as I pressed the buttons. I wondered whether the gift signified anything more than kindness. I had been quick to notice the kiss added to the end of the text, but that wasn't an abnormal way to sign off. It would though, I thought as I wrote the text and coughed, be rather lovely if Jason did like me. I was aware that I liked him, that it wasn't simply loneliness that made me look forward to our over-the-fence activities. There was something good at the core of him, something that made me feel safe, and it was, I realised, a very long time since I had felt safe.

Another coughing fit overtook me. I decided it was too soon to risk a walk. If I coughed when anyone was in sight, they would notice me—coughing in public had become an indecent thing, something to be avoided. Instead, I turned to the chocolate, my stomach rumbling from eating tiny meals, and my mouth watered as I began to peel back the wrapper. I would read the book again—the pages had been read a few times now, it was the only book I owned, and although there were things online to amuse me, I found the holding of a real book, the turning of pages, to be comforting. I opened the book at random, somewhere near the middle, and began to read again about the hapless Lucie and her shoemaking father. . .

Chapter Twelve

I woke shivering. For a moment, I couldn't remember where I was, or why I was lying on a bare mattress, evening sunlight shining through the window. Gradually I remembered my day, trying to read, nibbling chocolate, then feeling tired—an exhaustion that made even reading an effort, so I had abandoned the downstairs and come to bed for a nap. I felt cold, frozen right through as though I had been standing in the wind for too long. A coughing fit overtook me, and I felt a pain, deep in my lungs. The cough had changed, it wasn't a dry a cough now, and I felt mucous stirring in my lungs. I got out of bed and went to the cupboard. Another paroxysm of coughing delayed me, then I pulled down a second duvet and another pillow. Perhaps if I could sit up slightly, it would ease my lungs. I lay, shivering, feeling the cold in my bones, icy feet, frozen hands.

I don't know how long I lay there, but I was aware of the light fading, and the sky outside the window turning indigo. I could hear the sea, very faint as it pounded the shore, and the wind stirring the trees. Every few minutes a white light swept past, the reflected light from the lighthouse brightening the sky. It penetrated my dreams, which were peopled with coronavirus patients going to the guillotine, and crowds watching, while a spotlight swept over them.

I woke with a shock, my heart thumping because I had been forced to the front of the line, the guillotine was before me.

"She never studied anything at school," the crowd were jeering, *"she doesn't even understand storybooks."*

I lay for a moment, letting the nightmare subside, the ancient people gave way to the outline of furniture in the bedroom, the person pushing me forwards was just the lumpy mattress, digging into my ribs. The lighthouse lit the sky, a sweep of bright, fading to grey; I could hear the sea and wind, mingled as one whisper. Gradually my heartbeat slowed, my dream faded. I had warmed up slightly, though when I lifted my hands to my face they were still very cold; everything ached, my bones hurt, my head hurt, I felt sick. I realised I had a temperature. This was not good, it was definitely a turn for the worse, and I had thought I was almost better. I coughed, and the fit lasted longer than usual, and the pain in my lungs was hard and uncomfortable. I turned onto my right side, but that made the coughing impossibly bad, it was better to lie on my back or my left. My neck ached from lying on two pillows, but when I pushed them to the floor and tried to lie flat, the pain in my chest was unbearable, and the cough consumed me. I tugged the pillows back into place, and leant against them, exhausted.

My heart began to race again, my thoughts a jumble of worry—if the virus was getting worse, then what would happen if my symptoms grew severe, and I needed hospital care? Could I phone a doctor when I wasn't registered with one? What if I couldn't breathe and there was no one to phone for an ambulance? Could I expect Jason to help, when our relationship mainly consisted of jokey texts? Would I die, alone in a borrowed house, not discovered until the cleaner next came to prepare the house for visitors?

I took a breath. There was no point in trying to solve anything, I needed to be sensible, do what was necessary. My mother—oh! how I longed for my mother at that moment—had always been cautious about temperatures, telling us it could be dangerous to let one rise unchecked. I had pills, they were stowed in my bag downstairs. I needed to get them.

I reached for my phone, feeling the need for someone to know I was ill. It was a foolish need, a childish reaching out for another human simply because I felt rotten. My cough made texting difficult, but I managed to write a message, and before I could reason with myself that perhaps it wasn't wise, or ask myself what good purpose it could possibly perform, I sent it.

"Hi, are you awake? I am feeling rotten and need someone in the world to know. Cough back. Hurts. Charlie x"

I eased to a sitting position. I shivered, and considered wrapping the duvet around me while I went downstairs. But I knew I might trip, and a broken ankle would be more serious than whatever was ailing me. I told myself it wouldn't take long, I could take a couple of pills and be back in bed in less than a minute. I hunched my shoulders, forcing myself to stand, and moved over the moonlit floor, through the door, across the landing. I grasped the bannister as I walked downstairs, one step, then another, down to the hallway. My steps were silent, I was worried someone might hear me, and I realised the tendrils of my dream still clung to my mind—there *was* no one to hear me, I reminded myself, no one is waiting to judge me, to hurt me. The floor seemed unsteady, like a boat at sea, and I reached for the wall, using it to guide me. The tiles were cold on my feet.

The kitchen door was open, and I slid through, glad of the moon, which was uncannily bright, casting shadows as I moved to a cupboard, smelt the stale smell as I opened it, pulled down a glass. The room spun, I waited, grasping the solid edge of the sink for support. When my vision cleared, I turned on the tap, filled the glass and set it on the work surface.

The room felt airless, I went to the back door, fumbled with the key, pulled it open. Icy air rushed inside. I trembled pushing the door shut, shivering violently. I then struggled to the washroom for my bag—leaning on the table, the wall, the doorframe, the worktop around the sink unit, bending down to heave the bag from the cupboard. I carried it to the kitchen. The pills were in a side pocket, I found the battered packet, slid the capsules through the foil seal, turned to the water, was disturbed by more coughing, that reached into my lungs and stole my oxygen. The world spun again, a kaleidoscope of fuzzy sparks, and I grabbed at the work surface to steady myself, my flailing hands fell short. The pills fell, I saw the top of the work surface, heard the crack as it made contact with my skull, the floor rose up to slap into my knees and bang hard into my side, and all was black.

The first time I woke I was aware of the floor under my head, the hardness of it pressing into my ribs. I tried to rise, but the dizziness swamped me again, the kitchen fuzzed before my eyes, the queasiness churned in my stomach. I lowered my head, slowly, slowly, told myself I would wait a few seconds, collect my thoughts, then try again.

I could hear the guillotine, rising with a creak, crashing down on the neck with a bang. Another head rolls onto the floor. Creak as it rises, bang as it falls.

"That's not real," I tell myself, there is no guillotine. I heard it creak again, rising to the top of the scaffold. "The door," I tell myself, "it must be the door blowing in the wind."

More coughing, I turned onto my side, waited for it to subside. I could hear the tap, I must have not turned it off properly, and it was dripping, rhythmic plops into the sink, blending with the wind, and the guillotine—which is the door—and the sound of the sea; drip, drip, drip. The sound changed, the drips fall faster, "Like rain," I think, "it is raining now," and I wasn't lying on a cold floor in Norfolk, I was in London, and it was the worst of times. The very worst. . .

***

It is raining. That light, grey rain that only seems to happen in England, when the sky lowers and the world reduces to what can be seen immediately in front of you and to the side. As it becomes stronger, turning from drizzle to proper rain, I start to pull my umbrella from my bag, struggling with the mechanism which refuses to raise the umbrella. With a sigh of frustration, I dip under the shelter of the restaurant next to me, and stand for a moment, struggling with the catch and shaking the umbrella hard, as if to teach it a lesson. It flaps uselessly in my hand, spraying water and refusing to open, the metal struts somehow tangled together so that none can unfold.

The restaurant whose doorway I am sheltering in, is one of those exclusive London ones, full of dark wood and over-weight businessmen. The doorway is curved, allowing a small area of shelter under an overhanging porch, with a long thin window to the side, and a revolving door in front. A man in a green jacket is standing just inside the door, waiting to greet diners, and I turn my back on him, so that I can't see him, while continuing my fight with the umbrella. I glance instead at the long thin window to my side, as I shake my unhelpful umbrella, staring at my reflection, noting the lank hair now wet with rain so that it hangs either side of my face like a limp curtain, one ear protruding. A movement within the restaurant catches my eye, and I find I am looking beyond my own, damp, reflection, and into the restaurant itself. I see round tables and white cloths, and there, one table removed from the window, is Timothy.

Even now, even while the shock causes my mouth to fall open like a simpleton, I am beginning to raise my hand. Part of my mind is thinking to tap on the window, or make a movement that he might notice, to wave a greeting. But before my stupefied body can respond, before the greeting is sent, I see him lean towards his lunch partner, place one hand on her shoulder to draw her near, and I watch him kiss her.

Something in my stomach churns. A sharp point presses hard on my sternum, then twists, winding all my emotions into a tight whirlpool that become tighter and tighter until I can hardly breathe. For some reason beyond logic, I feel that I must not be seen, and I slip from the shelter and hurry towards the station.

The whirlpool inside has tightened into a lump now, that sits heavy in the area between my stomach and my chest, something hot and heavy. It is raining properly but I hardly noticed, moving as an automaton towards the station, passing my ticket through the machine, hurrying onto the platform. I carry my umbrella uselessly in my hand, barely conscious of what I am doing, though my actions to the casual observer would appear rational and normal. I stand for an interminably long wait on the cold platform, waiting for the train to arrive, stepping back to let other passengers pass. All the time the weight inside is pressing down on me, and I can feel a reservoir of tears waiting, patiently, until I allow them to fall. But not yet. While I am here, in public, I must suspend all feelings, ignore the horrible lump inside, behave as if all is normal. The station and passengers and squawking announcements are something from a dream. Only the ball of hurt inside is real, pressing against me. I wonder if I will die. Is this what death feels like?

My train arrives, I sit in the carriage, my face turns to the window, seeing nothing, my mind whirling.

Could I be mistaken? I know I am not. Is there a rational explanation? For eating lunch in a restaurant when he told me that he only ever ate sandwiches at his desk—very possibly. But for meeting and kissing that woman, that cannot be explained away with excuses or reason. There is no doubt, my eyes have not lied, that kiss was not a polite exchange between colleagues, that was the embrace of lovers.

The word lover makes the tears rush into my eyes, and I blink away their sting, staring up at the ceiling so that none can fall. Not here, not on a train, where onlookers will see me and form opinions, or worse, someone known to me might happen to arrive, see the betraying red-blotched face, ask what is wrong. No, I must keep everything inside, held close, until later.

We reach my station, I find the car, mercifully seeing no one who I recognise in the car park, and I slide into the driver's seat. I throw my bag onto the seat next to me, and find I am still clutching the umbrella, as though it could somehow solve something, perhaps magically open and everything I have witnessed will fade away like a dream. But it is not a dream, it is horribly real, and when I am home, when I am hidden and safe, I will allow myself to react, to think about it, and what it might mean.

How I drive home, I do not know. I must pause at traffic lights, indicate around corners, avoid other cars, but although some part of my body drives, my brain is not involved. I cannot tell you whether I pass anyone, or how I manage to leave the car park and pull into our driveway unscathed—but I do.

I walk into the empty house, peeling damp clothes from my body as I walk. Along the hallway, shedding shoes and coat; dumping my bag and umbrella at the foot of the stairs; up the steps, my cardigan hangs on the bannister, my skirt stepped out of on the landing, tights ripped as I tug them off in the bedroom, blouse is discarded next to the bed, underwear abandoned on the bathroom floor.

The shower is too hot, steam rising, my skin scalded under the flow, as I huddle on the plastic base and clutch at my stomach. Great heaving breaths rise up, forcing their way from my mouth as sob after sob is heaved from me, as though they will rip my body apart, while torrents of tears flow unchecked down my cheeks, washed away by the shower, ineffectual even in their passion.

I have no idea how long I stay in that shower, waiting for the anguish to subside, for the lump inside to dissipate. Neither happen, the only result is a headache from the intensity of my emotion and a sore throat from the sobs that wrack forth. Eventually, as the water becomes tepid and unwelcoming, I realise that crying does not alleviate my sadness, neither tears nor the shower can wash away the hurt. I step from the shower and pull a towel from the rail. A red-eyed stranger stares at me from the mirror, grey-skinned and puffy. No wonder, I think, he was looking elsewhere for love—can there be a plainer woman in the country? I walk to the bed, pull the duvet over my damp body, and will myself to sleep. Perhaps, if by some miracle I can sleep, can fall from consciousness, things will seem better when I wake.

But my whirling thoughts and the pain inside will not allow me to sleep. I am wondering when he met her, whether their affair is a long-term thing, how many lies I have believed during the forming of their relationship.

I glance at the time. He will be home in two hours. Some sense of self-preservation warns me that I should say nothing, reveal no trace of my pain. A confrontation will achieve nothing, especially as I am unsure as yet, what I want. I cannot turn back time, undo what I have seen, obliterate the past. Timothy is having an affair, and the world is different and can never return to what it was. I will never be the same person again, and talking will not change that. If he apologises, tells me it is a casual thing, easily ended, I will still be this grotesque figure, forever warped inside. But I don't think that the conversation will flow that way.

I know Timothy will turn his anger on me in his defence. It will become my fault, I should never have been in London, should never have seen him. He will insinuate that I have been spying, that my jealousy has clouded my judgement and that what I think I have seen is not true. And I might, after the slow drip of constantly being told this, week after relentless week, begin to believe him. My mind will begin to accept his words as true and deny what I have seen, what I am now feeling.

Yet I know that my feelings are justified, and I hug them to me, determined to remember, to not be persuaded into some altered truth where I am the transgressor. No, it is better to say nothing, to hide the hurt, to behave as if all is normal, until I decide what to do.

I am an actor, an empty shell that plays a part. My mouth smiles, my body responds, my brain engages; but inside I am dying, carrying a burden of burning hurt. It never leaves me, the lump lodged somewhere between my stomach and heart, a bitter ball of distrust and wariness. It infects what I see and hear, making me ever aware, looking for evidence that I had seen correctly, wanting to understand the facts, needing to know that I had not imagined what I saw, or mistaken a stranger for my husband.

Although my head acknowledges the truth of the events, for some weeks afterwards, my heart rebells, makes excuses, tries to convince me that I am mistaken. But over time, as I analyse his responses, measure the time when he is absent and compare it to how long his errands should take, I begin to feel more certain. The prisoner observed has become the watcher.

I know of course, that my own surveillance is still in place, and that everything I do is monitored. I use what I saw him do to turn spy, to collect my own data. I spend long hours at the shared computer, clicking unused icons, discovering how to access the computer history, how to destroy items already deleted so they couldn't be examined by someone else, how to view the computer's internet history—to see which sites have been visited. I then research how to reinstate deleted files, visit folders on this computer and view emails which survive on the server after they have been removed from the device. I am practising.

I study online, I discover that a WhatsApp message can be retrieved, even when deleted from a device, by deleting the entire app and then reinstalling it—all the previous messages restored for me to read.

I become adept at walking soundlessly, at entering rooms unnoticed, my eyes straining to see passwords as they are entered, to silently record them in my mind. Whenever a phone or computer is left unattended, I hurry to check whether he has logged out, whether on this occasion he has been careless, allowing me access to his private files, to scroll through his emails. He is careful, I have few opportunities. I learn how to appear disinterested whilst watching what he types. Gradually, I learn the password to open his phone. I commit it to memory.

One sunny afternoon, while he mows the lawn, his phone lies forgotten in his coat pocket. I pull it out. I can hear the mower, droning across our tiny lawn. I do not have long. I enter the password, the home screen appears. I begin to search.

I discover his phone has a facility that suggests addresses to email—those that he uses most regularly, and I plan to use the internet cafe in the town to write an innocuous correspondence, waiting for a reply, to discover who is in communication with my husband. I write down the addresses.

I delete his WhatsApp, then reinstall it. I am careful, making a list first of each message, so that when I have read the freshly installed messages I can delete the ones he will expect to have disappeared. I am thorough, a cautious spy. The mower stops. I rush to return the phone to its original settings, and slip it back into his pocket. I hear him calling me. I kneel down, pretend to be searching for an earring that I lost earlier. He stoops to help me, ever the attentive husband. I want to believe him, want for what I saw to not be true. But I know I must continue to gather evidence, to be sure, to verify facts and learn what can be trusted.

I know to block the camera, the watching eye in the corner of each room, easily covered with a square of muslin that I keep in my pocket. I hear Timothy mutter late at night, and know he is checking the footage from the cameras, angry that they have an intermittent fault and blank for a few minutes occasionally.

On one occasion, while he is occupied for longer than usual in the toilet, I find his laptop has been left running, the screen still open. There is no need to enter a password, he has already done that, the applications are available for use. I begin to press keys, desperate that the screen shouldn't lock after a period of disuse, all the while my ears straining for sounds of the washroom door being opened.

I scroll though his accounts, scanning his emails with my eyes, the figures and letters swimming before me as I try to absorb as much information as possible. I glance through his emails, pausing over the ones sent to individuals rather than groups. I open his deleted mail, go to 'folder,' click on 'retrieve deleted emails.' The computer whirs. I listen beyond the electronic noise, listening to the house, for warning signs of his approach. All is quiet.

The retrieved files appear in a box, and I begin to scroll down the list, opening any sent to an individual. They do not make for easy reading. I am never mentioned, our life together does not exist, instead there are appointments, he will collect her from her office, or meet her in the restaurant—she can choose this time, it's her turn, they always eat at X, his favourite place, would she prefer somewhere new?

Times when I thought he was working turn out to be time with her: walks in a park, coffee in a cafe, a snatched lunch between meetings. I read on, learning how he writes to her, eavesdropping on their online conversation, which is formal in style, perhaps a work colleague would read nothing untoward in the exchange, yet I know, I know because I have seen, that the formality ends when they meet.

I pause. Still no sounds from the house.

I then stumble on the icon which controls the house cameras and open the files. They are all there, listed in date order, the image and sound from every camera in the house.

I turn, glance towards the door. There is no noise from the washroom. I turn back to the computer, and begin to open the files, my fingers flying to mute the sound. I watch myself preparing meals, dressing, cleaning. But other cameras have captured Timothy's image, as he read the paper, checked the post, replaced my tablets with new ones.

My heart is racing. Still no sound from the bathroom. I return to my investigation, find an image of him using the telephone. On the screen, I see him frown, glance towards the door and move to close it, before speaking. There is something furtive in the gesture, his face is tense, he pushes his hair from his eyes. I recognise the signs of his tension, know that he had not wanted me to overhear that phone call.

I turn again towards the bathroom. Still silence. My mouth dry, I press to rewind the video, and gradually, hardly daring to breathe, I raise the volume, single click by single click, until at last my straining ears can discern the metallic recording of Timothy's voice. It is a call to a lover, the arranging of a liaison, the voicing of endearments. As I listen to *my* husband, *my* lover's voice as it caresses another, as he laughs—oh how that laugh cuts through me —that lump inside contracts still further.

On the video, Timothy glances up as he laughs, his eyes shining, his expression joyful. He sees the camera—is now looking straight towards it, towards me, and I read happiness and contentment in his face. He reaches out, towards the camera, towards me, and places something against it, so the screen I am watching goes blank. He didn't want his special moment recorded, and it feels as though he hadn't wanted *me* to see. Even though he wouldn't have suspected that one day I would view the footage, it still feels personal, as if I have been purposefully excluded.

I press stop. I had thought that I made my husband happy, and perhaps I did; but I am not alone. Others make him happy too and that laugh, that carefree laugh which I associate with our special times, with memories when we were alone and having fun, that does not after all belong to me. His expression in the video is one I have seen often, one I bask in, when I know that he is truly happy and having fun, an expression I thought was shared only between us, but I was wrong. It is shared with another, and I wonder if anything that I had thought was mine, reserved exclusively for me as his wife, was ever mine alone.

Sounds of flushing come from the bathroom, the running of water, the faint tap of a footstep on tiles.

I hasten to close files, shut programs, return the computer to its previous state.

A door clicks open as my fingers fly over keys, I lower the screen.

Footsteps come nearer. I glide from the office, leaving the door ajar, run into the lounge, flop onto a sofa, lift a magazine. I look up and smile as Timothy enters the room, and wonder if he can hear the thud of my heart, the catch in my voice, as I tell him that dinner will soon be ready.

Chapter Thirteen

I felt Timothy kneel beside me. His hands touched my hand, then my forehead. I can feel him, next to me on the hard kitchen floor, and I want to sit up; I try to speak, to explain that I just came down for some pills and I didn't mean to wake him. But my throat is too dry, and I cannot speak, my brain can't make the words come.

I heard him move away, and I imagine him looking round, I hear his footsteps as he walks to the doorway, the light snaps on. I gasp, the light wounds my eyes, blinding me and stabbing into my brain.

"Sorry, sorry, but I need to see," he says.

I stop breathing and listen. It is not Timothy's voice, it is Jason. I am not at home, I am in someone else's holiday cottage, and I am on the floor because I fainted. Did I leave the back door unlocked? I must have done. My past and present are mingling, I am too weak to keep them separate, the memories and the current situation are tangled together, I can't be sure where one ends and the other begins; reality and thoughts have morphed into one uncomfortable lump. I cough and try to focus on Jason's face. It is obscured by a cloth, which he has tied across his nose, so it covers the lower part of his face. He looks like a cowboy from an old Western movie.

"I think I fainted," I say at last, then I can't think of any other words. I know that I should say more, try to explain, but my body is rebelling, refusing to even let me lift my head.

"You're burning up," he says, "have you taken anything?"

I wait a moment, summoning energy.

"Charlie! Charlie, you have to help me a little here. Have you taken anything?" His voice is persistent, there is an edge to it and I wonder if he is angry.

"That's not my name," I start to say, then I stop. It's the name I told him. I need to focus, to sort out what is real and what is not. Jason is not Timothy. I am not at home.

"I didn't take anything," I manage to say. "I dropped them."

I have a moment of clarity: "You shouldn't be here, I might be ill. You'll catch it, I should self-isolate."

"It's too late now," he says, something determined in his voice. "Besides, you need help and there's no one else here."

I listen to his footsteps as he crosses the floor, then returns, and places his arm under my shoulders.

"Here," he says, passing me a glass of water and two paracetamol. "Take these, then I'll help you upstairs."

I am obedient. I swallow. I allow myself to be helped to my feet. I cough, bending forwards, the pain wracking through me, the world spins; but his arms are very strong and he supports me, waits until I am steady, then helps me to walk. I cling to the bannister as we ascend the stairs, and I am aware of the weirdness of the situation, of me guiding an almost-stranger to a bedroom that doesn't belong to me.

We enter the bedroom and I feel Jason pause, as if taking stock of the room. I realise the bare mattress and the uncovered duvet are not what he expected to see, and I wonder what I should say. But my head is too muddled, and my body is aching to lie down. He helps me across the room, and I slide onto the bed. I feel embarrassed when I'm lying down, and I wonder, for the first time, if I might have misread Jason, and if he will take advantage of the situation, and I realise how vulnerable I am.

Jason drapes the duvet over me and steps back.

"Charlie," he begins, his voice soft, barely more than a whisper and very deep. "We need to talk about. . . all this." He gestures, a wide sweep of his arm that takes in the room, with its neat furnishings and complete lack of personal items.

"But not now. You need to sleep now, and get better. I'm going now, but I'll be back soon." His voice fades.

I hear him walk away, and then I sleep.

I wake again when I feel the duvet being gently lifted, and I start to sit up, alarm surging through me. Another duvet replaces it. It smells clean, and it has a cotton cover. I cough. I sleep on.

***

When I woke properly, the sun was streaming through the window. There was a sound and I turned. I could hear footsteps coming upstairs, there was a tap at the open door, and Jason peered round. He smiled when he saw I was awake.

"Have you joined the land of the living?" he said.

"Yes. . . I don't know what happened last night. I think you rescued me? Thank you. . ." I didn't know what to say, how to explain the situation.

"Do you think you could manage a cup of tea? Or some toast?"

I shook my head. I felt clearer this morning, and I realised that if Jason made tea, he would notice empty cupboards and wonder about the lack of food.

"I'm fine thanks, much better. Water is fine, thanks. You shouldn't really stay. . . I'm probably contagious, and. . ."

Jason came fully into the room. He took a small white wicker chair from the corner and moved it closer to the bed, then he sat on it, swinging back slightly so the front legs lifted.

"I checked you a few times last night," he said, "—didn't want to find a dead body in the morning!" He grinned, then looked serious. "If I was going to catch it, I would have it already, so too late to quarantine I reckon."

I didn't answer, not sure what to say. I needed to remove him from the house, before he noticed something amiss.

"We need to talk though," he continued, "if you're up to it?" He leant forward, and peered at my face, assessing.

I felt myself blush under his scrutiny, not sure how I could answer his questions. If he had noticed the odd situation, then the only explanation was the true one. I was too tired to be creative, to think of plausible reasons why the house had no food, why all my personal items were hidden, why I had been sleeping on a bare mattress under a smelly duvet that I couldn't wash because there was no way to dry it.

I waited.

"Charlie?" he said. "I think you ought to explain what's going on, because I might be able to help. If you don't want to, then that's fine, none of my business, and I'll go back to my side of the fence and that'll be an end to it. But. . ."

He paused, as if choosing his words.

"But Charlie, I like you, and I think we could have more good times together, and I'd like us to keep being friends. But that can only happen if you can trust me with the truth. I don't think I can cope with lies, not if we're going to be friends. . ."

I looked at his face, his wonderful open, genuine face, and I knew that he was someone different to Timothy, someone who said what he thought, who didn't manipulate me or lead a double life—but in return he needed me to be honest and not lead a double life either. We were barely friends, and although the weirdness of the lockdown had meant we had got to know each other much faster than we would in normal times, he was still just a friend, someone who I could walk away from, as easily as I had walked away from all my other friends.

But I didn't want to. I wanted to continue getting to know this person who was so at ease with himself, so *honest*. There was something trustworthy about him, an artless sincerity that I longed to be part of; I yearned to leave this life of deceit that I had created, to step out of my life of shadows and start again. There were some aspects of my past that were better left unsaid, but most of it I could explain, admit to the tangle I was caught in, and hope that it didn't drive him away. I took a breath, and a sip of water, then pulled myself to a sitting position. I was aware that I needed a shower, that my clothes were crumpled, and that I was under a duvet that he had provided. I hugged it to me, as if it could shelter me from my words, and then I began to explain.

"Well, for a start, Charlie isn't my real name."

I told him as much as I could. I gave him my real name, and he repeated it, trying it out for size.

"It suits you," he said, "though I expect I shall think of you as Charlie for a while."

I decided to start at the beginning, was tempted to quote: *It was the best of times, it was the worst of times. . .* But there was nothing humorous about this story, and the best times had quickly soured to nothing but the worst of times. There was no morally pure Charles Darnay that I had fallen in love with, I had given myself to the 'baddie' and fallen in love with the Sydney Carton of the story. I shook my head, as if to chase away the daydream. That book had become strangely dominant in my mind.

Interspersed with coughing fits, I began to explain about Timothy, the teacher who had noticed me, offered me private consultations during lunchtimes, then clandestine meetings after school. "I was very young when we met, though that's not really an excuse, because I don't feel like I was 'groomed' or anything. I knew what I was doing, and it was what I wanted."

Jason's face darkened, and he made a sort of growling noise. "Doesn't sound right to me," he muttered. "It was grossly unprofessional, if nothing else. I'm surprised he didn't get fired over it."

I paused, not sure that I liked this picking-over of my past, being evaluated by someone who hadn't been there. I decided I would only provide an edited version, the parts that were relevant.

"No one knew," I explained, "not until I had flunked my exams and left school. Once I was working in a shoe shop I was deemed an adult, he could do what he liked and it was no one else's business." My tone was warning him, it was not *his* business either, Jason had no right to moral judgement over my past, only my present.

I told him about the gradual restrictions of freedom, how I became a virtual prisoner.

"He controlled all the money you see. He had always said he would 'take care' of me, and that I needn't work after we got married. I thought that would be a good thing, to be looked after, a sort of extension of my dad looking after me. I thought it would still be equal, him earning the money, me supporting him, making sure our home was nice, sorting the meals and stuff. But it wasn't equal at all, it soon started to feel like I was trapped. He had all the credit cards, and he checked everything I spent, he chose my food and clothes, and decided who I should see and who I shouldn't, and it all got too much really, and then when I found out about. . ."

I stopped. I didn't want to tell Jason about my husband's unfaithfulness. It felt like failure, proof of my inadequacies as a wife, an inability to satisfy my husband so he had needed to look elsewhere for company and sex and possibly love. I sipped the water and tried to plan my words.

"There was someone else," I said.

Jason nodded, and leant forwards, and touched my hand, very lightly.

"I wondered if there was," he said. "I thought that might be where all this was leading."

I paused again, my eyes filling. I didn't want to explain why I had left, I wasn't sure I could trust anyone with that information. But if I didn't explain, if I didn't make Jason understand why leaving had been so important, then my actions would make no sense. I had to continue.

"I think I could've stayed," I said, my voice husky now, the emotion clouding my words. "I still loved him, you see, even though I'd found out, I still wanted to be his wife. But I began to realise that it wasn't normal, the way he was deciding everything, controlling every aspect of my life. And it felt. . . I don't know, *unfair* I suppose, once I knew he was, you know. . . *cheating*." It was such an inadequate word, summoned visions of schoolboys cheating at games or poker players counting cards; this was bigger than that, this was about destroying the internal structure of another human being so that they ceased being themselves, so that every piece of self-confidence was wiped away, and they were left doubting who they were and whether they had any worth as a human being at all. But it was the only word

I could think of for now. In a classical novel it might be called *adultery* or *unfaithfulness*. But *cheating* was what we said today, or *playing around*, or some other weak, almost comical phrase that took away the sting and made the perpetrator vulnerable and foolish rather than immoral and destructive.

I forced myself forwards, ground out the rest of my narrative until I reached the end.

"But then he, Timothy, started saying he wanted a child, that we should have a baby. I was already taking the pill." I felt myself colour, embarrassed to reveal intimate details to a comparative stranger, but there was no way to tell my story without being specific. "But when I saw, on the videos, that he was changing the pills, substituting them—he always put them out for me, you see, put them into this little pill box each day for me to take, and checked that I had—but I saw him change them, for something else, and I realised that he was determined, even though I told him no, I didn't think a baby was a good idea, he was trying to force the situation.

"I had stood up to him, you see," I explained. "I could cope myself, with all the rules and boundaries, but I couldn't let him do that to a child. I had chosen to live like that, in a way, because I had chosen him as my husband. But I knew he would be the same with a baby, that he would never let my baby have any freedom, and I couldn't allow that. Even if it meant he would be angry, and punish me, I couldn't risk getting pregnant."

"He punished you?" said Jason.

"He never hit me," I said, racing to clarify, not wanting, even now, for someone to think badly of Timothy. "But I meant that he would be angry, and then he sort of punished me by being very cold. . ."

I think back to those days.

***

Timothy is annoyed, but he will not shout or argue. He is icily polite, thanking me for meals, answering questions, but not really talking, never chatting about his day or the news or what might be happening. He will start to bring his phone to the meal table, and read messages while we eat, often snorting with laughter over something he has received, but not telling me, not sharing the joke. I am excluded, he wants me to know that by resisting him I am not to be included in the intimate part of his life.

He spends long hours in his study, saying that no, thank you for the offer, he does not want to spend our usual evening together watching the television or playing scrabble. He stops asking me about my day, and although I know that he has seen every detail on his cameras, he usually asks, and I enjoy telling him some meaningless snippet about a nest in a bush, or the new car the neighbours have bought. But not now, now he is cold, and letting me feel his displeasure by removing everything of himself except for his body, which arrives with dominant regularity in my bed to claim his 'rights.'

His dark eyes are hard and icy as he peruses my body, takes his due. Sometimes I cry, even as he touches me, turning my head away so that he can't see my tears, so that he will not stop to interrogate me, to find out why I am not happy. I don't know whether he sees my tears—choosing to not interrupt his pleasure by commenting—or if he never actually looks at my face, and is perhaps pretending my body is *her* body.

***

"So I had to leave, I had to escape, to avoid a baby," I said, hurrying to finish my story, wanting to leave it in the past now, to live fully in the present. "I didn't have any money, all the bank accounts were in Timothy's name, and I knew he would follow up on credit card bills, and trace where they had been used. I wasn't sure what he'd do after I'd gone, but I thought he might well go to the police, list me as a missing person. I worried I might be on the news or in papers, you know, one of those 'has anyone seen this person, we need to check they're alright' sort of things. Like they do when they think someone's been murdered."

"I think they only do those for children," said Jason, frowning. "I expect adults leave home all the time, and the police wouldn't be interested unless they thought there'd been a crime."

"Really?" I felt myself blush again. Had I been foolish, shown my immaturity by thinking people were looking for me when in actual fact, no one had even been told? I stared hard at the duvet cover, tracing the yellow geometric shapes with my eyes. I felt like a fool.

"Anyway," I said, forcing myself forwards, "I left. And I didn't have anywhere to go, but I had this idea that out of season, when there aren't any holiday-makers, all the holiday cottages would be empty, and they would be a good place to hide. They're always fitted out really nicely, everything you need really except for food. So I went to one in Blakeney, the one we had been to for our honeymoon, and I hoped like crazy that the key would be hidden in the same place, and it was, so I stayed there for a bit." I was hurrying now, my words chasing each other, scurrying from my mouth in my desperation to get past the next bit, to finish my story.

"Then, when I saw on the telly about Spain and Italy having a lockdown, and I saw the numbers in England start to go up, I figured it was on the cards for here too, and Blakeney seemed too small. I realised that if I kept going to the grocery shop there, people would notice, and I thought they would probably stop buses and trains—even though actually they haven't, so I could've stayed there after all. But I didn't know that, and I thought somewhere bigger would be safer, so I came to Cromer, and that's it. That's why I'm here. Do you hate me now?"

Jason shook his head, but didn't speak. He stood and walked to the window.

I stared at his back, watching the wide spread of his shoulders. He lifted a hand, pushed back his hair, and breathed a long sigh.

"Wow!" I heard him whisper.

I waited. I had no clue how he would react to my story, whether he would inform the owner of the house, or worse, the police. Whether he would be angry, or even frightened that I might be a criminal and want nothing more to do with me. I had told my story in the hope that we could remain friends, but now that it was out, having listened to my words as I spoke them, I realised how unstable I sounded. The slim chance of a continued friendship now seemed ludicrous.

Chapter Fourteen

When Jason eventually turned to face me, I couldn't read his eyes. His face was solemn, and he looked older, as if I had placed a burden on him, trapped him with my story. I had nothing else to say, my future was placed irretrievably in his hands; I waited.

"I don't even know what to say," he said, and I glimpsed a bewildered boy beneath the veneer of the dependable man. "I've never encountered a situation like this—though I suppose I've read about them, about battered wives and stuff. . ."

I wanted to correct him, to clarify that I had never been abused, but I was prevented by more coughing. When I was still again, Jason came towards me, and I saw his eyes were clearer, and he had come to a decision.

"You obviously can't stay here, not if you're basically an illegal squatter. I think that's the first thing we need to sort out, and that's relatively easy. For now, you'd better come next door and stay with me. I have a spare room, you can stay there. I notice there's no food in the house, have you not been eating properly?"

I nodded, feeling ashamed, as if this is something I have chosen due to perversity rather than necessity.

"That might be why you're so ill then. Maybe eating proper meals will get you back on your feet. You can stay with me until lockdown ends—I can't think of any other option really.

"I saw there's a window broken at the back—was that you too?"

I nodded again, saved from answering by coughing, but still his disapproval reached me.

"Right, well we can sort that too. I know a handyman, I'll phone him, see if he's still working, arrange for him to fix it. Is there anything else *here?* Anything to do with this house that needs sorting out to make everything legal? My feeling is that we need to fix that first, make sure that at least you can't be prosecuted for anything."

"No," I said, my voice faint, feeling like the criminal that I knew I was. "I haven't stolen anything, nothing like that. Just being here, that's all I did wrong."

"And lying to you," I wanted to add. For surely, I thought, that is the very worst thing; that is the thing I regret the most.

Jason helped me to move house. He collected my paltry possessions, and under my guidance, returned items in the house to their correct places. The smelly duvet he brought with us, saying he would return it when it had been washed. He also brought the backdoor key, and we walked round the outside of the house, to the front. I felt neighbours' eyes watching us from the blank windows, but perhaps I imagined it, perhaps the guilt I felt made everyone else seem like a judge. I could only manage to walk very slowly, stopping regularly to cough, feeling the pain deep in my lungs. I felt light-headed, and was grateful for Jason's hand under my elbow, supporting me. I wanted it to feel affectionate, but I didn't read any fondness in his expression, only duty.

Jason guided me upstairs, and into a small bedroom at the back. I sat wilting on a chair, watching while he sorted bed linen: making the bed and bringing a glass of water for the bedside table.

"Right, you get into bed, I'll go and make some breakfast. Keep drinking," he said, nodding towards the water. "Everything I've read online says that it's important to keep hydrated. If you drink enough, we can probably manage to keep you out of hospital."

I understood that going into hospital would add even more inconvenience to his life.

"Do you want to shower first?" he asked.

I hesitated. I knew that I needed a shower, that sweating all night and wearing the same clothes for several days in a row was not going to be smelling great. But I felt too weak, I thought I might faint again if I tried to stand unaided, and I could hardly ask him to wash me. Now that I had told my story, passed the burden of knowing who I was and where I was from, onto him, I felt more of an intruder than I had when I'd been living in a borrowed house. I had no inkling of what our relationship had now become, and to show any weakness, or ask any favour, felt wrong.

I shook my head. "Maybe later," I said.

I watched him leave, the door closing with gentle determination behind his departing back, and I lay back on the pillows. It was nice to be in a clean bed, with sheets and duvet covers and pillow cases, yet I felt more uncomfortable than I had since my escape. I needed to make a plan, to decide what the next step was, how to untangle myself from this new burden of obligation, but I was overtaken with coughing, and the pain in my chest made breathing almost unbearable, so I tried to relax, and concentrated on drawing air into my lungs, and after a while, I slept again.

I don't know how long I slept for, but it was several days. Identical days of fitful sleep, woken by the hard stone of pain in my lung, or the sound of Jason when he replenished the water next to me, or the dizzy, holding on to the wall for support, trips to the bathroom. Sometimes my sleep was dreamless, sometimes they were populated with jeering creatures, as I was led to a guillotine, or running, as fast as I could, while knowing there was no escape.

The times of wakefulness were worse, lying in the bed at night, staring into the darkness, the pain almost unbearable, feeling exhausted yet unable to rest because of the coughing that shook my body and rattled my aching head. I wanted to die in those times, and I told myself that as soon as I was strong enough to walk from the house, along the cliff edge to the path that sloped down to the beach, I would leave. I would stop at the bench half-way down the ramps, and crawl into the gorse bushes, and die there, listening to the sound of the waves, shivering with the animals that crawled into the sandstone, until my life ebbed away. I didn't think it would take long in my weakened state, and I longed to leave behind all my stupid mistakes, my spoilt life, the absolute failure in everything I had attempted. I had failed at school, failed at friendship, failed in my marriage, failed my parents, and now I had even failed at staying healthy and living independently. I wanted it to end, the physical agony of my full lungs and the emotional agony of knowing that I had nothing, was nothing, and my life was worthless. I didn't believe in eternal damnation or heaven or anything, I believed everything would end with my death, and oh! how I craved that ending.

But in the daylight, when the sun filtered through the patterned curtains, and my eyes rested on the pictures and books in the room, my mind was clearer, and I knew that I would never do it. Although the thought of finishing my life was wonderfully attractive, I knew that someone would find my body and be traumatised, the police would trace me—because I was more noticeable when dead than alive. I knew the news of my death would affect people, my mother would feel guilt, even Timothy would be impacted and although I needed to escape from him, I wished him no harm, I didn't want everyone blaming him, I didn't want him to have to cope with the trauma of a suicidal wife. I decided that to kill oneself, a person needed to not only feel completely desolate, but also must feel some anger towards the world, and want to cause hurt and inconvenience and guilt. I felt none of those things, the guilt was all mine, and without the anger, I could not inflict an inconvenient death upon the world.

Chapter Fifteen

It was more than a week before I began to feel better. I lay in bed, coughing and feeling wretched, while Jason replenished my water, and fed me paracetamol and sips of soup that made me want to gag. Sometimes I would wake, and find him standing in the doorway, the lower part of his face covered with a scarf, watching me, and I knew he was wondering if I might die in his house, and at which point he should phone for an ambulance.

But I continued to live, and when I woke up, aware the sun was already high in the sky, and the birds were busy in the tree outside the window, I understood for the first time that I wouldn't die, my body had won the fight with the virus that had invaded it. I used my hands to push myself up, nudged a pillow to support me, and sat up. I felt weak and dizzy, and my lungs were still clogged with muck that made me cough every few minutes; but I was better in myself, my temperature was normal and although I was light-headed it was due to hunger and weakness, not disease.

The room I lay in was pretty, traces of the woman who had designed it lingered in the flowery curtains under the pelmet, and on the lace cloth on the dresser. There was a print on the wall, of a lighthouse looking out to sea, and a collection of shells littered the window sill. In the corner was a pile of boxes, and I guessed that the room had been designed as a guest room, and used by Jason as a dumping ground for things he planned to sort later.

There was a tap on the door, and Jason appeared, carrying a jug of water.

"Hey, you look better!"

"Yes, I feel better today, I think I have rejoined the land of the living!"

He grinned, and I could see he was pleased, satisfied that his nursing skills had been effective.

"Thank you," I said for the thousandth time, "really, thank you for having me here. And risking catching it, and everything else. . ." My voice faded. I could see he was uncomfortable, was pouring water into the glass and going to fiddle with the curtains.

"I think," he said, turning and going to sit where he always sat, on the little wooden chair next to the door; "I think that perhaps it's time to stop saying thank you now. You've said it enough, every day in fact, since I brought you here, and I understand—I know that you're grateful—but now you're feeling a bit better, let's move on. Don't you think? We were friends—I think—before you got sick, and I think it would be good if we could be friends again. Which means we need to sort of iron-out the relationship again, and you need to behave like an equal, not some wounded little bird that I found in a bush and put in the shed to recover. Do you know what I mean? I'm not a hero, or a saint, or anything like that, so let's just go back to how it was—when you were insulting my cooking and beating me at every sport we attempted over the fence."

He looked at me, and I felt his eyes staring at my face, searching my mind, trying to peer inside and make me understand. I *did* understand, I knew that my being beholden to him was uncomfortable, and I realised that he wasn't going to throw me out on the street, not yet, and that perhaps I should relax a little, and concentrate on getting strong again.

"Talking of food, how about some breakfast? Could you manage something solid?"

I was hungry, properly hungry for the first time in days, and I nodded, my mouth watering in anticipation.

"Do you think you could manage some porridge?"

"Porridge?" I said, thinking of lumpy gruel.

"What do you normally eat then?"

I thought of Timothy, on the first morning of our honeymoon.

***

I have set the little table in the kitchen, laying spoons and knives and plates and bowls, delighting in the domesticity, loving being *his wife*. I fill the toast rack, and stand cartons of cereal in the centre of the table.

"What's that?" he asks, picking up the packet of *Crunchy Nut Cornflakes*.

"Those are what I always eat," I smile, waiting for his praise of how nice the table looks, with the egg-cup of flowers I have picked in the garden, and the cafetiére, which I have never used before so I am hoping I spooned the correct amount of coffee in before I added the boiling water.

My husband looks at me, an indulgent smile plays around his eyes as he shakes his head.

"We don't eat cereals like these. Cereals high in sugar are what ignorant people, who don't know any better, eat." He walks to the bin with the unopened packet, and throws away the cereal. "We will manage with toast," he says. "I will come to the supermarket with you next time, and show you the sort of food that you should be buying. After all, my love, I want you to be healthy. . ."

For the next few weeks, Timothy always accompanies me to the shops. He removes food from the trolley that will be bad for me, or anything he tells me is *"horrible"* even if it's one of my favourites. I am his wife now, and I must learn to eat the things he likes me to eat. Because he is older, and he knows best. . ."

***

I looked up at Jason and smiled. I haven't eaten porridge in years.

"Yeah, well, that's what my mum always gave us, when we were hungry," he said. "To *fill your belly and stick to your ribs!*" He stopped, and grinned. "But I could burn you some toast if you prefer."

"Porridge sounds great."

The porridge wasn't great, but it was hot, and it filled me up. As I swallowed the last salty, slimy mouthful, I licked the spoon clean and took a long drink of water.

"Do you think I could have a shower?" I asked.

Jason nodded. "I thought you'd never ask!" he said.

***

During one of our chats, when I well enough to get up, and was making an attempt to be helpful by washing up, leaning against the sink for support, I happened to mention how much I hated the dress I was wearing. I held a knife under the tap to rinse away the bubbles, and some of the water shot sideways, soaking the skirt of my dress. I laughed, placing the knife on the draining board and dabbing at my skirt with a tea-towel. Jason came in, and asked if I was okay, and whether my dress had survived the deluge.

"It's okay, I always hated this dress. In fact, I don't really like wearing dresses at all, but it's what Timothy wanted me to wear. He was paying, so it seemed reasonable that he should choose."

I turned back to the sink, aware that Jason had come next to me, and was staring at my face. He picked up a tea-towel and began to wipe it across a wet plate.

"What do you mean? Are you telling me that your husband chose all your clothes?"

I nodded, then shrugged. Compared to other restrictions, it wasn't such a big deal.

"Then I think you should buy some clothes that you like wearing," said Jason, his voice serious. For a while he was silent, wiping plates and stacking them in a tower next to him, carrying them to the cupboard when they were all dry.

"In fact, I think it's probably important." His voice echoed from inside the cupboard, and then I felt him turn, and I knew I was being watched, I could feel his eyes scrutinising my back. I continued washing the saucepan I was holding, scrubbing the dried sauce from the base, rinsing it in the bowl of bubbles, attacking a stubborn lump that cleaved to the edge.

"Yes, the more I think about it, the more it seems important. People express their identity by what they wear, and if you're a closet. . . I don't know. . . a closet *goth* or a *punk* or something, then I guess I'd like to know." I heard him chuckle. "I might regret this, of course, when you start to wear something outrageous, but honestly, I think we should leave the washing up and go and choose you some clothes. Shops are still delivering, even if you can't go in person."

I turned, shaking my head.

"I can't, Jason, I don't have any money, you know that. And to buy online I would need a credit card."

He made an impatient gesture, a flapping of his hand as if what I said was inconsequential rather than an absolute barrier to my freedom.

"I'll lend you the money. When this is over, you'll get a job, and I'll keep a tally of everything you spend. You can owe me. Up to a certain amount—I think ordering stuff from *Harrods* is out. But if you want to buy a few clothes from a high street shop, then I can just pay now, and you can reimburse me in the future.

"What do you *like* wearing, by the way?"

"Jeans," I said, my heart racing at the thought of wearing them again. "And baggy tops, over-sized teeshirts and sweaters. Nothing goth or punk or super-expensive, I promise."

I was smiling, excited to think I could stop wearing the flowery dresses and frumpy court shoes. I would feel like me again. I didn't like the thought of owing Jason even more than I owed now, and something nagged in my mind, that I was becoming beholden to someone else, another man was replacing Timothy in holding me to debt. But I pushed the thought away, and hurried to look online.

***

My new clothes had arrived, and I wore them immediately, walking into the sitting room in tight jeans, a baggy top hidden by an over-sized sweater. Jason had been watching television, and he looked up when I entered, his expression frozen as his gaze swept my hair, my clothes, down to my bare feet. He said nothing, but I saw the glimmer of something in his eye, and I knew he was seeing me as someone different, someone less odd. I walked to the sofa, and sunk into it, lifting my legs—ah! the freedom of not fussing with skirts and modesty—and tucked them under me. This was how I liked to sit, curled up in a chair. Jason had been right, the clothes *did* matter; I felt more like myself.

"Nice clothes," said Jason, his voice very light, as if he had barely noticed. He turned back to the television, told me it was a documentary about coronavirus—because everything on television was about coronavirus. As he spoke, I detected something new in his voice, something self-aware and not quite as relaxed as previously.

I smiled, knowing that my new appearance had unsettled him, and for the first time in a very long while, I felt again the power that a woman feels when a man is *noticing* her. I settled into the chair, and stared at the screen.

***

We were sitting in the garden when Jason asked his first questions. It was sunny—spring was lovely that year, almost as if nature was in defiance of lockdown, showing off that a virus couldn't stop the blossom drifting in the breeze, or the hyacinths holding their heavy-scented heads above their hunched-shouldered leaves. Jason had pulled a couple of chairs next to a hawthorn bush, and I could smell the perfume of the delicate white flowers, stark against the green leaves. A bird was fussing because we were sitting too close, and Jason said he thought there might be a nest in there.

Jason had spent the morning working, as he spent every day working. The house had been filled with loud phone calls, and online meetings, and the crackle of productivity. He had suggested that we should sit in the garden while he had his lunch, and the empty plates rested on the grass next to us. I sat back in my chair, still exhausted easily, the tendrils of the virus sapping my energy. I glanced across at Jason, and noticed that his hair was growing even longer and had taken on a shaggy, untamed look. I wondered if I could offer to trim it, but dismissed the idea as too familiar, too intimate. He would have to wait until the barber shops reopened, or cut it himself. I turned to the sky, shutting my eyes and enjoying the feel of the sun on my skin.

"We need to make a plan," he said, interrupting my revery, and there was an old tension to his voice which I thought had disappeared, and I realised that the recent long days of pleasant chatting and playful teasing, had only been an interlude, and the questions and judgements that had waited until I was healthy had never gone away, but rather been put on hold until now.

I looked up, and looked into his blue eyes, and nodded.

"Yes, I know. I've been wanting to put it off, because it's so lovely here, but you're right. I don't belong here, and I need to make a plan, and get out of your hair as soon as the government releases lockdown."

His eyes darkened, and I saw anger in the lines of his face.

"That's not what I meant," he said, his voice short now. He turned away, and reached to pull a dandelion from the ground. "I do actually *like* you being here."

His tone was measured, and I knew there was a *but* hanging unspoken.

I waited. In my dreams, I saw a future where lockdown eased, and I found a job in a local shop, so I could pay my way, and contribute to the household expenses. But in my dream, which I knew was simply a dream and not something to be relied upon, I remained living with Jason. Our friendship was an easy one, there was no sexual contact to confuse it, no obligation, no friends or relatives watching and offering advice. We were cocooned by the lockdown, safe in our own little world, and the aims were very simple: I needed to get well, Jason and I developed our friendship while we isolated from the world so the virus didn't spread.

"But you need to sort things out, with your family, and your—husband."

He stumbled over the word *husband* as though it was an awkward thing, and as I looked at him, I saw something new in his eyes, something conflicted and uncertain.

"I'm not sure there's anything to sort out with my mother," I said, choosing the easier subject to address. "She has always put my sister's needs first, and even when I was growing up, I always knew that we had to do whatever was necessary to help Gracie. Which was fine, I understand. And I love Gracie, I really do. I always thought that one day, when my parents couldn't look after her, that I would, and that she'd live with me—or at least, somewhere that I could look out for her. It was one of the things I found difficult, when Timothy separated me from my family, not being able to see Gracie.

"But now my dad has gone. . ." I paused, and even now, after all this time, I felt the words stick in my throat like something viscous, and I heard again his words: *"It'll be okay,"* and I knew that my feeling at the time, that nothing would ever be okay ever again, was correct. I looked up at Jason.

"I didn't even go to his funeral," I whispered, and I heard in my own voice all the anguish and regret and self-loathing that I could have let such a thing happen.

"And I know my mum," I said, forcing myself to continue, to wade through the emotions that were threatening to weigh me down, the sorrow clinging to the footsteps of my conversation so I could hardly make my way through it. "My mum never wanted me to marry Timothy in the first place, she saw it as me deserting her, turning my back on Gracie, some massive teenaged rebellion designed to injure her." I shook my head. "Mum will never want me back, I'm sure of it. Otherwise, surely she'd have come, wouldn't she? I mean, my address was never a secret, but she never attempted to see me, to make contact, even if she couldn't get through on the phone, I'd have thought she would have come. . ."

And without warning, the burden of those years washes over me, and I remember looking from the window, wishing that she would come, and I am lost again, with nowhere to go, and no one I can turn to, and I long with a passion to feel my father's arms around me, and to know again the touch of my mother's hand as she strokes my cheek, and presses her lips to my forehead; and I want to turn back the clock, and be a child again.

I was aware the Jason was standing, moving across the small space between us.

I felt a hand on my shoulder, tentative at first, then firmer, as Jason touched me, trying to reassure me. It was the first time, since that evening when he rescued me, that he has made any physical contact, and I felt the warmth of his hand through the cotton top I was wearing, and I leant towards him, taking comfort from the proffered hand, his strength. I rested my head against his arm, bare where the sleeve had been rolled up, and felt the whisper of fine hairs against my cheek as I absorbed the warmth of him. It had been *so long* since I had felt the contact of another human being, and even that slight touch—his hand on my shoulder, my head rested on his arm—was like a tonic, something revitalising.

After a long moment, he spoke, his voice gentle.

"I think you might be wrong, I think perhaps mothers are built to forgive their children far worse things than that. From what you've told me, I think your mother did love you—*does* love you—and she will want to see you again. Don't forget, your husband has been drip-feeding you misinformation for years. It will have warped your sense of what's right."

He paused, and I heard a hard edge to his voice as he spat: "It was a form of abuse you know. It might not have been physical abuse, but emotional abuse is still abuse, and it will have damaged you, I'm sure it will. So, I'm not sure you should trust your feeling that your family will reject you."

He stopped, and moved back to his seat.

"I think it's worth a try, at least. When the lockdown has eased, I think you should plan to go back to your family home, and try to see your mum, and try to explain to her everything that you've explained to me. Because I believe you," he said, looking at me, holding me with his gaze. "I believe you."

I nodded, my heart lifting at his words, and I realised just how very much I needed to hear those words, and to know that Jason, of all the people in the world, believed me.

***

Our next conversation of any weight was on a Sunday evening. We had been chatting to some of Jason's friends on zoom, people who he knew from the pub, and they were planning to have a pub quiz, each couple would do a round of questions for the others.The screen dissected into tiny squares, a person in each one. Jason introduced me, which was embarrassing, and everyone called hello, or waved, and although I was nervous and had wanted to sit out of sight, I discovered that they were friendly, and their faces were open and honest, and there was a sincerity which was very attractive.

Everyone had outgrown haircuts, and the women who dyed their hair had great tramlines of grey down their partings. They were all older than me, some looked almost the age of my parents, but I found that I liked them, and their jokes were funny, and when they discussed an old woman that one of them was shopping for, and a couple of old men who were having food delivered during the lockdown, I realised that they were basically *nice*. They were good people, like Jason.

I mainly listened, not sure whether I should actually join in with the general chat. It was odd interacting with people outside of our 'bubble.' I felt relaxed living here with Jason, but the absurdity of the situation became real when it was explained to other people. Jason introduced me as "a friend who's staying here," and no one commented, or asked questions. But I could see the surprise in their eyes, and I knew that after the call, couples would turn to each other and wonder who I was, and why was living there, and was their friend being taken advantage of?

It also reminded me that Jason had a whole life that I was not part of. He had lived in Cromer for years, and he had friends, and colleagues and neighbours who were part of his life, and I was separate from all that. Although I knew Jason better than I had known almost anyone other than my family, our relationship was in seclusion, and I wondered if that somehow made it less *real*. When all this ended, when the lockdown was eased, would our friendship continue? I loved living here, with this man, but it wasn't *normal*, and when we attempted to have a 'normal' exchange with other people, albeit via the internet, it was impossible to ignore how precarious my position here was. I tried to ignore the nagging worry, and concentrate on what was being said.

"I'll do a picture round," Jason was saying, "or is it meant to be a secret?"

"Well it's not a secret now, is it!" laughed an older man with a big nose.

"I don't know what kind of round I'll do," said a woman with very blonde hair and a dark line of roots. "Can't we just agree to do ten questions each, and decide what on later?"

"We might all do the same questions though," said Jason.

"I'll be Quizmaster," said a thin man with a mass of fair hair that he kept pushing back from his face. "You all tell me what category your questions will be, and I'll let you know if there's a clash."

Everyone nodded, and I wondered who he was, this man who had so easily taken the lead. He reminded me of Timothy, he was very certain.

We couldn't chat for very long, as there was due to be an announcement from the Prime Minister, so we arranged a time for the quiz to happen, and everyone promised to have their questions ready. Then there was a lot of waving —which felt like we were at the end of a sixties pop-group sitcom, and we ended the zoom meeting. Jason flicked the screen to the news and we sat, side-by-side, staring at the screen, waiting to hear what the government would now allow us to do. There was a confusing list of rules.

The Prime Minister said that although the lockdown must continue, people could return to work. People should avoid public transport, and instead drive or cycle, but wherever possible, everyone now needed to work—at home if possible, otherwise at their place of work. The government's slogan had changed: from a red-bordered *Stay at Home,* to a green-bordered: *Stay Alert.*

"Well, not much information there," said Jason, turning off the screen at the end of the speech. Maybe we'll learn more tomorrow, when the actual document is published. It does sound though that we're now able to meet other people, even if it's just outside, in a park or something. It sounds as if the 'single household' rule is going to be relaxed.

He shuffled in his seat so he was facing me. I realised there was something important he wanted to say, and I felt my muscles tense.

"Have you thought any more about your family? About what you're going to do? Especially about—"he coughed, as if the words were hard to say, " —about your husband."

I stared down at the carpet, tracing the swirls of green and crimson with my eyes, wondering who had chosen the patterned rug, and whether, if it was his wife, he thought about her whenever he vacuumed it.

"No," I said, "not really." I glanced at him. His eyes were distant, staring blankly at the wall opposite, and when he spoke it sounded as though he had rehearsed the words, tried them out in his mind before voicing them.

"You need to go back, and sort things out," he said, and his voice was very low as he measured his words, weighing each one to see whether he meant it. "I want for our— " he paused, and I knew the right word eluded him, and he was keen to not say the wrong thing, to not insinuate something that was not yet there. "Our friendship," he said at last, "I want for our friendship to continue, and to develop, and if it becomes something more, something deeper—well, I don't want anything to stand in the way of that.

"But at the moment, that cannot happen, even if it would. Because you are married, and that's not something I can ignore. I don't know if you still love your husband. . ."

He looked at me, but I lowered my head again, because I didn't want him to see. I didn't *know* whether I still loved Timothy, my feelings were too muddled. I longed to be that child again, the innocent teenager who had so eagerly joined her life to the older, sophisticated adult who beckoned. I didn't know if Timothy was the same man; if I was the same girl.

"But even if you don't, even if you never want to see him again, I can't be *the bit on the side.* I'm just a normal person, you know that, and part of that means I need things to be. . . sorted. I can't be *the other man,* even if you're sure the marriage has ended in everything other than name. Before we can even start to find out who we are, whether we have a future together, you have to go back, you have to discover what you want, and make it right.

"Do you understand?"

I nodded. I did understand, and I knew how much the words had cost him, I knew that he wanted to waive his conscience, tell himself that the emotional abuse annulled the marriage, nothing else was important. But the deceit of that would simmer, under the surface of our happiness, and in time, perhaps when we least expected it, it would rise up, and sink in its teeth, and wound us. If we wanted to be together, in whatever form that might take, I must first go and face Timothy.

I wanted to cling to Jason, to plead with him to come with me, or to not let me leave. But I knew he was right, I knew I couldn't run from this forever, and now was the time to turn and face my past. I knew I must go alone, without distraction, and make my choice.

"Yes," I said, and my voice was so quiet that he had to lean forwards to hear. "I know that you're right, and that I need to sort it out. I've been sort of putting it off, until I felt stronger."

"Well, there's nothing wrong with that," he said, sounding now as if he wanted to take back the words, was regretting voicing them and forcing an issue that he also would prefer to avoid.

"Perhaps you should wait until you're properly strong again. Certainly you shouldn't meet your husband yet, I think that would be foolish while you're still weak from the virus.

"But your family is a different matter. I know you think they won't want to see you, and maybe you're right. But you should ask them, let them say how they feel, not just assume something that your husband convinced you to believe. After what Boris has said, it sounds like you could arrange that now.

"I'm not suggesting you should move back with them, nothing like that. Like I said, I like you being here."

I felt a smile grow inside when he said that, and I wanted to curl up next to him, and ask him to say it again, and demand to know what, exactly, he meant by that. But I didn't, and although a smile may have played around my lips, I stayed in my seat, and allowed myself the smallest nod to indicate that I'd heard him.

"Why don't you phone them? You could speak to your mum tonight, get it over with. Ask if she wants to meet you, maybe in a park or somewhere—does she live near a park? Not sure whether a garden is allowed, probably it would be, somewhere outside anyway. You can maintain social distance, keep to the two metres apart rule, but you can at least see each other, have a conversation, sort out a few things that are better said face-to-face.

"I'll drive you," he offered, sounding more certain now, as though the plan had formed in his mind and he approved. "I'm pretty sure you've had the virus and are immune, but you're still weak, and just in case it was something else, I can drive you, take a book to read for an hour while you talk to your mum, then drive you home again. It'll be a start anyway, you can decide what to do after that, when you know how the land lies."

I was smiling and nodding, and trying not to focus too much on the word "home" and that he had included me, very firmly, within that noun, as if I belonged here with him.

"Okay," I said again, and stood up.

Jason put out his hand when I passed him, and our fingers touched, very briefly, as I left to phone my mother. As I walked away from him, into the hallway, I could still feel the trace of his fingers where they had trailed my hand.

I stood for a moment, staring at the front door, and I lifted my hand to my face and let it rest against my cheek, wanting it to be his hand touching me. My eyes scanned the ornaments on the little shelf next to the front door, and the picture of flowers hanging next to the mirror—things that I knew Abigail, his wife, had placed there, and I felt the ghost of her, watching me, and I knew that the only way to extinguish the ghost was to deal with my past and move forwards to the future.

Chapter Sixteen

Jason drove me to the park. Although public transport was running, he said the risk of mixing with other people was too great, and the hassle immense, and it was easy enough for him to drive me on Saturday.

"It seems daft to risk catching the virus," he said, waving away my objections with a smile and a sweep of his hand. "I know we both *think* you've already had it, but without a test, it could potentially have been something else, especially as you weren't eating properly and I imagine you were pretty stressed by your living arrangements at the time."

I nodded, torn between not wanting to accept another favour—having to *owe* him for something else—and the knowledge that to catch trains from Cromer to Kent, even if they were all running, would be hours of hassle.

"Look, I really don't mind, especially as it was me who nagged you into meeting your mum in the first place. I'll drive you, we can eat a picnic on the way because I'm assuming all the services will be shut. Then I'll sit in the car and wait while you talk. We can take it from there, and you can tell me how it went on the way home. Honestly, I don't mind at all. I'm pleased, actually, that you're sorting it out."

I nodded again, the plan was made.

The journey was faster than I'd anticipated, as very few other cars were on the roads. As we drove along the lanes towards Norwich, I strained to see the railway line, to try and work out if we were travelling near to the route I had taken when I arrived in Norfolk, a lifetime ago. But although there were glimpses of the line, I couldn't match the scenery with what I had seen, so I settled back in my seat and let my mind wander. Fields of green, dusty acres with barrel-shaped shelters and routing pigs, hamlets dwarfed by ancient churches.

The traffic thinned even more when we joined the main roads. Even though, since people were encouraged to return to work if they couldn't work from home, the roads around Cromer had been noticeably busier than during the lockdown, the motorways were empty. It was strange, driving along three lanes of emptiness, the odd car hurtling down the fast lane, an occasional emergency service vehicle overtaking us, but hardly anyone else driving. The surreal impression of having stepped into a science-fiction movie returned as I stared through the window.

We passed closed shops, empty car parks, bollards forming a short orange barrier on the slip-roads to eateries. I wondered where the chefs were, how the serving staff were spending their days, whether the roadside cafes had enough saved up to reopen one day. Or would those squat buildings gradually disintegrate, the windows smash, the grass grow over the tarmac outside, as nature reclaimed the space that humans had stolen for their businesses.

"By the way, I keep meaning to ask," I said, piercing the silence. "In that book, *A Tale of Two Cities,* all the stuff about the French Revolution begins when that man, the rich cruel one, runs over and kills the child by the fountain. Is that true? I mean, did the revolution begin with one child dying?"

"No, I don't think so," said Jason, his voice warm and interested, as if he was pleased by the distraction, happy to discuss the book again instead of thinking about driving, and why we were returning to my home town. "I think, if my memory serves me correctly, the revolution began with the storming of the Bastille, when the peasants broke into the prison, and then it escalated from there. But to be honest, I don't really know what triggered that event."

I saw him smile as he considered, and I settled back into my seat, thinking of those long-ago times, when people behaved so randomly, when society seemed to disintegrate into chaos.

"I expect it could have been something like that," I said. "I mean, the people had been abused for years, and there must have been a trigger, a single event that set off their protest. And at first, I suppose, the protest was justified—I mean, the poor people were treated awfully, weren't they?

They didn't have any rights, were pretty much worthless in the eyes of the rich."

"Ah. . . *his contemptuous eyes ran over her and all the other rats. . .*"

"You saddo!" I said, laughing. "You can actually quote passages, like for an English Lit class?"

Jason was laughing too, his deep chuckle filling the car. "I knew it would impress you," he said. "I can't help it, it's just the way my brain works, if I read something carefully, I remember it. It's useful at work, but I agree, slightly nerdy.

"However, getting back to the book, I'm not sure how historically factual some parts are, though Dickens would have heard stories from the old people he met whose parents lived through the revolution. But it could have been a single event, a single person being killed, that sparked the trouble. When society has been repressed, when it has suffered injustices for long enough, it often seems to ferment until one day, something starts a sequence of events that becomes almost unstoppable.

"When you think of the revolution, it's deplorable how poor people suffered, abused by the rich and with no 'rights' at all. Even the laws were rarely upheld, not when they should have been protecting poor people, only for the convenience of the rich. So in theory, for a carriage to kill a child was illegal and should have been punished; in practise, no one cared enough about the poor to do anything. You can understand why they rose up, turned against their oppressors, tried to change things. The trouble is, they lost all sense of proportion, started to attack people who weren't really to blame—anyone considered rich was at risk, hundreds of people were sent to the guillotine who didn't deserve to die, and there was no one to speak up, everyone was too worried about the tide of emotion, their personal safety, to stop it happening. It's scary, when you think of it, the things that societies, regular people, can do when they're put into certain situations. It doesn't even mean the starting point was a bad one, but things get out of hand, one things leads to another, until the whole thing has turned from 'justified' to 'evil' and no one really knows how they ever got there, or how to stop it. . ."

I was silent, as I wondered whether our conversation had moved on from the story of long ago and Jason was now talking about me, and my situation, and my complete inability to alter something that had crept into my life, a combination of events that had caused an unstoppable evil. I frowned, not sure that Timothy had been *evil,* or that the events were inevitable. I glanced at Jason, but he was concentrating on driving, edging past an old Volvo, indicating back into the slow lane. Perhaps I was reading more into his words than they merited, perhaps he was simply chatting about the book.

We left the motorways and drove through countryside to the town where my mother and sister still lived, the scenery becoming evermore familiar. There were a few car parks nestling within a wood we drove through, and I remembered parking there as a teenager, donning wellies and mixing with dog-walking couples in waxed jackets as I strode through the trees. The car parks were full, Land Rovers and BMWs jostled for space on the hard mud, red tape fluttering on the bank next to the road, abandoned when the car park reopened. There was a dead fox, and a fallen branch, and then we rounded a steep bend, drove down the angled street of a last village, and we reached the town.

I directed Jason past various small industries that sat scowling next to the road, refusing to appear anything other than stark and functional, unwelcoming in their ugliness. There was a mini roundabout, and a new building with a bank scattered with white flowers and red, red, poppies dancing in the wind, then a railway bridge, and we turned right, into the leisure centre, and parked.

"Right," said Jason, leaning over to the back seat and retrieving a book. "I'll sit here and read about psychopaths. You go and find your family. There's no rush, but if you're going to be much more than an hour, come and let me know. I might drive around a bit, and come back later if you want to be ages."

"I won't," I said, opening the door. "They might not even show up."

A few other cars were there, but mostly there was space, and litter, and a sort of betrayed air, as if the car park was offended that all the people had left. A man was in the corner, throwing bottles into the recycling bank. There was a crash, the tinkle of shattering glass, a pause, then the next crash. I glanced across at him. He was removing bottles from a box in his boot and throwing them, over-arm, like an athlete pitching a ball, a wide sweep of his arm, releasing the bottle, a crash, tinkle, repeat. There was something destructive about it, and I moved away.

I kept the red-bricked leisure centre to my right and headed towards the little park. Usually a constant smell of chlorine wafted into the car park, but everything was closed, even the smell had gone. Blank windows stared back at me, weeds were growing in the cracks of the path. There was no line of excited swimmers waiting to go in, no straggly-haired lines of school children heading back to their coach, no athletes with rolled towels heading to the gym. It could have been any building—an office, a library, a gallery—without the people it had lost its identity.

There were a few people in the park. Couples wandered up the path from the shops, bags of shopping heavy in their hands. Two elderly women were talking, standing the prescribed two metres apart, speaking in unnaturally loud voices. I wondered if they were friends who had arranged to meet, or strangers so starved of conversation that a chance encounter in a park was all the excuse they needed. Everyone was careful as they walked, detouring round each other, no one daring to walk too close, to pass within reach, within coughing-distance.

I headed towards the pond. A family of ducks was waddling over the path, looking expectantly at a woman and child, hoping for crumbs. On the bank, next to warning signs about slippery banks, and a Dalek-shaped waste paper bin, was a wire seat. I perched for a moment, looking round. It reminded me of the duckpond in Blakeney, and those ducks behind the tall fence which was meant to keep them safe but which actually kept them captive.

There was no sign of my mother, and I began, for the first time, to wonder if she would come.

We had spoken on the phone, and she had surprised me by crying, and saying my name over and over, as if she couldn't believe it was me. Once she was sure I was real, something suspicious came into her voice, and she asked why I was calling, and was Timothy there? When I said I had left him, she muttered something I couldn't hear, and then asked—before I could even suggest it—if we could meet.

But now I began to wonder whether, after she had thought about it, weighed my transgressions against her desire to see me again, she had thought better of it. Perhaps, I thought, she realised that she didn't want to see me after all. Perhaps my journey had been a waste of time. I wondered whether, if she didn't come, I would direct Jason to her house, the house I had lived in as a child. Would I seek her out? I decided I wasn't brave enough to face the rejection, if she didn't come to the park, I would simply leave. I tried to tell myself it was 'her loss' but there was something heavy inside, something that felt as if it might break, and I knew that the loss would be mine, and almost impossible to bear.

A rat swam across the pond and scurried to a hole at the foot of a tree. There was something dirty about it, the way the red tail trailed behind, the determined way it moved past me, and I shivered and stood up. Even on a sunny day, there was nothing pleasant about sitting next to a pond and watching rats.

I followed the path round to the children's play area. A chunky orange barrier blocked the entrance. It looked inflated, as if it would be light enough to move, and I considered squeezing past it, to sit on the abandoned slide, or swing, while I waited. But the apparent puniness was deceptive, and it was firmly screwed onto the posts either side of the entrance, denying me access. I considered jumping the low fence, but there were too many middle-aged women with sensible haircuts and comfortable shoes, and I knew they would be of the type that interfered with a stranger when they broke the rules, and one would be sure to shout at me, while another phoned the police.

I wandered round the perimeter of the pond, under trees that reached ancient branches across the sky, over grass that was dry and firm. I stood staring at a cedar tree, the majestic layers of branches almost like floating clouds, the kind of tree that prompts stories of other worlds, and fairies, and magical beings. The leaves were dense and green, the branches stretching horizontally at impossible angles, and I wondered how often they fell, crushing whatever was beneath them. I had almost decided to go back to the car, to admit defeat, when I saw them.

My mother was crossing the road at the lights, Gracie was holding her hand and scowling. It took me a minute to recognise my sister, she had grown, was now as tall as me, and it wasn't until the sun caught her curls, so they shone with the familiar deep auburn, that I recognised her.

Without warning, tears rushed to my eyes, and I felt sick, and something inside was churning and I couldn't walk towards them, or force a smile, or wave. I simply stood there, waiting for my mother to notice me. The moment was suddenly significant and I realised that I had been waiting my whole life for this one moment, and all I had done, and all my mistakes, were somehow wound up with this one desire, this overwhelming need, for my mother to notice me.

The light was red, and they stared at the passing few cars, then waited, even though the road was clear, until the light turned green, allowing them to cross.

My mother saw me when they reached the other side. She turned to speak to Gracie, and as she turned back towards the park, she saw me, and froze. I watched her stop, her face began to twist, and her mouth turned down, and for a moment neither of us moved and I held my breath, waiting to see whether she would come to me or turn away.

She came. She dropped Gracie's hand, and took a step towards me, then collected herself, and grabbed the hand again, pulling my sister along as she hurried along the path, and over the grass, and then her arms were around me, and she was crying, and her tears were tickling my neck and I felt the huge heave of her sob as she held me fast. She moved slightly back, but kept hold of my arm, and her other hand was stroking my hair, and as the tears ran unchecked down her own face, she moved her hand from my hair to my cheek and started to wipe my tears away.

Gracie was standing next to us, her body stiff with disapproval.

"You are touching," she said, and I remembered the sound of her voice, slightly too robotic, as if she couldn't quite manage the correct, the *normal* inflections.

"People shouldn't stand near," she repeated, giving her judgement and finding us wanting. "You two are breaking the rules. The Prime Minister said we mustn't stand near each other. Because of the germs. You two are touching."

"It's your sister, Gracie," said my mother, smiling through her tears. "She isn't a stranger. Mothers can touch their children," she said; although both of us knew this wasn't true, and we had broken the law and taken a risk, and my sister, as she often was, was completely correct.

"She doesn't live with us anymore," said Gracie, the disapproval finite. "But mothers can touch their children," she said, as if testing this new idea, wondering if it was true. "Mothers can touch their children, even if they have left."

She moved away, towards the metal bench, and sat on it, staring at the pond.

"But not sisters," she said, sounding definite. "Sisters don't have to touch."

"No Gracie," I smiled, sitting near her but resisting the urge to drape an arm over her shoulders. "Sisters don't have to touch. Not if they don't want to."

"All seems like a lot of silly fuss to me," she muttered, making me smile in spite of myself, the wonderfully familiar awkwardness of my sister reaching through the sweeping emotions of meeting my mother.

"Why don't you go and look at the stone snake?" said my mother.

Gracie nodded, and headed towards the entrance to the leisure centre.

"She's grown," I said, watching her back.

"Yes, it's hard now, to get the right balance between letting her be independent, and keeping her safe. I'm trying to teach her to explain to people what she doesn't like, like being touched, or if they change the supermarket round— you know the sort of thing. If she can explain she doesn't like something, then hopefully we can stop it escalating into a complete meltdown. It's harder now she's big. I can't just pick her up and move her when she loses it." She looked across to where Gracie was standing, staring at something on the ground.

"There are painted stones," explained my mother, coming to sit next to me on the bench and taking my hand in both of hers. "Local people paint them, and put them there, in a long line, like a snake. Gracie likes to count them each day, check none are missing." She looked at my face, and reached up to place a hand, very lightly, on my cheek.

"You have no idea how much I have missed you," she said, and her voice was thick with tears again.

"About Dad. . . the funeral. . ." the words came slowly, my reluctance at saying them, of possibly causing a row, making my mother withdraw again, was difficult. But they had to be said, it was why I had come.

"Clear the air," Jason had said. "Before you assume they all hate you and never want to see you again, best to check, don't you think? Just in case you're wrong? You might be surprised you know, mothers in my experience are more resilient than you think."

But clearing the air was no simple thing, it involved touching things that had never healed, peeling back a scab that had formed over a deep sore. I could guess at the hurt I had caused my mother, at the depth of her anger, and now I was attempting, stumbling word after stumbling word, to try and face that. To try and apologise involved first raising the issue.

My mother shook her head. She turned slightly, lowered her gaze to the ground in front of us, so it was impossible to read her expression.

"It was difficult," she said, "and I couldn't reach you. Every time I rang, *Timothy* answered." She spat his name, the hatred raw in her voice. "I didn't trust him, I never trusted him, with all his smooth ways, and lovely manners. I knew he was whispering in your ear, turning you against us, and you weren't very old, barely more than a child."

Her voice changed, and suddenly I realised she wasn't accusing, she wasn't angry with me—she was apologising, trying to help me understand.

"But I wasn't coping, I had Gracie, and there wasn't the support for her that I needed, and then your dad got ill, and I sort of lost the plot a bit, and it was all I could do every day to get up and put on my clothes and get through the day. Day after day, plodding through the impossible balance of caring for your dad, keeping Gracie on an even keel. There were days when I could barely force myself out of bed, when all I wanted to do was pull the covers over my head and stay there. . . So I do know," she twisted back on the bench so she was facing me again, her red-rimmed eyes staring straight into mine, the tears again rolling down her cheeks, one after the other in a damp race of emotion.

"I do know that I failed you," she whispered. "And I was so frightened, when you stopped answering and only *he* answered, telling me that you didn't want to see us any more, that we had failed you as parents. Well. . ." she paused.

"It was true, wasn't it? I *had* failed you. Gracie and your dad had used up everything I had to offer, and I needed you to help me. But when it came to mothering, I just didn't have anything left. So when *he* said you wanted to be left alone, well, I understood, really I did. So did your dad."

The breeze stirred the tree above us, and my mother shivered, even though it wasn't cold. For a moment we just sat there, holding hands, listening to the ducks as they plopped into the water, watching a moorhen as she swam across the pond, three chicks in her wake.

"Your dad told me you went to see him," she said, her voice low.

I turned with a jolt, surprised he had mentioned it.

"It meant a lot to him." My mother took my hand again, her thumb moving over my skin in an affectionate stroking motion that I recognised from childhood. "He said he thought you were okay, that there was a lot you weren't saying, but that you were okay."

Something new entered her eyes, something like fear, and I knew, in the pause that followed, that my mother had her own ghosts, her own nightmares that she was forcing herself to face; whilst inside, something was loosening up and swelling and filling me. It was freedom, a sort of release from the prison of my own fears. *It wasn't all my fault.*

"But were you?" she whispered, and in her question I heard the dread, and I knew that part of her still did not want to know, part of her was too vulnerable, too hurting, and wanted to hide from knowing what might be an even worse truth than the one she had accepted.

"Sort of," I said, my new-found freedom making me generous, and I realised that I was still trying to shield her, still felt a strange duty towards my mother; that first-born duty felt by every oldest child, that mutual bond of caring for the parent who cared first for us, that special binding emotion that might be denied but which continues to exist throughout our lives. I could see that my mother was anxious, had worried year after year about me, while feeling impotent to change anything, and that anxiety now expressed, was as much as she could bear. This was not the moment for retelling of hurts, or remonstrance. It was a time to reconnect and heal, to reassure and forgive.

I gave her the barest facts, the explanation of my reduced contact, the unhappiness I had felt, the loneliness when I decided to leave. I told her about my escape, the days hiding out in holiday homes, being rescued by Jason. She stopped me then, wanted to know more details, how old was he? Was he married? Did he have a job?

She frowned when I mentioned his age, muttered that I had always liked older men, she hoped I was being careful.

I explained that our relationship was platonic, and she sort of snorted, gave me a knowing look, but made no comment.

"He's here, actually, waiting for me in his car," I said. "Do you want to meet him? I should probably go back soon anyway, let him know that you came."

"Of course I came," said my mother, squeezing my hand again. "You should never have doubted that, even if I made huge mistakes. You will never stop being my daughter."

I nodded, still coming to terms with this shift in perspective, this idea that perhaps the burden of blame lay with both of us, that I was not completely to blame in the fiasco that has been my life.

We stood, and walked over to where Gracie was standing, staring at a line of stones next to the path. There weren't many, and they were all different, some obviously painted by children, some advertising local events—which I doubted would happen unless the lockdown lifted soon— some were varnished, and delicately painted, perhaps by artists, certainly by someone who knew how to paint. Some advertised books, others were simply patterns.

"Two are missing," said Gracie, reproach in her voice. "I expect they've been stolen."

"That's a shame," said my mother, and her voice was brisk again, matter-of-fact. She was back in charge, coming to meet my friend before she took Gracie home for lunch, which must be served on time because that would make the afternoon easier to live through.

Gracie and my mother walked with me to the car, and stood at a distance when I opened the door. Jason climbed out, speaking to them across the bonnet. I watched him as he smiled a greeting at my mother, and listened patiently while Gracie told him about the stones, and that two were missing, and that someone must have stolen them. I watched the sunlight make his curly hair shine, and how he had tiny lines at the side of his eyes when he squinted to keep the light out. I listened to his voice, hearing the slight Norfolk accent underlaying the cultured education, knowing that my mother would like him solely because he had listened to Gracie and not because he was being polite to her.

I hugged my mother, and she held me as if she would never let me go and I wondered if my ribs would crack under the strength of her arms.

"Think about my offer," she said. "You ought to come home really, it's where you belong. And it's even legal, the government have said people can move house. . ."

I promised I would think about it, and would phone her later today, when I was home.

Then I waved from the window as we drove away, and we left my home town and headed towards Cromer, and home—which wasn't my home at all, but rather somewhere that a kind stranger was allowing me to stay—and the muddle of emotions and thoughts and complete indecision was immense, so for many miles I said nothing. Jason drove in silence, giving me space, waiting until I was ready to talk, and I thought of everything there was to say, and how I did not want to say some of it, because there was something about this life, this suspended reality, which I didn't want to end. But I now knew that it must end, and soon.

Chapter Seventeen

I made pancakes for breakfast. The first one was in the pan when Jason came into the kitchen, his hair ruffled from the shower. He was wearing jeans and an old tee-shirt, and he smiled at me as he came to the stove and peered into the pan, his hand touching my shoulder.

"Smells good."

"Yes, thought I'd better make an effort, for my last breakfast," I said, my voice carefully light. But the words reminded me that I was leaving, and they echoed too much with the idea of a last meal for a convicted prisoner, and I thought again how much I wanted to stay, and how it was impossible because now I had an alternative and I had no *rights* here, I was an uninvited guest.

"There's not much flour left," I said, forcing the conversation on, towards less emotive topics. I used the spatula to ease the pancake from the sides of the pan, smelling the eggy aroma as it cooked.

"I hope they get some in the supermarket soon, there was nothing there on Saturday when I went—well, only some expensive looking bread flour, and that's not much good for anything other than bread, obviously.

"I don't know why," I said, musing the problem as I flipped the pancake, watching the shiny pale brown surface as an air bubble formed underneath, pushing up like some strange moon crater. "I mean, I understand why they ran out of stuff at the beginning, when everyone was panic buying, and I'd understand if it was stuff from abroad they couldn't get—like rice, or out of season fruit. But flour? Why has everyone run out of flour? I can't think of a reason for that."

I slid the pancake onto a plate, warm from the oven, and passed it to Jason.

"Thanks. Looks good." He moved back to the table, and started to pour maple syrup onto the pancake. I watched his hands as he snapped the top shut, reached for a knife. I loved his hands and they had become an expression of affection between us. We never kissed, or hugged, and I knew—because he had told me—that this was because I was still married, still *belonged with* Timothy. But in recent weeks, the affection between us had grown, expressed chastely through the odd squeeze of an arm, the touching of fingers.

I turned back to the pan, pouring more creamy batter onto the fat, hearing it sizzle as I swooshed it around. "Maybe everyone's cooking more," I said, "now that they're stuck at home for longer. They can't go to the pub, so they're making sourdough instead!"

Jason chuckled, and I smiled in spite of the ache inside. He had a good chuckle, a sort of natural bubble of deep laughter, that spurted out of him whenever something amused him. It reminded me of a child giggling. There was something honest about Jason, if he laughed, it was because something amused him, not because he felt he *should* laugh.

"Not much of a trade-off," he said. "Sourdough instead of the pub. Don't expect that one will last."

I carried my pancake to the table and began to slice a banana, watching as the slices fell onto my plate.

"You know you don't have to leave," Jason said again, his voice serious.

I nodded, pretending to concentrate on drizzling syrup over the banana. I wanted to tell him that I would stay, that meeting my family, reconnecting, had been enough. I could continue to maintain contact through emails and online chats, I felt no desire to go back home—it was like going backwards, returning to my childhood, and it underlined my failure.

But I didn't really have a choice, I knew that. The lockdown was easing, people were allowed to mix—last week in gardens if the number stayed below six people—now whole 'bubbles' could combine. Single people were allowed to go and stay overnight with one other family, to join the 'bubbles' of their quarantine. Although I was not, strictly, living alone, I sort of was. My mother had offered me a place to stay, and whilst every part of me wanted to stay with this man, with the person who had generously given me so much, I knew it wasn't right to stay. I was a parasite here, not able to pay my way, and his very generosity made me feel under an obligation, not equal.

Also, I wanted, so very much, for our relationship to develop, for us to become more than friends. This could only happen if I spoke to Timothy and ended our marriage properly. Something inside of me understood that I should not be living with Jason when that happened, I had almost a premonition that if I were to meet Timothy whilst living with Jason, he would know, and would search for anything sordid or nasty that could be smeared on Jason.

"I know, you already said," I replied, taking a bite of pancake and chewing. "And it's kind of you."

Jason sort of growled, an annoyed sound of contradiction.

"But you know that I shouldn't, it would be wrong. I need to get back on my feet, and become independent again. As soon as I can, I need to start looking for a job, earning my way again. I want to repay you what I owe, and then for us to start again—as equals. It's important to me. I want this to be right."

Jason stopped eating and took my hand. My heart jumped, and I swallowed, an unchewed piece of pancake scratching my throat as it went down.

"I know all that, and I understand, and like I've said before, the money doesn't matter—there's no hurry, I hardly even care if it never comes back. But I do care about you—about us. You've made me realise that my future could potentially be as bright as my past, and I don't want to see that walking out of the door. Just promise me, before you leave, promise me that you'll come back."

"I promise," I said, and my voice quavered, full of unspoken emotion and longing.

"I hope this feeling doesn't fade," I thought, *"I hope he doesn't change when I've gone, when life becomes normal again."* I knew I was risking so much by leaving, but there seemed no other way.

Jason released my hand, and stared at the wall behind me, as if lost in thought.

I took a swig of coffee, and turned back to my pancake.

"I met Abigail when I was a teenager—did I ever tell you that?"

I shook my head. Jason hardly ever mentioned his wife, even though her presence whispered from every ornament and rug and carefully placed table. There were photographs of her around the house, laughing in her bridal gown, smiling on a beach, windswept in a field—I had picked them up when alone in a room, stared at her face, compared her prettiness with my plain features, her slender figure with my own—wondering how we compared. She looked as if she had been fun, which annoyed me because I found that I wanted to dislike her, for her to be a bad person and best forgotten.

"We were just kids really, but we started out as friends, and then became a couple soon after we went to university, which wasn't the best timing really as it meant travelling across the country every weekend so we could be together. Everyone said it wouldn't last, that the distance would mean we finished, but we didn't. We got engaged a year after graduation." He grinned, remembering.

"Everyone said we were too young, but it's what we wanted." He glanced at me and smiled in an embarrassed way.

He looked back at the wall, at a spot somewhere above my head, and I knew he was thinking of her, recalling times and events, the touch of her, the smell of her, the sound of her voice.

"We had too short a time together," he said at last, something bitter in his voice. "It wasn't the perfect marriage or anything like that—we argued, and she wanted kids right away and I thought we were too young and what was the hurry when we had loads of time—except we didn't, did we? It was a car accident—did I tell you that?"

I shook my head again, not wanting to speak and interrupt the thoughts and emotions that were filling his mind. His face had a new expression, one I hadn't seen before, a hardening of the lines around his mouth, something angry in his eyes.

"A drunk driver, on the Overstrand road, going too fast and lost control at a corner. It all felt so random at the time —one minute earlier or later, and she wouldn't have been in that exact spot at that exact time. It made no sense. . ." he dipped his head and rubbed the back of his head. "It still makes no sense."

For a while we were silent. I folded my knife and fork, no longer hungry, the pancake on my plate growing cold and unappetising, the banana beginning to brown and soften in the air.

I waited.

"Abigail was more than a wife," he said, his voice soft. "She was my best friend."

I felt myself tense, and I knew he was saying things that I did not want to hear. I didn't want to face this, and for the length of my stay I had managed to convince myself that his wife—I never used her name because then she was less real—his wife was firmly in the past, an ethereal being from dreams and memories. The thought of her as a real, flesh and blood human, was uncomfortable. Jason was speaking again, voicing his memories, wanting me to understand.

"But it got better, after a while. I stopped forcing myself out of bed in the mornings because it started to be natural again. And I stopped wanting to punch the rude person in the supermarket, because it wasn't so annoying any more, and I realised that I was even able to laugh again, that things were still funny and interesting and worth doing— even without her.

"Eventually, I even stopped seeing her. It sounds weird now, almost like I was a bit insane, but for the longest time afterwards, I kept thinking I saw her. I'd be shopping, and catch sight of her in the next queue, or I'd drive past her in the street. It was never her, of course, I don't believe in ghosts or anything. But it was as if my mind was trying to replace her, to make me see similarities in other people. Weird thing, the brain. Has a mind of its own!"

He grinned, and for a moment his eyes cleared, and I knew he was with me again, directing his words to me. But as I watched, his expression became wistful, and I realised he was only partly here, his thoughts were still lost in the memory of his wife.

He reached out, and took hold of my hand again, but in an absent way, almost as if he was unaware of doing it.

"I still miss her," he said, and I saw tears fill his eyes, and hang there for a moment until he looked up at the ceiling and blinked them away in a gesture I guessed he had learned to do in the days when crying was a frequent thing. I wanted to move closer, to take his sad face in my hands, to comfort him. But I didn't. I sat very still, waiting until he had regained control, until he could finish what he wanted to say.

"I miss her every day, but less now, sort of less sharply. When I think of her, and remember things we did, something she said, then mostly it makes me smile now rather than cry."

He looked at me, and grinned in embarrassment.

"Blokes aren't meant to cry, are they?"

"I think," I said, not wanting to break the spell of his reminiscing, "that after your wife dies, crying is very much allowed, for as long as you want to. Even for blokes."

"Well," he said, taking a breath and sitting up straighter, but still holding my hand in his.

I sat very still, feeling the warmth of his fingers and wanting to curl my own hand around his but not daring to, not wanting to do anything that might make him aware that he was holding my hand and make him stop. I craved the physical contact, even though I was fairly sure it was an inadvertent gesture, an unconscious act.

"You'll be relieved to hear that I am much better now, and my Kleenex bill has reduced considerably!" He grinned, then turned to face me, his expression serious.

"Most of that is down to you. These last few weeks, life has been so much brighter again, laughing has been something normal again, I've woken in the morning pleased to be awake, not dreading another day. It feels ironic, amidst all this death that the virus has brought, I've personally felt more alive than I thought I ever would again. I like being with you, laughing with you, teasing you and being completely thrashed whenever we play a game. . . I think. . ." he paused.

I waited. The clock on the wall was ticking very loudly, and I realised I was holding my breath. I swallowed, my mouth felt dry, and I looked into his eyes, lost in the deep blue of their gaze.

"I think I might be in love with you," he said, "but. . . it's complicated, isn't it?"

I nodded. It *was* complicated.

"I don't think I can be *the other man,*" he said. "I can't have an affair with a married woman, and you *are* married, however much I tell myself that it was your husband's fault, and he has in fact nullified the marriage by his actions, which makes you free. But you're not free, not properly. Not until you sort it out."

He dropped my hand, and stood up, as if suddenly restless. I watched as he paced the kitchen, unsettled by his thoughts.

"And I don't even know what will happen in the future. I mean, I know how I feel now, but this is such a weird time, nothing is normal. We don't know each other that well, not really, not like being friends for years and years. . ."

"Not like you and Abigail," I thought. And I realised that I would *never* compare with Abigail. I could never go back in time, and be the girl he grew up with, never be the one who had shared his adolescence, been there when he graduated, planned his first house with. I would never be her—but could I still have a place in his life?

I watched him, as he began to clear the table, moving crockery to the sink with a roughness I hadn't seen before. I knew he was angry, frustrated because he was too honest to make promises he couldn't keep, too honourable to ask me to leave my husband when he didn't know yet what he could offer in return. I understood.

I also knew, felt a stirring inside, that there was a chance, however tiny, that we might be happy together. We *did* have a connection, the beginnings of a relationship. But that could not deepen into proper love, a real bond, unless I was free. And to be free I must confront Timothy and sever those ties properly. And to do that, I needed to be living somewhere else. Which meant that whilst my heart longed to stay, I needed to leave.

"I know," I said, and stood too, making him look at me.

He stopped pretending to clear up and came back to the table. He stood very close, looking down at me, and I felt something swell inside, and longed for him to reach down and kiss me.

"I know," I said again. "I know that you can't make me any promises—we aren't at that stage yet, and unless I sort things out, we never will be. And I know that I need to sort things out *for me*. So that I can get on with my life and move forwards, whether that's with you or not. Which is why I need to leave. I need to live somewhere independently, I need to go back to my mum, at least for a little while, and get myself sorted out. Perhaps after that. . ."

I left the words, not able to say them, not wanting to vocalise something that might be too much, might make him retreat.

"Yes," he said, "Perhaps after that." He sighed, a deep sigh of frustration, almost despair. "There's so *much* in the way," he said, "There's your husband, there's the age gap, your history, my history. . And yet, even with all that between us, all I want is for you to stay, for us to be together. It makes no sense, I know that, but it's what I want."

Jason placed his hands on my shoulders. I could smell his soap, and noticed he had a tiny spot of syrup on his chin, and I longed to reach up and wipe it away, but knew that I mustn't. I didn't have that right, not yet.

"I don't like the risk—of you going—I don't like the risk that you might not come back," he said.

"I will," I said. And at that moment, I meant it.

***

I packed my few things into three crumpled carrier bags, stripped the bedding from the bed and left it washing in the machine, then told Jason I was ready to leave. I wanted to leave a gift—but I had no money to buy one. I wanted to leave a note—but there was nothing I hadn't already said. So I simply filled a tiny vase with flowers from the garden, and left them on a window sill, hoping he would see them when he returned to the house, and think of me, and smile.

Jason had insisted on driving me again, saying it was too much hassle to take trains, and more risk for my family. I craved the extra moments with him, so accepted willingly, but we didn't talk much on the drive. I think we were both wary of saying the wrong thing, upsetting the fragile equilibrium that we seemed to have arrived at. We chatted about inconsequential things: the weather, if anyone would be able to have a holiday this year, whether the announced quarantine for people entering the country was even slightly sustainable if they wanted to boost the economy—and what would that mean for lorry drivers carrying essential supplies from Europe.

Jason turned on the news, and we listened in silence to a debate about whether a government advisor should resign—he had broken the lockdown rules and visited his parents, citing the need to sort childcare as his excuse. Jason glanced at me.

"I guess everyone has stretched the rules to suit their own situation," he said, "not just us."

I nodded, thinking of how we had combined our households, and Jason had risked catching the virus from me, and how my mother had hugged me, insisting that was allowed, and now, even this drive, this joining yet another household, was sort of against the rules. I was not in a position to judge someone else.

"The thing is," said Jason, easing into the flow of traffic at a junction, "someone in authority has to be more careful than everyone else."

"But he's not an MP or anything, is he?"

"No, but he is an advisor, and we all feel like he has a lot of influence. When you think about people stuck at home in an inner city, perhaps with kids, obeying the rules, not seeing people who they love, not going to parks for exercise even though they'd love to. Or people watching their business going to pot, or not able to attend the funeral of someone they love. Maybe not even able to visit them when they were dying in hospital, so that people have died alone, without family round them—all because they're obeying the rules and doing what the government told them to do, protecting the NHS and vulnerable people. Well, you can see how they must be pretty livid when someone who probably has it a lot easier than them, goes and flaunts the rules. You can't do stuff like that, not when you're seen as one of the rule-makers. It makes people feel foolish, as if they were idiots for obeying the rules when someone else doesn't."

He shook his head. "Pretty stupid of him really, considering he's meant to be such a clever guy. . ."

I nodded, but didn't respond, knowing that Jason was talking for the sake of something to say and the things we were really thinking about, and wanting and feeling, couldn't be discussed, because they might take us back to the same dead-end of all our other discussions. Neither of us wanted the conclusion we had come to, but neither could we find an alternative solution.

I stared out of the window, watching the scenery moving like a film in front of me, feeling the miles as they passed, knowing that they were miles that would separate us. It felt much further this time, the journey from Cromer to Kent, and I knew it was because each mile was taking me further away from him, and was another obstacle—a physical one amongst all the emotional ones—that would need to be overcome if we were ever to be properly together.

The news changed topics, the reporter describing the latest response to some protests against racial inequality, the desecration of a statue in Bristol.

"I'm not sure what I think about all that," said Jason, indicating to over-take a lorry, checking his side mirror. "I mean, I get the whole racial inequality argument, and it's terrible what black people in America have had to put up with, the police abusing their rights, people not educated properly—things that should have changed in the last century. But these protest marches in England, changing names of places because the person who paid for the hospital also had slaves, writing on Churchill's statue because he made racist comments—I'm not sure about all that. In the past, society *was* racist, and that was wrong. But I'm not sure destroying things today changes anything."

"But surely you accept that England still has a racist problem?" I said, thinking of Charlie, and all the *rubbish* she had to deal with, just because she happened to have a dark skin. I thought about the name-calling, the teachers who never picked her when she raised her hand in class, the trouble she'd had in finding interesting work. I reached into my bag and pulled out a bottle of water, then held it up, offering some to Jason, but he shook his head.

"Well, it all started with the police killing that black man in America, didn't it," said Jason. "That seems to be the single event that has set off the protest. I mean, black people have been abused forever, and that's wrong and needs to change. But I worry that the protest marches will get out of hand, will start to be about a different issue. When a mass of people starts to move in a certain direction, sometimes that can become dangerous, sometimes the wrong people get hurt. . ."

I nodded, thinking about the crowds I had seen on the news, their shouts of glee when the statue toppled, the violence as they hauled it to the quay, threw it into the water, as if their actions could obliterate the past, as if destruction could remove the hurt. I wondered where it might end.

The news headlines finished, music filled the car, and we stopped talking.

As I watched the passing scenery, I thought again of the book we had read together, musing over the descriptions of the French Revolution. That too had started with the death of an individual, after years of oppression towards one sector of society. The story had described scenes where the masses, a churning tide of people, had risen up and swept through a city, uncontrolled and powerful. I shivered, wondering whether this new phenomena, like the virus, something unconnected to me, would somehow affect the course of my life. Where would it end, this tornado of public outrage?

I glanced at Jason. He was tapping a beat on the steering wheel, lost in the rhythm of the song on the radio. I decided I was being melodramatic, and stared out of the window, watching the scenery become more familiar, as we neared my home town. A sense of dread filled me, and I wanted to stop the car, change the direction of our journey, stop going back to where I had started.

"I have to do this," I reminded myself. "I have to confront the past so that I can make the future how I want it to be."

When we arrived, I pulled my bags from the car and then stood there, staring at my mother's front door, but not wanting to knock. When I knocked, I knew that she would answer immediately, and that I would instantly be back where I had started, and my time with Jason would have finished.

I felt again that sour weight of failure, the knowledge of wasted years—I was arriving right back at the beginning, returning to my childhood. I had failed utterly at being an adult, failed at being a wife, failed even at being an independent human. I swallowed, determined not to cry, to push away those feelings and get over the hurdle of starting the next chapter of my life.

Jason stood next to me, waiting. He looked at the front door, and I wondered what he thought, whether he was surprised by the smallness of the house, the untidy garden next door, the general tatty air of the location. He rubbed the top of his head, in a gesture I knew so well, and I knew he was feeling awkward, unsure of what to say. He turned to me, leant down, and very lightly, kissed my cheek, the briefest touch of his lips on my skin, but it warmed the very core of me.

I turned, and was about to leave, when he reached out and picked two stray hairs that had collected on my sleeve. He looked at me, as he twisted them round his finger, round and round, so they made a circle.

"Do you remember, the old man in the story?" he asked, reminding me of the book we had read together, and the father who had waited in the North Tower for long years until his daughter had arrived to rescue him.

I nodded.

Jason took his wallet from his pocket, and slid the circle of hair into a corner, next to the photograph of his dead wife.

"I'll be waiting," he said, and his eyes were full of love. "Whatever you decide, I'll be waiting."

Chapter Eighteen

While I was saying goodbye to Jason, another man, in another town, had just said goodbye to someone whom he loved. His name was John, but I didn't know that, I knew nothing about him or his work partner, and I would have been shocked if told of how they would alter my life.

John was driving home, barely noticing the cars he passed because he was thinking about Di.

"Such a good body," he thought, smiling to himself as he thought of her sleek limbs, the way she walked, almost as if she was walking on tip-toe, like a model. She was very tall, some people would be nervous of that, but for John it was ideal. He smiled again, thinking of the afternoon they'd spent together, how much he enjoyed working with her.

He yawned, stretching his mouth wide. He was tired now, hoped he could have an easy evening in front of the telly.

John parked in front of his block of flats, and pulled his bag from the boot.

"Better try and get into the shower as soon as I'm inside," he thought.

Di's perfume probably lingered on his clothes, some trace of her absorbed by his skin. His wife Ali wouldn't like that. He'd try to be clean before she greeted him—it would make the evening smoother.

***

I was also unaware of Benjamin. As I was walking to knock on my mother's front door, Benjamin was stepping from his shower.

The shower curtain touched his damp body as he stepped from the bath, and it clung to him, cold and slimy, smelling faintly of mould. Benjamin shuddered.

He detached the plastic shower curtain with a grimace, and moved towards the mirror, wiping away the steam with his hand. His face stared back at him, his eyes dark pools of despondency in a pale face.

"I look normal," he thought, staring at the short hair, the thin cheeks. "No one looking at me sees the agony inside, all the pain is hidden."

The sadness welled up inside, and he reached for the knife. It was one from the kitchen used to slice through potatoes and carrots, kept sharp by the little silver sharpener someone had bought from Lakeland—probably Carl, he was a stickler for having decent kitchen equipment. They all were, they all cared more about the flat than the people sharing it, than Benjamin.

He looked at the knife, and lay it on his arm, against the damp skin. He had so much pain inside, so much unresolved sadness, and there was nowhere to put it, no way to get it out. Maybe, if he used the knife to hurt his outsides, it would help the world to see the pain that was suffocating him inside. He needed a way to express the sadness, to feel physically what was happening emotionally.

Slowly, slowly, Benjamin moved the knife away from his flesh. He wasn't sure he wanted to feel pain like this, didn't think he could force himself to endure the sting as the knife slid into his flesh.

As he lowered the knife, his eyes filled with tears again, flowing down his face, dripping onto his damp chest. He wasn't even brave enough to hurt himself, to allow his agony to take a physical form. He was a coward, not fit for anything, even this.

The knife dropped to the floor, and Benjamin lay next to it, and curled, shivering, onto his side.

Part Two

Chapter Nineteen

Timothy first met her in 2014, when he took the job at the nearby comprehensive school. It had just been taken over by a local trust, who were pushing for academy status and anyone who had different politics either jumped ship or was, ever so gently, pushed overboard.

In the world outside, Ebola was ravaging West Africa, the first Malaysian aircraft had disappeared, but the second one had not yet crashed, and Germany was training to win the World Cup in Brazil. None of these events touched Timothy even slightly, he noticed them in passing and continued to prepare for his new role teaching apathetic students with snagged tights and trousers worn half-way down their underwear.

Timothy saw her on his second day at the school, when he was beginning to feel more at home with the end of lesson bells that sounded like an emergency and the slow-motion arrival of his next class. He noticed her because she was sitting very still, and her back was completely straight, and when he spoke to her, she blushed as though on fire. He noticed her, and would have let it remain at noticing, if they hadn't met so often at so many random events. She turned up at school concerts, and appeared in the dining room at the same time, and happened to be wheeling her bike up the driveway as he was unlocking his car. She was hard to ignore, with her tangle of long brown hair, the green pools of her eyes, and the pale skin that coloured whenever she saw him.

She was funny too. He realised, when he politely greeted her or her friend Charlotte—who seemed permanently glued to her side—every conversation was smattered with ironic comments and amusing anecdotes, so that in spite of himself, he laughed. He began to look for her, when he entered the hall, or walked the corridor, and he knew that he was smitten, and there was danger in obsession; but he hadn't looked for danger, only for her.

She began to come to him under the pretext of needing extra tuition. That her maths needed help was as obvious as the fact that she didn't care in the slightest. Her work was sloppy, inaccurate, as if she had scribbled the answers under duress and was hoping for his pen to cross things out, correct numbers, show her different formulae.

"I can't work out why this one is wrong," she would whine, the buttons on her blouse indecently revealing lace and pale, pale skin. "I did everything you showed us, but my answer is still different."

He stole his eyes away from her skin, and avoided her eyes, and stared at the scribbled answers.

"You're out by ten," he explained, showing the number she had carried forward but forgotten to add. "Everything else," he looked at her, met her eyes, smiled very faintly, "is perfect."

"Out by ten" became a regular saying between them, a special phrase, the *"everything else is perfect"* understood but never said. After a while it became her nickname, the special label he called her by, which gradually became shortened to *Ten*. "Hello Ten," he said when he saw her in the corridors; "Thank you Ten," when she handed him her homework; "I'll collect you later Ten," he whispered over private tutorials.

She came often, stealing into his tutor room at break times and lunchtimes and occasionally after school—though that was more noticeable and therefore more risky, so he suggested she should stop. He always behaved with discretion, he never did anything that could cost him his job, but he knew they were sitting slightly too close, and that under the table he could feel her leg touching his, and that sometimes when he was explaining some tricky formula or algebraic equation, she would lean against him to watch as he wrote, and he would feel the warmth of her skin through his sleeve, and smell her soap and shampoo.

The concert was the first time he broke protocol, and suggested they meet outside the confines of what was appropriate. He had known he was taking a risk, but his obsession by then had taken hold, she was all he thought about, dreamed about, saw when he ate or drove or worked. She was always there, sapping his resolve, enticing him with her innocence. He had bought the tickets in a moment of abandon, regretted it, decided to return them, then invited her anyway and hoped she would refuse. But she hadn't refused. She had not refused anything.

He had started to see her outside of school, and the private tutorials stopped, as he deemed them too risky. He would ignore her now in the assembly hall and corridors; no one watching would suspect they were anything other than formally acquainted. But when she stole from her home in the evening, walking to the corner where he was waiting in his car, he would watch her, and listen to her, and absorb her. She was all he ever thought about, and as he learned more about her, it only increased his hunger, and his need to own her.

She was mature for her age, and when she had overcome her blushes enough to speak coherently, she told him about her life, and he listened for long hours. Her younger sister had special needs and it seemed to him that her own needs had been constantly denied, soaked up by her parasitic sister. The mother always sided with the sister, desiring life to be as smooth as possible, which lead to the sister being denied nothing, she had only to shout— or even to widen her eyes and hold her breath in a precursor to shouting—and whatever she demanded was provided. This meant that he wanted nothing more than to protect *Ten,* to steal her away from this neglectful household, to take her where she would be adored and prized. He began to make a plan.

When she failed her exams, the school agreed there was little point in continuing her education. If her father resisted, suggesting that perhaps further qualifications were worth pursuing, Timothy argued harder. As her father whispered in one ear, Timothy whispered in the other; and Timothy had more practice than the father.

"Why don't you find a little job in a shop?" he whispered, "something to earn a little cash and be independent until we can be together."

"Won't that be boring?" she had asked, sliding her blouse from her perfect white shoulder.

"It won't be for long," he promised. "As soon as your father gives permission, we can marry, and then I can look after you. I'll work hard enough for both of us *Ten*, you won't need to ever worry about money again."

Timothy promised he would look after her for ever—something her dying father, with his regular trips for failing chemotherapy, and his weary eyes, could not offer. Timothy would always provide a home for her, he would set her free from the parasitic sister, and the neglectful mother and the dying father. He knew they were hard things, things that any girl would want to escape from, and he was right. She fled her past, and went willing to him.

Timothy took her to his home—the house he had bought with hard work and careful saving. He was very proud of his house, bought when he was younger than most of his colleagues, in a quiet part of town. It was a three-bedroomed semi-detached red-brick house, with a sunny sitting room, and a small office that overlooked the square garden. He lived there before he met her, and had fitted the kitchen cabinets himself, and papered the walls and dug the garden. It was his special place, and when he brought her there as his wife, he thought that his happiness was complete. But euphoria does not last forever. He began to have doubts, to fear her rejection, to wonder if he had given her too much.

For a while, she continued to work at the shoe shop, going each day to measure feet and arrange displays. Timothy would go sometimes, in his break times and on a Saturday when her shift fell at a weekend; he would stand across the street, simply so he could catch a glimpse of his wife as she worked.

One summer's day, as he stood in the shadows, he recognised the cotton dress she was wearing, one of several he had bought for her when they first got married, and he had explained how he thought her jeans were too tight, and slightly common, and she wouldn't realise that, growing up as she had on a council estate, but he could teach her things like that, now they were married. He had put her clothes into big black bags, ready for the charity shop, saying that she could, of course, remove anything she particularly wanted to keep, but the clothes he had bought for her were ones he loved to see her wearing. They were so elegant, so feminine—but if she wanted to wear clothes he hated, of course that was her choice. Did she want to remove anything from the bag?

He had watched her expression, torn between wanting to please him and the desire to continue with her old way of life, wearing the same clothes as her contemporaries.

"No, no, I love the dresses you bought, and it was so kind of you. Of course I won't wear jeans any more, not if you don't like them. Though, I might keep one pair. . ." she went to the bag and rummaged down, past the tight tee-shirts and cropped tops to where her jeans were folded. "For when I'm gardening, or doing something dirty," she explained, smiling up at him and hugging the jeans to her, like a talisman.

He had smiled at her, loving the look of her in the simply cotton frock, so like one that his own mother had worn when he was young. It was the same dress she wore now, as he watched her stoop to measure a child's foot. He wondered if the neckline gaped when she bent, and whether men sometimes brought their children to have their feet measured, and if they stared at her body. It made him feel uncomfortable, and he turned away, thinking that perhaps he would suggest she stopped working.

"It's so boring," she moaned later in the evening, curling her beautiful body into the sofa, staring into his face while he listened. "I am beginning to hate children, they have such sweaty little feet! And they never keep still while I'm trying to measure them, and then they never like the same shoes as their mothers do, so I have to stand there, like a complete lemon, while they have a row about what kind of shoes they came for in the first place. Half the time they just leave, without buying anything, so it's all a waste of time anyway."

"Do you want to stop?" he asked, wanting her to be happy. "I can afford for you to stop, if you want to. It might be nicer for you to just stay here, to read, and look after the house and stuff. You could cook dinner for when I get home, and sometimes I could pop home at lunchtime, so you wouldn't be too lonely I think. Do you want to? I want you to be happy."

She had nodded uncertainly, and Timothy saw she was torn, not wanting to give up her tiny slice of independence, but also hating her job, the tedium of her days, the futility of her labours. The idea had grown on him, the thought that if she didn't work, he wouldn't have to share her with anyone else, she would be his alone, for him to nurture and keep safe. He began to ask her regularly, every time she came home moaning, he would say it was her own choice, why was she still bothering? He belittled her income, calling it 'pin-money' and making it seem insignificant, not worth her effort to earn it.

"Look *Ten*," he would say when checking the bank statement, "there's the money you earnt. It hardly seems worth it, does it? Perhaps you could spend it on a plant for the lounge or something! Or buy the sandwiches one day for lunch. That can be your own little contribution to the family coffers."

Gradually her demotivation grew, until she was ready to accept his kind offer, and she handed in her notice, and stopped leaving the house five days a week to waste her time with shoes.

However, she still had her friends, and when her job ended, her social life increased. Sometimes, they met her friends together. On one occasion, they all met at a pub, Timothy and her arriving first, sitting in an alcove while they waited.

"Do you know why they're late?" asked Timothy, handing her a fat glass of white wine. The bar behind him was busy, young people jostling to buy pitchers of cocktails and sickly drinks with invisible alcohol so they could get drunk on the culinary equivalent of orange squash. The lights were low, hiding the migraine-inducing patterned carpet and the dusty curtains and the faded cushions on the seats. He slid onto the bench beside her, and avoided touching the sticky table.

She shook her head, her eyes shining. "They're always late!" she shouted above the overly loud music.

Timothy looked around. Everyone was shouting, adding to the already immense noise; shouting and laughing, as though they were all part of some hilarious joke. He guessed most people were in their late teens, though some were younger, he noted, seeing a boy from his GCSE class. The girls wore tight clothes, tops that revealed more than they hid, skirts that gave glimpses of thighs or trousers painted on to their chubby thighs or stick-thin legs. The boys wore crumpled shirts or faded tee-shirts and jeans that refused to cover their underwear. Timothy took a mouthful of wine, then stood as Charlotte arrived. She was his wife's best friend, and Timothy worried about her influence, and whether he was ever the topic of their conversations.

"Charlie! Great to see you—what will you drink?" Timothy was smiling, the welcoming host, not showing any resentment at having to spend money on drinks for her friends, drinks that half of them would guzzle, barely tasting them, in their quest to spend Friday night inebriated.

"Sorry we're late," Charlie shouted towards him as she slid onto a chair. She leant towards his wife, as though trying to exclude Timothy, even though she needed to shout above the general noise to be heard, and her words could be heard by anyone near.

"My brother Trevor gave me a lift, and we were stopped *again* by the police. Honestly! That's the tenth time now since he bought that car. They said a brake light wasn't working, which is a load of bollocks, because it was serviced last week, and when they finally decided that we hadn't stolen the car and let us go, the light was magically working again. I don't know. . ." she paused, her face hurt, as if mystified by the world she found herself in. "I said to Trevor, I said, it's just not worth the hassle. The police see him—a black man in a fancy car—and all they think about is that it's probably stolen and they need to check. I wish he'd sell the thing and buy some battered old car, the type everyone expects a young black bloke to be driving. Then maybe I wouldn't be late for things all the time when he gives me a lift."

She glanced up, as if only just realising that Timothy was hovering, waiting for her to finish her story.

"Vodka and coke please Tim, make it a nice strong one. I'm here now, the party can begin!"

By the time Timothy had made his fourth trip to the bar and spent the money he would have preferred to spend on a weekend away, all her friends had arrived, and were discussing where they would go next.

"Let's try that new club in Bromley,"

"Bromley! I'm not going all that way, we'd have to get the train. Can't we go somewhere nearer?"

Timothy wanted to suggest that perhaps they could all simply stay in the bar they were in, that the whole idea of drinking—*prelashing*—before going to their final destination was a silly one, the next venue would have the same sticky floor and loud music as this bar.

"Oh dear, look at him!" said Charlotte, leaning against Ten, *his Ten,* "Someone should stop him!"

Timothy looked to where she was pointing. A man, older even than Timothy, was dancing, his beer slopping onto the floor, his fat behind wiggling in time to the music, his elbows awkwardly bent.

"He looks like my dad dancing!" giggled *Ten.*

Timothy turned to her, saw the sloppiness in her mouth, the gleam in her eye. He wanted to take her home, away from these children who were playing at adulthood.

"I'm tired, and have some marking to do before tomorrow," he said. "I might head home."

A couple of *her* friends looked at each other, their eyes laughing at his age, the reference to marking. They leant closer to each other and he caught snatches of their conversation, whispered too loudly because the alcohol had affected their senses and their discretion was compromised.

"Mrs Black in geography was a right bitch this afternoon," he heard and, *"the staff in that place don't know what real life is for."*

"I'm not ready to go home yet," she said, her arm slung over Charlotte's shoulder, her eyes darkening like a stubborn child speaking to a parent.

Timothy did not want to be her parent, nor did he want her friends to think he was like her parent, didn't want them to whisper things in her ear that would pull her away from him.

"No, my love," he heard himself saying as he forced a smile and pulled notes from his wallet. "Here, you take some money, have a fun time with your friends, but if you don't mind, I'll head home now. Is that okay?"

He waited for her to refuse, to thank him but say she wanted to stay with him, her friends could go on without her, he had been generous, paid for all their drinks, of course she wouldn't just abandon him now.

But she didn't. She folded the money into her bag, and giggled at Charlotte, and looked *pleased* that he was leaving. It was almost as if she relished time alone with her friends, as if he was an encumbrance, perhaps as embarrassing as the man on the dance floor, who was now turning in drunken circles.

Timothy left. He drove home, let himself into the empty house and sat in their little sitting room alone. The hours ticked past, he finished his work, tried to watch a film, then sat, waiting.

"You're home late," he said, when the front door eventually clicked open and his wife staggered into the room. He looked at her face, saw the glow in her eyes, smelt alcohol on her breath. "I was waiting for you."

"You could have come," she called over her shoulder, casually, as if it was no big deal.

But it was a big deal. It felt like a taunt, as if she regretted tying herself to someone so much older. Timothy raced from the chair and caught her at the foot of the stairs.

He pulled her to him, and kissed her. "I love you *Ten,*" he whispered, holding her close. "I miss you when you're not here. You're my wife now, not a silly school kid. . ." He paused, knowing that to suggest her friends *were* silly would be a mistake. "I want to spend my evenings with you. I don't need anyone else, you're my world, my complete world."

She nodded, and relaxed into him, and he took her upstairs.

Chapter Twenty

Timothy knew that too much time spent with her peers would undermine his influence; she might grow to regret her decision, and slide away from his grasp. He had waited too long, those long months while she was his pupil, and then while he waited for her father to give permission for them to marry. He couldn't bear to lose her now to her friends, for them to laugh at his age, to pull her back into their circle.

"I don't like you spending every evening with your friends," he told her one day, holding her close. "They're different to us, and when you've been with them, you're different too. I want you to be all mine, I love you too much to share you."

He found things to ridicule when she told him what her friends had said:

"Toby said that? You mean Toby-of-the many-spots? Goodness! I didn't realise he had political views—or do you think he borrowed them from his father?"

Gradually he put obstacles in the way of her arranging to meet them. He came home from work one evening with a bag full of special food, a bunch of flowers, and some Prosecco.

"I thought we'd share a romantic evening," he told her, unpacking the food onto the kitchen table. "I even remembered strawberries—your favourite."

He went to her with the flowers, and kissed her cheek: "For my special wife."

He saw her eyes cloud, watched her struggle for the right response. The flowers were a mixed bunch, roses and chrysanthemums and stems of delicate gypsophila, rolled into a paper cone.

"But. . . I was going out tonight with the girls. Did you forget? We arranged it ages ago. . .for Charlie's birthday."

"Oh!" he let his face drop, his expression dejected. "I had completely forgotten," he lied. "I remember now you mention it—weren't you all going to that tacky club where all the school kids use fake ID to buy drinks so they can throw-up on the pavement outside afterwards? I'm sorry, I'm not sure you ever told me the date."

He watched while she decided whether or not to protest, to say she had reminded him several times, and he knew she had bought a gift because he'd watched her wrap it at the weekend. She bit her lip.

He began to arrange the things on the table, to stick a candle into an empty wine bottle, to carry the food to the worktop and start to unwrap it. There were tiny portions of salmon mousse, and a bag of salad that he tossed into a bowl. He pulled out a frying pan, and laid two steaks on a plate, sprinkled them with salt and pepper, then paused, stared at them for a moment and then with deliberate movements placed one on a separate plate and put it in the fridge.

"No worries," he said, his voice sounding hurt and full of disappointment, as he tipped the strawberries into a sieve and washed them. "You go ahead, have a lovely time with your friends. This won't keep really, I'll just eat it myself." He managed a bitter laugh. "Not quite what I'd planned, but hey-ho, that's life."

He glanced up at her stricken expression, knew that she was in an agony of indecision.

"You go, really, I don't mind," he said, bowing his head as if to hide his hurt.

She came to him, reached arms around his shoulders, rested her head in his neck.

"No, of course I won't go. It was a lovely thought, really kind, and I'd love to stay and share it with you. I'll just go and phone Charlie, try to explain that I can't come. . . maybe say I've got a headache or something."

He poured Prosecco into two glasses while she went to phone her friend, waited until he heard her voice: "Hi Honey, happy birthday! Listen, I'm really *really* sorry, but. . ." then he went to her, offered the drink, kissed her just loud enough for her friend to hear, whispered that he loved her. He knew it would be obvious to Charlotte that there was no headache, simply an excuse to not attend her birthday. He knew it would cause hurt, hopefully a rift between them. But it didn't matter, he felt that it was time that she chose, either her friends or the man who she said she loved. It couldn't be both.

On other occasions he would arrive home with a film, or tickets to a show, or pretend she had forgotten a date they had arranged—each time when he knew that she had planned to meet her friends. She became the unreliable one, the one who was likely to cancel at the last minute. After a while, she saw her friends less frequently, and eventually, never at all.

Timothy loved knowing that she was fully dependent on him, and he sought to care for her properly. He would often pop home to see her during his free lessons, and most days he ate lunch at home unless there was a staff meeting he couldn't avoid.

Her phone was an old one, with slow responses and limited abilities, so one day, when a promotion enabled him to have money for treats, he bought two matching smartphones, one for each of them. It had cost him more than he'd realised, but he wanted her to be happy, and he knew that sometimes she was lonely.

"Look, now you can text me, whenever you want. And I've downloaded an app, so you can see me, and I can see you, so I'll know when you're shopping, and if you get stuck somewhere, I'll be able to come and rescue you."

"Where am I going to get stuck?" she asked, laughing at him. "Honestly Timothy, you think I'm a numpty!"

He laughed, sharing the joke, delighting in her laughter, but knowing that he couldn't bear to lose her, and this would help to keep her safe.

Almost on cue, her old phone rang, the tune calling from her pocket. She fished it out.

"I need to change my number to my new phone," she said, glancing at the screen. "Oh! It's Mum." She stood and walked to the window, talking as she went. Timothy watched her.

"Hi Mum, yes thanks, we're fine. Timothy has been promoted—isn't that good?

"Gracie? Oh dear. Yes, I guess I could come and sit with her on Thursday afternoon. . ." she turned, raising her eyebrows, asking him is that was okay.

Timothy frowned. There had obviously been no discussion about his promotion, no asking what his new role was, whether he was pleased. Her mother only ever seemed to phone when she needed someone to look after Gracie, and her interest in both his wife and himself was minimal. He knew that her mother disapproved of him, of their relationship, and although she had never actually said as much, he felt that if she could separate them, she would. He disliked his wife spending time with people who might weaken their special bond. He sat and listened while *his wife* finished making arrangements with her mother while he set up her new phone. He passed it to her when her call finished and she came back to the table.

"That was Mum," she said unnecessarily. "She wants me to watch Gracie on Thursday, so she can do some shopping in peace."

"She isn't offering to take you with her then?" said Timothy, handing her the phone and showing her how to record her thumb print as a security measure. "She's not suggesting you meet for coffee, so she can spend time with you?" he said, taking her thumb and rolling it over the sensor on the phone. "Not suggesting that she could perhaps come here, and see where you live, or that you go to watch a film together or something?" He heard the bitterness in his own voice, and coughed.

"Honestly *Ten*, she only ever phones you when she wants you to watch Gracie. I know your dad is still ill, but she could pay a sitter occasionally, it shouldn't be your responsibility all the time."

He watched as her head drooped, and he knew that she hated these conversations, disliked hearing him criticise her family. But it was his responsibility to care for her, and not to allow her mother to keep abusing their relationship. He picked up her hand, and ran his thumb over her palm, stroking her.

"I don't like them taking advantage like this," he said. "To be honest, I think it would be best if you didn't give your mum your new number. If she calls your old phone, then obviously you can chat if you want to, but it means you won't be 'on call' all the time, you can take time off from being the dutiful daughter sometimes, live your own life rather than always being her back-up."

He saw her nod, and decided that later, he would phone her mother himself. It was time for him to step in, and stop this constant one-sided asking for favours. Yes, he decided, it was time. He would block her mother's number on the old phone, reduce the possibility for contact, and he would phone the mother himself, tell her his wife had a new number and they would prefer she stop phoning. That should do it.

***

Timothy had become rather adept at viewing events through the light of his own optimism, and he never paused to wonder whether his view was possibly skewed. He thought back to when he had first learned that her father was seriously ill. Her mother had sent the text, saying that she was unable to reach her daughter on her old number, and perhaps he could relay a message, as it was important. Timothy decided as soon as he read the message, that this was not information he should share, and he deleted the text.

"She's happier with me than she ever was with her family," he reasoned, "and if I tell her, then she has such a strong sense of duty she'll go rushing off to see her father, and he'll put all sorts of doubt and worries in her head, and then die, leaving her in turmoil."

He had a mental image of his wife, clinging to his arm as they walked from a church to a cemetery, her face blotched with tears, her sorrow dumb as she went to bury her father. Timothy imagined her pain, the blame he knew she would heap upon herself. No, he would save her from all that. The mother was a parasite, would use emotional blackmail to get childcare for the retarded sister, and once his wife was back in her mother's clutches, the demands would increase until they dominated her life. No, he thought again, I'm not going to allow her to go back to that family, I'm going to keep her safe because that's what I promised to do when I married her. I can save her from the heartache of losing her father, there's nothing she can do to prevent his dying, no good can come of her being upset. Why make her suffer unnecessarily?

Timothy had therefore hidden the information, never mentioned the texts that arrived with irritating regularity from the parasitic mother, and even when he learnt the father had died, he said nothing to his wife. He knew she would be devastated, blame herself for losing contact, would feel she should have visited while he was alive. Going to the funeral would benefit no one, decided Timothy, deleting the information. It was something he could mention later, at the right time, when he would be able to manage his wife's distress and ensure her upset was lessoned.

Months later, when he did pass on the news, he was surprised by her lack of emotion.

"Darling, there's something I need to tell you," he said, sitting beside her on the sofa and draping an arm over her shoulders.

"I'm afraid I've had news that your father died several months ago. I am so sorry."

He kissed her cheek, and held her close.

She turned and looked at him, staring long into his eyes, her expression completely blank.

"Oh," she said, then turned back to her book.

For a moment he wondered whether she had misunderstood, whether the shock had been too much. But as he watched her, slowly turning pages which he was fairly sure she had not read, he realised that he was being shut out, that she wasn't turning to him, seeking refuge in his embrace, leaning against him for strength. She had retreated even further into her inner self, and he was as excluded as if he was banished from the room.

"Right," he said, standing and taking a deep breath. "I'll be in my study if you need me."

He was certainly not going to sit and be ignored all evening. She could cope with her grief on her own.

**

Timothy monitored the *find-a-friend* app regularly, keeping his phone on his desk while he taught, noticing when she left the house, saw which shops she visited, how often she went out for coffee.

One day, as he dismissed a particularly difficult class, he noticed the blob of her face moving over the map, and he knew that she was approaching a coffee shop, and he wondered who she was meeting. There had been nothing on their shared calendar that morning, and she had not mentioned meeting anyone when he'd asked about her day. Timothy frowned. Was she having coffee alone, or meeting a friend?

He sucked in his lips, and felt that familiar knot of insecurity. He glanced at the time. He had time, if he managed to find somewhere to park, to pop into town before his next lesson. He wouldn't disturb her, he would simply walk past the window, glance inside, learn who she was with; because, he reasoned, when you love someone, you want to know everything about them.

Timothy drove to town as fast as he dared, driving through an orange light, his speedometer hovering just above the 35 mark. There was a space—not quite big enough—at the end of a line of cars on the High Street, so he abandoned his car at an angle, scoured the street for traffic wardens, and set off at a jog towards the coffee shop. There were butterflies dancing in his stomach, and he could feel the tension rising inside as he wondered what he might find, who his wife might be meeting. He slowed as he neared the cafe window, and stopped when he reached the door.

He peered into the gloom. At first, he couldn't see her. He checked his app again, and the photograph representing her position still hovered over this position. He opened the door and stepped inside. There were two areas of seating, one at the front of the shop, and another round the corner, at the rear. She wasn't in the front, so he walked to the corner, and peered round.

She was at the back, right in the corner, hunched forwards across the table, her coffee resting in front of her. He couldn't see who was opposite her, so edged slightly nearer. A woman with a pushchair asked him to move so she could pass, he stepped back, waited for her to leave, then peered again, searching to see who his wife's companion was. His mouth was dry, and he swallowed, leaning forwards slowly, inch by inch, not wanting her to see him, to know that he was following her. He saw her back, rounded at the shoulders, the edge of the table, her coffee—he stepped forwards, almost fully in the room now —beyond her coffee, on the other side of the table, was a book. She was reading a book. There was no one else there.

He backed away, quickly, not wanting her to glance up and see him. She might misunderstand if she saw him. He smiled. She had been there for a while, there was no possibility that someone was meeting her and she had arrived first, she must have decided to read at the coffee shop for want of a change of scenery.

Timothy hurried to his car, smiling with relief, his tension replaced with happiness. It was, he felt, rather foolish of her to drink coffee in public, never mind the extravagance when she could drink coffee at home, there was always the risk that someone so young and attractive might be approached by a stranger. She might find herself the target of a stalker. She would be safer at home, but he knew this wasn't something he could insist upon. No, the money would be a better tack. When he checked the money at the end of the week, he would comment on the receipt when he saw it, suggest that they couldn't really afford to go out for coffee, not unless it was a treat, at the weekend, both of them, together.

***

"I've bought some monitors," Timothy said, carrying the brown package into the kitchen and setting it on the table.

She moved the cereal box, and sat opposite him, expectant, interested by what he'd bought.

He opened the box, passing her the rubbish so she could place it into the recycling bin. Inside was a ball of bubblewrap, and when he unwound it, there were four small boxes. Each box contained a white plastic monitor, with a recharging point at the back and a lens at the front.

"They're cameras," he said, passing one across the table so she could examine it. "I've been worrying lately, about whether you're safe while I'm at work. I can put these around the house, and link them to my phone. Then if you fall down the stairs, or if someone breaks in, I'll know."

"Why would I fall down the stairs?" she asked, her forehead creasing into a frown, her voice bemused. "And how would you watching me prevent me from falling down the stairs, even if I did one day wake up and decide to fling myself over the bannister?"

Her voice was teasing, and he felt annoyed, irritated by her lack of appreciation. Timothy began to put the monitors back into their boxes, and collected them all together in his arms.

"You can mock if you must," he said, angry now, wanting to hurt her for her rebuff. "I shall be in my study, connecting these to my phone, and then deciding where to put them. If there are things you do in this house that you would rather I did not see, then kindly let me know, and I will refrain from placing the cameras in rooms where you want to do underhand actions. Otherwise I shall assume that in a loving relationship"—he emphasised the word "loving" to make his point—"there are no secrets and therefore nothing to hide."

He stood, ignoring the hurt that he saw in her eyes. He knew that she hated when he was cold and formal with her, but sometimes she deserved it, she shouldn't challenge him, not when he was trying to keep her safe. He went to his study, closing the door behind him.

The telephone rang. It was Felicity. Felicity was one of his several female colleagues. None of them especially interested Timothy, however, they appreciated his mind, and his humour, and when—such as now—his wife was being inappreciative, it was rather pleasing to know that other women admired him.

"Hi Felicity," he said, allowing his voice to be slightly warmer than normal. "No, it doesn't matter at all that you've called on a Saturday, really, I wasn't doing anything important. What can I help you with?"

He listened to the woman's voice, telling him some problem that was easily solved, listening to her thank him, feeling his confidence return as he basked in her thanks.

"Really, it's no problem," he said, and then, because it was polite and he liked to appear sociable with his colleagues, he asked: "So, what are you up to today, anything interesting?" and settled down for a chat, even though he knew that he had left the kitchen in a bad mood and she was probably waiting for his return; because it was good for her to wait sometimes.

When Timothy finally left his conversation and his study, he found her peeling an orange. He watched for a moment, as she stuck her nail into the edge of the orange, making a hole large enough to start pulling off the peel.

"That's not how you do it," he said, smiling, his bad mood forgotten. "You'll damage the fruit inside. Look," he took the fruit from her and turned it, indicated the dimple where the stalk had been. "That's where you should begin to peel." He held her hand in his own for a moment, noticing the soft skin, the delicate fingers. He stooped, and kissed the top of her head, breathing in the smell of her shampoo.

She nodded, and satisfied, he went upstairs to check she had folded the laundry correctly.

Chapter Twenty-One

When they had been married for two wonderful years, Timothy applied for a new job, and was again promoted. The work involved overseeing the mathematics curriculum of several schools, and there was an amount of travel between them. It was also where he met Celeste.

Celeste was a maths professor from the states. She was tall, with blonde hair that she wore tightly secured with a clip, and she had a trick when tackling a particularly knotty problem of undoing the clip, and shaking her hair in a golden cascade down her back, twisting it back into a knot and fastening it again—all apparently unconsciously, whilst studying the problem in hand. It was difficult to ignore.

Celeste was married, to a husband who she managed to portray as ineffectual, and they had two children, who she described as "simply awful." Timothy never heard her mention their names, and he knew nothing about them other than that they interfered with Celeste's work, and she was happy to leave them for a two months secondment and thought that they were probably happy to see her go.

She managed to make it plain, with her casual: "Oh, he'll be as glad of the break as I am—goodness only knows what he'll be getting up to!" that the time in England had separated her, albeit temporarily, from not just her home country.

She wore silk blouses, buttoned to the collar, but they clung to the shape of her, and showed the smooth curve of her rather large breasts encased in their expensive lace bras, and she had a way, again completely unconsciously, of stretching her back, so that her arms were outstretched behind her and her eyes were shut and those rather large breasts in their lace bra, strained forwards, as though beckoning to Timothy. He always averted his gaze, of course, and concentrated on the problem in hand. But he was aware. And he knew that she realised he was aware.

Timothy did not particularly *like* Celeste. He found that he was fascinated by her brash dismissal of her family, the aggression of her conversation with other colleagues and the obvious attraction of her body. But when he was at home, he could honestly describe her as someone he disliked.

"She's very rude to people," he said, after a day when Celeste had phoned several different schools and given less than encouraging feedback about their curriculums. "She's probably quite clever, but the way she talks to people is horrible sometimes."

"Is she married?"

"Oh yes, has a husband and children waiting for her in the States. Doesn't seem to like them much though, she's always swearing when she talks about them, said the youngest child is a complete brat—I don't think I've ever heard anyone be quite so rude about their own children," he shook his head, smiling.

"She sounds horrible."

Timothy had watched his wife as she served their dinner, and then carried the plates to the table. Even though he had started the conversation, he found he wanted to defend Celeste, he wasn't keen on hearing her criticised by someone else. But he stopped, feeling that perhaps it was better if his wife thought badly of the other woman. They were never likely to meet, and a distorted view of Celeste's bad features might make life easier for him.

"Yes, she's not an easy person," he agreed.

"Is she pretty?"

An image of Celeste's thick blonde hair, her voluptuous body, her very white teeth flashed through Timothy's mind.

"She's rather over-weight," he said, "and she wears much too much make-up, she plasters it on like war-paint. It makes her face look horrible, a sort of orangey colour. Not at all natural. And she's old, not young and beautiful like you. . ."

Timothy turned to his dinner, feeling it was time to change the subject.

"This looks delicious and I'm starving, and I don't want to talk about work—there's nothing interesting there. Tell me about your day instead," he said, turning the conversation to safer topics as he acknowledged, deep in his subconscious, that there was something a little dangerous about Celeste and his growing awareness of her.

***

Celeste wore sophisticated perfume and an air of self-assured intellect that was impossible to resist.

When they were asked to attend a weekend conference at a centre in Guildford, Timothy packed all his best clothes and was careful to explain that it was purely a work-related conference, and he would phone home whenever he could but he would be busy, and he didn't know what the signal would be like, so his wife, who he loved, wasn't to worry if he was unreachable.

"You could always come?" he offered, trying to appear open. "I mean, I'll be working all day, and then I'll have to attend some boring dinner in the evening with all the frumpy mathematicians that will be there—but if you want to come, so you have company at night—then it would be lovely. I can smuggle you in through a fire door or something!"

She had reached up to him, her eyes huge, and he had felt her wonderful body against him, and had almost changed his mind, almost decided to stay at home. But the conference really was essential, and part of his job which he was doing for both of them, so they could afford to live in their lovely house together; and if there was a frisson of danger, of an unknown possibility in the air—well—it wasn't something he had engineered, he wasn't looking for trouble, he was simply deciding to not try too hard to think about the consequences. And perhaps he was imagining it all anyway, so it would be silly to refuse to attend an integral part of his employment, he wasn't making any decisions, he would just wait and see what happened.

Of course nothing happened during the actual conference, which was full of interesting lectures and boring feedback sessions where Bob-the-boring answered every question and spoke at length about how *he* would solve every issue. Timothy found that Celeste was sitting next to him during the dinner—which was a social affair, lots of overly loud conversations where everyone tried to prove that they had exciting social lives as they extended their egos with stories of foreign travel or extravagant purchases. As they ate the rather limp prawn cocktail, and chewed dry chicken and drank too much wine, Timothy felt the soft warmth of Celeste's leg against his, and it reminded him of those sessions of private tuition a few years ago, and the promise whispered by a hand not moved away quickly enough, or a knee that rested overly close, a shoulder that leant for a mere second against his. When Celeste turned her face up to him, and looked full in his eyes, and laughed for too long at one of his jokes, then it was *her* eyes that he saw, and it was the tantalising forbidden contact with *her* body that he was responding to, and his past and present were mixed up with the alcohol and the day-after-day of trying to appear impervious to Celeste's sophistication and unspoken invitation.

When they rose from the table and followed everyone into the bar, they avoided the main area of stained green chairs and sat in the corner, at a sticky round table, on lumpy chairs that brushed the dusty curtains. They ordered brandy, which Timothy didn't especially like, but it suited the moment, and he swirled the orange liquid around the glass and sipped the medicinal alcohol, and wished that he smoked so he could go outside with her under the pretence of needing a cigarette.

Timothy watched Celeste's mouth as she talked, her accent grating on his nerves as she criticised one member of staff after another.

"She thinks she's witty," thought Timothy, watching her crimson painted lips, "but really she's just rude." He stopped listening, and concentrated instead on her lips, moving as she spoke, the flick of her tongue as she licked away a grain of salt.

"I wonder what they feel like to kiss," he wondered, having never before kissed anyone wearing lipstick. "For clowns and hookers," his mother had said, and her words lingered in his mind, so whenever his wife had worn lipstick, he passed her a tissue and suggested she wipe it off. He thought that Celeste would probably laugh in his face if he were to suggest such a thing.

They left the bar together, and when she invited him into her room, to look over the numbers again, he was very aware that it was not the numbers he would be looking over, and he followed dumbly, deciding that he could think about it tomorrow, when he felt less fuzzy; this evening was all about being led, and shutting off his mind, and allowing the inevitable—because it was inevitable—to happen.

Timothy never slept with Celeste again, though their affair—if it could be called that—continued for several months, until she returned to her native Ohio. Timothy told himself that it would be rude, given their liaison, to simply stop all affectionate gestures. They would slip from the office to drink coffee in a park, or arrange to meet for lunch.

But Timothy felt uncomfortable, he wasn't sure he even *liked* Celeste, with her too-strong perfume and expensive shoes. She was often intense, the lilt of her accent grating on him as she explained her position on a certain issue, a little too confident as she flaunted her body. He began to regret his actions, though justified the conference by reminding himself that it had been a learning experience, which would enrich his marriage.

"And I learnt something about myself too," he admitted to himself when the guilt churned in his stomach late at night. "I realised how much I love my wife, and that no other woman, however sophisticated, can ever compare to her. I know now that I'm not married because I fell in love by chance, I'm married because what I feel for my wife can never be replaced by anyone else."

Timothy never mentioned his home life at work, and although Celeste knew he was married, she never asked after his wife. His relationship with Celeste was confined to work times, and work topics, and they only ever visited places encompassed by work. Their lunches could have been between colleagues discussing an issue, their coffees could have been a necessary break from the office. Timothy was confident that no other work colleagues suspected their liaison. He was not so sure at home.

Chapter Twenty-Two

Timothy became aware of a change of mood at home, a subtle turning away of her head when he was watching his wife, a little less enthusiasm for shared walks in the evening. When they watched films together, he was sometimes aware that her eyes were glazed, and although she was facing the screen, she wasn't really watching. He wasn't sure what had changed, and worried that his new enthusiasm with work, and the longer hours he was working, were beginning to add to her discontented air.

He also began to worry that due to his actions, some weird karma might intervene—not that he really believed in such things, superstition was for the ignorant, there was no logic to it. But if karma of some sort *were* to occur, it might mean she would be removed from him, perhaps some horrible accident would occur, to punish him for his mistake. He could no longer pop home to check she was all right, his time was tied to a schedule and he was frequently in other areas. What if he deserved to lose her? What if one day, while he was at work, the house should be broken into and she was attacked? Or perhaps there would be an accident, and he would return to find her crumpled at the foot of the stairs, her neck broken.

He tried to dismiss the ideas as ludicrous; he also struggled to not let his intrigue with Celeste turn to hatred for what the woman had tempted him into doing, because after all, he had been content until he met her. It was her fault he had strayed, and due to that, some horrible event might happen in consequence. It was a feeling he couldn't shake, and he began to think of ways to keep his wife safe, so that he wouldn't lose her.

***

As time passed, the guilt that churned inside Timothy began to intensify. During the day, he could forget about his indiscretion, or at least rationalise it, tell himself that most men strayed at least once, and it was not really his fault, Celeste had played the harlot and enticed him into actions that were against his nature.

But at night, while he lay listening to his wife's even breathing, the sickness of shame turned his stomach like a physical thing. He thought back to his actions, and what might happen as a result, and frequently had to leave the bed to vomit. As he retched over the toilet, his hatred for Celeste was powerful, and had he possessed the power to kill her, he would have done. He felt that she had ruined something precious, and he was unsure how to repair it.

The sense of doom, that something terrible would happen to his wife as a punishment, intensified. Timothy found he was watching her compulsively, his eyes glued to the monitors whenever he was out. When he was at home, he would listen to her phone calls (not that she had many) and check her internet history, and use Google maps to follow her timeline, checking the places she had been, comparing it to the data he could collect on the 'find a friend' app.

It became routine, checking the movements of his wife evolved into something normal.

"Hi *Ten*, I'm home," he said, kissing his wife as she emerged from the kitchen. "What have you done today, anything interesting?"

He followed her back into the kitchen, watching her back as she made him a cup of tea, noticing that she forgot to sniff the milk before pouring it into his cup.

"No, nothing much. I read some of that library book about Germany that you recommended, and I went to the supermarket, and I spent the afternoon watching a film and sewing—you know, all those missing buttons from shirts and holes in cardigans that I've been meaning to sort for ages. Then I started to cook dinner, it will be ready in about half an hour."

There was something flat about her voice, an almost toneless recitation of facts. He looked at her face for clues, but her expression was as bland as her voice, he was unable to detect any sadness or depression. She didn't seem *happy* but nor did he worry that she was particularly sad. He decided that she had spent an unsatisfactory day doing various jobs, and felt slightly fed-up, but that was okay, that was normal.

Timothy carried his tea into the sitting room. He picked up the library book, and found the bookmark was a few chapters further along than yesterday, confirming that she had spent some time reading. There was a pile of folded clothes on the arm of a chair, and a quick glance confirmed buttons sewn on—though some were rather too tightly fastened, he might mention that, no point in having buttons attached if they were too tight to fit through the buttonhole. He folded the shirts back onto the chair and went to the study.

Her phone was plugged into the recharging point, so he flicked to Google maps and found her timeline, staring at the history of her movements. Her route to the supermarket was traced on the map, though it looked as if she may have detoured into the next village on her way home. Timothy frowned. He knew the map was sometimes unreliable, occasionally the position of the satellite or something showed a phone as having visited a place it had never in reality been to. But was this the case today, or might she have visited someone on the way home, and not be mentioning it? He tried to calculate the timing, remembering when he had checked her position in real time on his app. He smiled, and shook his head. No, he was pretty sure the map was wrong, she did go straight to the supermarket and home again, she probably did not have a clandestine meeting with an unknown friend.

Timothy glanced at the time. He still had a few minutes, so he went to the computer and called up her internet history, checking for anything untoward. Everything seemed normal, there were no unexpected searches, no joining of social media chat lines, nothing that he needed to worry about. He smiled again, satisfied, and went back to the kitchen.

"This smells delicious, as usual," he said, sitting on the narrow yellow stool and watching her as she strained potatoes over the sink, clouds of steam wafting up. "Don't you need an oven mitt to do that?" he asked, watching as her skin reddened in the steam.

"It's fine," she replied, her voice dismissive—as it often was now.

Timothy felt something turn inside, that familiar feeling of dread as he looked at his wife. She was saying and doing nothing unusual, and yet there was a resistance in her attitude, a resigned attitude rather than one of reciprocation.

"Perhaps I'll buy her some flowers tomorrow," he decided. "That should make her smile."

He really could think of nothing else to do.

Chapter Twenty-Three

As Timothy struggled with his wife's seeming disinterest in life, he strove to protect her from anything that might upset her further, thinking that to maintain the balance of life, things would at least not get worse.

"She's going through a discontented stage," he told himself, "if I can keep things on an even keel, it will pass and we'll get back to where we were before."

The thought occurred to him that perhaps, *where we were before* might not be completely satisfactory to a young woman married to an older man, but he refused to consider that, and pushed the thought away before it could settle.

"It will be all right in the long run."

***

When the first reports about a new virus appeared, Timothy more or less ignored them. The virus seemed to be contained in China, and frankly he had always been suspicious of their eating habits. He barely noticed headlines about the gradual spread of the virus, not bothering to read reports which again, seemed to be only about Chinese people, even if they lived in Europe.

When the number of cases started to grow in England, Timothy was captivated by the numbers. He plotted a graph, showing the exponential increase of cases over time, and predicted the likely numbers in one month, two months, by the end of the year. He didn't bother to mention his interest at home, as his wife was having one of her distracted phases, and he had decided they would have a baby.

Timothy had realised now that his wife was moody. When she first started to withdraw from him, he had been concerned, and sought to find a solution. But he could never find the source of her discontent, and he decided that his wife was probably of a depressive personality, and her apparent periods of withdrawal were nothing to do with him but rather a personality flaw on her part. It was irritating, as he preferred the adoring wife of former years, but he loved her, and was mature enough to know that no one was perfect—if his wife had a propensity for mild depression, had times when she was less responsive, well he could live with that, she was his only delight in life.

Timothy thought that having a child would possibly break his wife's cycle of moods, and would be another factor binding them together. His feelings of insecurity following *"that bitch Celeste"* as he thought of her, had diminished but never fully disappeared. A baby seemed the natural solution, a way to secure his wife's dependence, ensure that she again leant on him.

"We'll make such good parents," he said, his voice excited as he broached the subject. "You'll make a wonderful mother, much better than most women because you've already sort of practised, haven't you? —Looking after your sister so much when you were younger, I mean."

She had looked at him, a long silent look, and her face had paled.

"I don't think. . . I don't think I'm ready for that yet," she said, and her voice had a finality about it, something wary.

He leant across the dinner table, and touched her cheek, moving her hair and tucking it behind her ear. "This needs a trim," he said, noting the fringe was almost touching her green eyes.

"We can talk about our baby later, I can see I've taken you by surprise. But really, I think it's time, I'm earning enough to support a child as well as you, so you needn't worry about that." He heard the pride in his own voice and smiled, immensely satisfied as he thought of his income, and how well he was doing at work for someone of his age.

"Is there a pudding?"

Silent, his wife stood, and began to clear the plates, moving cutlery to the side, scraping leftover scraps of potato and cabbage into a heap. He watched as she carried the dirty crockery to the sink, reached into the depths of the fridge, pulled out a flan and a carton of cream. He waited while she cut a slice and placed it into a bowl, passing it to him with the cream. Her movements were deliberate.

"I'm not going to change my mind," she said, her voice determined. "I don't want a baby. Definitely not now, and maybe ever. But definitely not now. I'm too young. . ."

Timothy paused mid mouthful. Was the reference to her age an insinuation that he was *too old?* No, he decided, pouring more cream into his bowl and continuing to eat. She was just a bit surprised, needed some time to get used to the idea. He glanced at her over the top of his spoon. She looked white, frightened almost.

He'd mention it again in a few days.

"Did you see anyone when you went to town?" he asked, knowing that she hadn't had time for more than a fleeting conversation even if she had met someone—he had been checking the app even more diligently since his good idea. He felt so much more secure now that he could see her every move, was confident that he knew every aspect of her life.

His wife shook her head, and he smiled, spooning heaps of fruit flan into his mouth. It was really rather tasty.

***

Timothy decided his plan to have a child was an excellent one, and began to move things further in that direction. At first he had wondered whether his wife was correct, whether now was the right time to have a baby, whether it perhaps might be better to sort his wife's mental health first. But after a little online research, Timothy decided his wife's depression was due to an hormone imbalance, and the solution was either to insist she visit a doctor, or, the more natural solution of pregnancy. He read that the surge in hormones when a woman was pregnant often brought about physiological changes in the mother, and not only did she incubate a child, but also her mental state might become altered. Timothy realised that this confirmed the perfection of his idea.

His wife was clearly not in agreement, so Timothy decided to act on her behalf. After all, she was his responsibility, and he wanted, more than anything else, for her to be happy. She took a daily birth-control pill, which Timothy helped to remind her to take, by placing a fresh pill each morning in a small plastic 'pill dispenser' he had bought for the purpose. It was one of the many roles he undertook to ensure his wife's happiness and ease of existence. He now needed to find a suitable placebo for the medication.

Timothy stood in the sweetshop, perusing the shelves of jars. The shop was in Rye, and Timothy had travelled here for the express purpose of finding an old-fashioned sweet shop in a place where he wouldn't be recognised. He didn't want someone to mention in passing that they had seen him, or he would need to explain to his wife why he was there, and he disliked lying to her.

The shop had a bell above the door, and it rang as another customer entered the shop. It was a woman, complete with shopping basket and headscarf, who looked as if she had arrived from another era herself. Timothy could see her bicycle, leant precariously against the shop window, and he mustered a smile and indicated that she should take his place at the front of the queue. He moved a step back, and waited while the man behind the counter served the woman. He started to pour barley-sugars onto his scales. The sweets clattered onto the metal pan, which began to lower, dipping to a point where it was level with the balancing weight, in a century-old method of weighing sweets. Timothy wondered why people enjoyed tradition, and the charm of old-fashioned sweetshops, then he shrugged, and began to search the shelves.

In his hand, smuggled from the tissue in his pocket, was one of his wife's contraceptive pills. They were small, round, peach-coloured pills, and he hoped to find a corresponding sweet that he could use as a substitute. There were sherbet pips, and he considered picking out the yellow and white ones, using the remaining peach-coloured ones. But the texture was wrong, and he thought perhaps his wife would notice the tang of sherbet when she placed one in her mouth. He hoped to avoid suspicion, otherwise, he reminded himself, he might as well simply insist his wife obeyed him and became pregnant.

There were jellies, and chocolate drops, and tiny sugar pearls—all of which were nearly right, all of which had some texture or size or colour difference that would betray him at first glance. Eventually, after the woman had wheeled away her bike and the shop assistant had coughed three times with impatience, Timothy settled on some tiny sweets made from boiled sugar, which had the correct colour and sheen, but were too round. He would, he decided, wait until the current box of contraceptives had finished, and then tell his wife the new batch were slightly different. He doubted she would question him.

The following day, Timothy added his sugary substitutes to the pill box. He watched his wife on the kitchen monitor when she came to take a pill, watched her cross the kitchen floor in her dressing gown, saw her shake the kettle before refilling it, reach into the cupboard for a mug, struggle with the tight lid of the tea tin before pulling it off, extracting a tea-bag, dropping it into the cup, fill the cup with boiling water, reach for her pill dispenser. Timothy held his breath. His wife flipped open the lid with her nail, shook a pill into her hand, then, with Timothy not daring to breathe, she tossed the pill into her mouth, stooped beneath the tap and took a mouthful of water, shook her head, and swallowed. Timothy smiled; she had not even noticed.

Chapter Twenty-Four

On Monday, 9th March, Timothy returned home after a relatively boring day at work. He parked the car, and reached into the back for his briefcase and newspaper. The paper's headlines were full of people being quarantined in Italy, and how the handful of cases that had reached England were being contained, and Timothy had no interest in any of it. He pulled out his keys as he walked to the front door, and called a greeting as he entered. There was no answering response.

Timothy left his case in the hall, hung his jacket on a hanger in the cramped cupboard under the stairs, and went to the kitchen. The surfaces gleamed, the sink smelt of bleach, and every canister on the counter top was perfectly aligned, exactly as he preferred. But there was no smell of cooking, no wife to greet him, no ingredients emptied onto the surface ready to be prepared. Maybe his wife was ill.

"*Ten? Ten?* Are you ill? I'm home sweetheart," he called, running upstairs. He hoped she hadn't caught a bug from somewhere, it was a busy time at work and would be hard to take a day off if he needed to stay at home and nurse her.

"Are you ill?" he said again, as he entered their bedroom.

The bed was made, the cover pulled tightly across the surface, cushions scattered over the bedspread, the fluffy throw covering the bottom three feet. His slippers were placed next to the bed, ready for later. The bathroom door was open, and Timothy could see the white shower cubicle, the closed toilet, the sink with a new bar of soap in the corner, towels hung on the rail, each one folded exactly in half. All appeared perfect, except for the empty space where his wife should have been.

Timothy frowned, and pulled out his phone. He looked for her on the app, and saw that she was still showing as being at home, as she had been all day. Perhaps she was in the garden. He dialled her number as he walked to the window, held it to his ear as he moved the curtain to the side, peered down into the tiny square patch of green attached to the house.

Next to him, from the depths of her bedside table, his wife's phone began to ring.

Something in Timothy's stomach contracted. This was not normal, something was wrong.

He sank onto the bed, wrenched open the bedside cabinet. There, stuffed above her library book and a box of tissues, was her handbag, the mobile phone ringing from inside. Timothy groaned, reached for the bag, tipped the contents onto the bed. Her phone rolled out, her purse bounced across the duvet and settled near a cushion, pieces of paper floated onto his lap, a pen rolled to the floor. He snatched her purse, looking for clues among the receipts, the folded photograph of himself, a faded picture of Gracie her sister, her credit cards filling their designated slots in the soft worn leather. No clues. He reached into the folds of bag, feeling the lining, searching for anything that might give him an idea of where she might be, knowing deep inside that he would find nothing. Everything was too neat, too planned. There was nothing.

Like a wild man, Timothy flung aside the bag and staggered to the door, leapt down the stairs, raced through the house. The sitting room was as picture-perfect as the bedroom, his study was exactly as he had left it. He wrenched open the back door, charged into the garden, three strides and he was at the tiny shed, almost ripped off the door in his hurry to open it, was greeted with cobwebs and tins of paint and their lawn mower and garden tools, but no wife. She was gone.

Back to the house, he walked slower now, checking as he went, staring around the sitting room, looking for signs of a forced entry, displaced items to indicate a struggle—nothing. Back into the kitchen, checking cupboards, flinging open the doors and leaving them gaping while he perused the contents, hoping something would direct him, then upstairs again, into the spare bedroom—of course! He had forgotten the spare bedroom in his panic—surely she would be in there, perhaps lying down with a migraine, perhaps collapsed, or. . . but no, the spare bedroom was as empty of humanity as the rest of the house. Back to their bedroom, dry-mouthed, heart thumping in his chest, stomach churning as he knelt, looked under the bed, returned to the bedside cabinet and pulled out the tissue box—perhaps something was hidden inside—pulling out the tissues in two handfuls, letting them fall like crumpled snowflakes to the carpet, feeling around the empty inside of the box, snatching her handbag again, running his hands over the lining, before leaping up, staggering to the wardrobe and flinging wide the doors. All her clothes were there, surely a sign she hadn't gone far? He began to search the clothes, turning out pockets, looking inside shoes, emptying the drawers so that knickers and socks and tights fell in a heap beside him, mute and unhelpful in his quest for answers. He sank beside the mess, his head in his hands, fingers tearing at his hair, a groan rose up, echoed round the room, stomach churned again and he rushed to the bathroom, reaching the sink in time to deposit the remains of his lunch. As Timothy rinsed his mouth under the sweet clear water of the tap, his mind began to understand what his eyes had been telling him: his wife had gone.

"This is my fault," Timothy groaned, the magnitude of the discovery seeping into his heart. "I drove her away, I only ever wanted to protect her, and I drove her away."

Timothy went back to the sitting room and sat on the sofa, his eyes unseeing, his back upright, as rigid as a statue. Inside, nothing was still as his emotions swirled and heaved, one thought chasing the next.

"She was unhappy, and nothing I did was able to reach her," he acknowledged. "But I tried everything, the fault was inside of her—I should have taken her to a doctor."

He sighed.

"Perhaps our ages were too different, she couldn't cope with the pressure," he thought, remembering seeing her with her friends, laughing over the rim of a glass of wine. "I shouldn't have left her alone all day," he decided, "if I was still popping home each lunchtime, she wouldn't have been bored."

Restless, Timothy began to pace the room, then went back upstairs. He started to return things to their places, stopping when he reached her purse. The credit cards remained in their slots, but when he slid open the zipper, there were no coins, no notes. "What is she doing for money?" he wondered. "How long can she survive without credit cards? How much cash does she have?"

Timothy went to his study and slid open the security drawer under his desk. It was packed with envelopes: his will, insurance documents, birth certificate, teacher number. The envelope fat with money, notes rolled together in case there should ever be an emergency and they needed cash in a hurry, was missing.

He pulled everything from the drawer, noting that every document was there, but not his cash. He sat back in his seat, shocked that she had stolen from him. There had been several hundred pounds in that envelope, weeks of wages, stored secretly in his secure drawer, ready for him to use if he ever needed to save her, protect her from an unforeseen crisis; and now *she had stolen it.*

Timothy shook his head, unable to process this new fact, not able to reconcile the dishonesty of the act with his compliant wife. He wondered, briefly, whether perhaps she had been kidnapped, if criminals could have entered his house and stolen his wife and his money. But he knew, even as he turned to the recorded footage of the security cameras, he knew that his wife had left willingly.

The cameras showed his wife tidying the house after Timothy had left for work. She went to the bedroom, and was hidden from the camera when she stooped beside the bed, and Timothy knew she was placing her bag in the cabinet. He saw her take her coat, and lift a back-pack from under the stairs, and then walk through the front door. It told him nothing he did not already know: his wife had left, and had been well prepared. This was no spontaneous, spur-of-the-moment thing, this was a premeditated action, something she had been plotting. He wanted to believe his wife had been involved in an accident, was unable to return home from an innocent shopping trip, that any moment the front door would open and she would tumble inside scattering apologies and needing his comfort. But the bag secured in her cabinet denied him that comfort, the abandoned phone shouted that she did not want to be found, the discarded credit cards were a statement of independence.

Timothy wondered if someone else was involved, if some man had persuaded her away, enticed her to leave. He shook his head. There had been no opportunities for her to have an accomplice, he would have seen the signs, noted the discrepancies in timings. No, the plan, the execution, the idea was hers alone; the loss, the sense of betrayal, was his. He leant back in his chair, eyes closed, and wondered whether the pain in his chest was sorrow or something physical, whether his heart might truly be broken. As the sun sank in the sky and long shadows reached out from the corners of the room, Timothy still sat, immobile in his chair, for all the world as though he had ceased to be human and had turned into stone.

***

Timothy stared at his phone for several minutes, not wanting to make the call. Eventually, with a sigh and a straightened back, he phoned Charlotte. If his wife had gone anywhere obvious, it would be to her friend Charlie. She answered on the second ring.

"Hello? Sorry to bother you, it's Timothy. I was wondering whether you know where Ten is?"

There was a pause.

"Hi Tim," Charlotte said, using the name she knew he hated before adding, ironically he felt: "You do know that's not her real name, right?"

He nodded, even though she couldn't see him, and coughed.

"Is she there?" he said, deciding to ignore her barb. "I'm worried about her, I want to know that's she's safe."

"Why wouldn't she be?" asked Charlotte, sounding confused. Her voice was clearer now, as if she had continued with whatever she was doing when she first answered but this new information was interesting, so she was now fully concentrating. "Have you phoned her? Isn't she answering?"

"Her phone is here. She left her phone at home when she left." Timothy was scowling, embarrassed to have to admit this information, but knowing that there was no way to learn anything from Charlotte unless he did. And she might know something, the girl might, if she actually spent a few minutes *thinking* rather than simply projecting an image, she might actually *know* something useful.

There was silence at the other end. Charlotte was clearly processing this, realising that Timothy wasn't calling from some over-anxious nosiness, but actually had a reason to suspect something was wrong. No one of their age-group would ever willingly leave home without their phone, not unless the action was highly significant.

"Oh, oh I see," said Charlotte, and the girl's voice was full of condescension, almost glee. "Well, I guess in that case, she wasn't too keen on you finding her Tim, was she?

"I suppose you've checked hospitals? In case she hurt herself," she added, something new entering her voice, something solemn.

"Yes," said Timothy, relieved that she was finally beginning to understand the seriousness of the situation. "I phoned the local hospitals before I rang you. And the police —in case there had been an accident. But they didn't know anything, were really quite unhelpful. . ."

Timothy paused, unwilling to reveal that the police had been almost rude, telling him that he could not file a missing-person report, it was much too soon, she could simply be visiting a friend. They told him that even if she didn't return, there was very little they could do, unless they suspected foul play, she was an adult, she had the freedom to leave if she wanted to, and the police were not in the business of searching for adults who were missing by choice.

"I thought you might have heard something?" he said, his voice hopeful despite his belief that this was unlikely.

"No, Tim, sorry," said Charlotte, and her voice was flippant again, with a hard edge. "To be honest with you, it's so long since we were friends, I doubt very much that she would contact me. But if she did—if by some slim chance she came knocking on my door—then I really don't think I'd be jumping up to tell you about it, would I? We never exactly got on, did we Tim? Never saw eye-to-eye as it were. I hate what you did to her, how she changed to please you, and if she's left—well, good luck to her, that's what I say. You had it coming I reckon. Leave her be.

"Was there anything else, or can I go now?"

"Thank you," he said, the sarcasm dripping from his words, "you have been most helpful. Goodbye."

But Charlotte had ended the call before Timothy finished speaking, and he sat, staring at the phone in his hand, shaking his head. He had been right to discourage that friendship, he thought, walking through to the kitchen and flicking on the kettle. Charlotte had never been a good influence on his wife, always been jealous of their bond, keen to pull his wife back to her childhood, the council estate, the lack of restraint and over-indulgence that marked those years.

He poured water into a cup, and waited for the teabag to brew, glancing at the clock so he could time it for five minutes. No, he had been wise to get rid of Charlotte, and he was pleased, in a way, that she hadn't known where his wife was. Although he was no nearer finding her, at least she hadn't abandoned everything he'd taught her, at least she hadn't gone to Charlie.

Chapter Twenty-Five

Three weeks later, and Timothy was no closer to finding his wife. He was standing beneath a tree outside her childhood home, staring at the front door, wondering whether he really wanted to knock. He knew her mother was inside, could see her through the unadorned window, moving around in her living room, wiping a duster over surfaces. While he stood watching, he saw another person enter the room, turn to speak to the mother, fling herself into a chair; he recognised the unpredictable gesture, and Timothy realised it must be the sister.

"Goodness! She's grown. The last time I saw her she was a child. The father's died, of course, so I'll have to deal with the mother, and she never liked me. Is it even worth knocking? Would she tell me anything anyway?"

The house was in the centre of a terrace, with other terraces joining at the corners, so they formed a sort of horse-shoe shape, with an area of grass in the middle, and the road where Timothy had parked beyond the patch of green. Sounds from the main road floated on the air: a few cars zooming past, a lorry reversing in the nearby industrial area, a siren. The sounds mingled with the call of a parent, shouts from a group playing football in the park, a bird tweeting, a dog barking, all muddled together in a timeless tangle of noise that could have come from any town, at any time.

As he stood, staring at the house, Timothy felt he was hearing sounds from bygone years, and he remembered those days, when he met her at the corner, waiting for her to emerge from this same front door, the anticipation of knowing they would soon be together. He recalled the nervousness of meeting her parents, his determination to defeat their disapproval, his desire to snatch her away, to remove her from this house in this neglected part of town and to place her in a home where she would be cosseted, valued, adored.

So much promise, such excited anticipation, an intoxication of tasting forbidden fruit. And now this, this waiting like a stalker outside of the house, removed from centre stage to the wings, not knowing whether he would be allowed to speak his lines.

Timothy moved back to the road and leant against the warm outline of his car. The sun was shining straight into the house window, lighting everything inside but he knew that standing where he was outside, he would be in the shade, they wouldn't notice him unless they specifically looked. He stayed there for a few minutes, staring at the front of the house, looking at the overgrown bushes in the small garden, the cracked path, the fence that needed painting.

The house on the left was tidier, people there enjoyed gardening and had filled tubs with flowers, early spring bulbs with bright heads and strong perfume, a miniature tree in blossom. The neighbour on the right was neglectful, the house was in disrepair with rubbish filling the garden— old bikes, a broken fridge and a tangle of weeds. The front door of the house on the right opened, and a man came out, staring at Timothy, clearly wondering who he was and why he was standing, staring at the terraced houses. He was a tall man, dressed in jeans and a shirt that hadn't been ironed, no jacket, hair that flopped over one eye.

Timothy avoided his eye, turned, opened his car door and eased into the seat. He watched in his rearview mirror as the man turned away, began to march up the road, his shoulders hunched against the cold air. It was the most noteworthy event of the morning.

Timothy stayed outside of the house for several hours, waiting and watching. Sometimes he got out of the car, walked up and down the pathway for a few steps to stretch his legs, never moving far from the house. He noted the litter in the gutter, the white stains of chewing gum spat onto the tarmac. Opposite the houses, on the other side of the road, was another small patch of grass, muddy where people had taken a shortcut over it, a red bin for dog waste standing guard.

Inside of the house Timothy saw the mother, moving around, leaning forwards to look at something the sister was showing her. He saw her vacuuming the floor, watched the shadow of her in an upper room and guessed she was cleaning up there too, saw the sister lift her head as she was called, then look back down at the book or magazine she was reading. It was boring, and uncomfortable, and when Timothy was convinced there were only the two of them in the house, he decided to leave. He could come back again, perhaps for a few hours each week, keep an eye on the house. It was his only link to her, the only place that he was sure she would eventually contact.

***

It was a Wednesday when he followed them to the park. Timothy had arrived on the estate in time to see them just leaving the house, the mother slamming the front door behind them, trying to make the sister hurry as they headed towards the town. It was months since his wife had left, and this was the first time during one of Timothy's visits that the couple had left the house while he was there. It was easier to visit more frequently now, his work was all online, lessons crammed into a few short hours, less marking, fewer meetings. The time for watching the mother had increased, and when he heard on the news that the lockdown was easing, his surveillance had increased. If his wife decided to meet her family again, now would be the time.

Timothy slowed the car, crawling behind the pair for a while, looking as if he was trying to find a place to park between the cars rammed against the curb. They didn't notice, and he didn't see anyone else so could follow for a few minutes, well behind them. At the end of the road, they turned right, away from the town, and Timothy guessed they were going to the park for their allowed form of daily exercise.

Timothy pressed the accelerator, and turned left, driving three sides of a square, arriving at the park ahead of the mother and sister. He parked behind a van, invisible from the entrance, and walked with long strides towards the park, staying close to the bushes, round the side of the leisure centre. There was a main path through the park, and as he marched, his foot kicked a stone and he glanced down to see a line of stones, all painted, stretching along the edge of the path. Timothy bent down, retrieving the stone he had kicked. Someone had painted a cartoon on it, varnished the oval surface so it shone. He stared at it for a while, thinking about the time spent on the design, wondering what motivated a person to produce something and then leave it in a public place, on the ground, simply so others could admire it. He weighed it in his hand, finding the shape of it pleasing, the roughness of the back contrasting with the smooth of the varnished front. Timothy slipped it into his pocket, and headed to the trees near the main road. He could watch from there, see most of the park and all of the entrances, whilst being shielded from view. He expected nothing. He was surprised when she arrived.

The car swung into the car park, and Timothy normally wouldn't have paid it any attention, but something, some karma perhaps, or the wheels of fate, or, more likely, the magnetism that had first attracted him and then had continually drawn him towards her so that even now, after months of abandonment, he was unable to turn from seeking her, *something* made him glance up. It was *her*. Timothy's precious wife—and a man—were parking. Timothy moved closer to the tree. He was separated from the car park by a low fence, standing in the shade, the comforting width of an oak trunk shielding him from view. He peered round the tree, feeling the rough bark against his sleeve, hoping no one was watching his strange behaviour, desperate to see her before she noticed him.

She was nodding, looked as if she was making plans, then she opened her door and climbed out. Timothy watched her stretch her back, and he longed to call to her, to go to her and hold her, to feel her hair against his cheek, to absorb the feel and smell of her. But he knew it would be unwise, knew she had left for a reason and the coming back to him might not be easy; he needed to analyse the situation, make a plan.

For a few minutes she stared at a man using the bottle bank, as if surprised that normal life existed during the lockdown, as if the man was doing something odd. Then Timothy watched as she turned away, and headed towards the park.

There was no real hiding place in the park, and so Timothy stayed where he was. He knew the mother and sister were headed this way, and deduced that the three of them had planned to meet. He was reluctant to be seen, not yet, and so he stood, sheltered by the ancient tree, watching the car with the man inside, wondering how long he should wait.

The man in the car was reading, he had adjusted his seat so that he was almost lying, and he held a book near the steering wheel, relaxed and at ease with the world. Timothy wondered who he was, whether he was a lover, or simply a taxi driver, hired for the journey to the park—she had never learnt to drive, Timothy felt it was unnecessary, he could drive her if she needed to go anywhere.

Time passed. Timothy walked a few paces left, then right. A passerby stared at him, and he stared back, his expression aggressive, discouraging comment; the passerby hurried past. Cars drove past, more traffic than a few weeks ago but not as much as before the world became surreal and everything was forbidden. Another car entered the car park, another person unloaded bottles from carrier bags in their boot, dropping them with a crash into the bottle bank. Timothy wondered how much the nation was drinking now, whether alcohol at home was becoming the replacement for friends in coffee shops. The woman at the bottle bank was wearing a mask and gloves, even though she wasn't near anyone, and she kept glancing nervously over her shoulder. Timothy wondered whether she feared the virus, or being seen with quite so many empty wine bottles.

Eventually, he saw his wife returning. She was walking with her mother and the sister, smiling, leading them back to the car. The man opened the car door when he saw the group approaching, and stood there, half in the car, leaning on the door, speaking to the mother. Then the sister started to speak, and even from his position next to the tree, Timothy caught the strange monotone of her voice, and knew that she would be rambling, on and on, about some random piece of boring information, unstoppable as she recited unnecessary details and ridiculous facts.

Timothy decided that he would go and join the group, he would throw caution away, force her to acknowledge him, make her agree to meet him, he was owed an explanation. This furtive stalking of the mother was ridiculous, he had rights, his wife must give him her contact details, at the very least. He walked quickly from the tree, almost jogging, as he hurried along the side of the fence towards the entrance. He would intervene, remind his wife that he existed, and he loved her, and he needed to know where she was living. The driver of the car was clearly *not* a paid employee, he was potentially a friend, possibly a lover, and Timothy felt the hot rage of jealousy forming in his stomach as his breathing raced with his increased pace.

How dare *the man attempt to steal his wife?* And what business had she with another man, when Timothy had provided everything for her, and worshipped her, and wanted nothing more than for her to be safe? *How dare* they laugh and smile and carry on with a normal conversation, introducing each other, when he, *Timothy,* was tortured by her absence, beside himself with worry?

His mind was racing faster than his legs, as he reached the entrance, strode along the path towards the group. A couple of elderly ladies stared at him as he passed, but he ignored them, rounded the corner, past the line of painted stones, striding beyond the entrance to the leisure centre, towards the start of the car park; he could see the edge of the car, the back of the mother, another step and *she* came into view. He stopped.

Timothy could see her face, her wonderful face with those huge eyes, and he paused, all the breath taken out of him, and his heart pounded, and he wondered if he might die, right there, in the middle of the path that lead from the park to the car park—because she was looking at the driver, watching him while he listened to the sister, and Timothy saw something in her expression. Her face was illuminated, that wonderful pale skin glowed, and her eyes were full of something wonderful, some intangible emotion, an overwhelming expression of love. Timothy felt his throat contract, and tears filled his eyes and the pain in his chest grew and grew until he staggered, back the way he had come, past the staring elderly women, out of the park back to the main road, to the safety of his oak tree. He leant his back against it, feeling the solid support as he fought for breath, staring up at the green canopy against the blue sky, tried to calm his breathing, waiting for the pain to subside; for as certain as Timothy was that the expression in her eyes was surely love, just as certain was the realisation that he had never, ever, seen that expression before.

Chapter Twenty-Six

It was July. The world was trying to reopen, scurrying to implement new laws so the failing economy could stagger back to its knees, anxious that people should feel safe enough to continue with their traditional summer holidays, that tourism might not completely crumble and die. Countries made pacts, agreeing to make exceptions to their quarantine laws, some even promising to cover the cost of medical bills if people fell ill while a guest in their country. Public houses and restaurants bought screens and ordered paper menus and disposable cutlery and retrained their staff, and tried to entice customers back inside.

Gradually, like hibernating animals creeping from their lair, blinking their sleepy eyes at the dawn of a spring morning, people began to withdraw from their houses. They slunk to the shops, in their ones and twos, cautious of contact, standing in line so their numbers inside were limited, many hiding behind face masks; coming to spend their money. Credit cards or smart phones were waved—cash was discouraged, became something dirty, to be shunned. Schools opened their doors to limited pupils, never all at once, specific entrances designated to small groups, parents directed into strict holding areas, tables within classes spaced, playgrounds segregated—even if this last stipulation was largely ignored by friendship groups who rushed towards each other, and smuggled snacks to each other, and passed pencils, which must not be shared, to the friend who had broken theirs. Society reopened for business, their vulnerable sheltered, their masses cautious but moving, mingling; production attached to the electrical leads that would bump-start the engine.

In his London flat, Benjamin was preparing to leave. He was ready; all he needed was a knife. He slipped it into his backpack, ready for when he would use it. The sorrow inside was eating through his soul—not that anyone cared. His psychiatrist hadn't seen him in months, saying that due to the virus they would need to have telephone conferences instead. How could he have a telephone conference in a shared flat? How was he meant to reveal his worries: the thought that life was not worth living, his anger at society—when everyone else was listening?

He shook his head, knowing deep inside that it was all an excuse. He didn't even know anyone who'd had this virus; he suspected it was all a government ploy, propaganda to ensure people stayed inside. All that fuss about government officials being seen breaking the lockdown, well, that was just proof, wasn't it? Proof that they weren't worried, because they *knew*. The virus wasn't real, all they had to do was announce lots of statistics, make up stories about people dying, and the population ran scared. It was clever really, he thought, shaking his head. People were so gullible, they had willingly locked themselves into the prison of their own homes, with no *proof* that it was necessary, nothing other than some cleverly made films and some fictitious newspaper reports.

Benjamin stood, and walked to the wardrobe. He would need to wear clothes if he was going to leave his room, venture from his flat. He could hear music coming from the room next to his, and he scowled at the wall. They didn't care—his flatmates—they didn't notice how tortured he was. After the first few days of suggesting they all ate together, they had left him alone, isolated in his room. They barely even acknowledged him when they happened to meet in the kitchen or walking to the bathroom. Sometimes Benjamin heard them whispering, and he knew they were talking about him, saying he was odd. He would like to show them how odd he was really, like to use the knife before he got to the protest march. But he must wait. Patience was a virtue. There would be journalists at the protest, maybe even television crews. No point in getting stopped before he was properly started. Maybe if he managed to come back here afterwards, maybe he would sort his flatmates out then.

But first, he reminded himself, he would attend the protest march in the London square. He would wield his knife, use it to express his anguish to some of those strangers he saw every day, the myriad of people who ignored him. His knife would release the blood of his sorrow, create a visual sign of his distress. There would be media, Benjamin would be seen, he would force people to notice.

Benjamin selected clothes from his cupboards, and then wound the towel around his waist again and set off for the bathroom. He must wash his hands before he dressed, to be properly prepared. He would wash them again after dressing, and again before he left the flat. He grinned. The government would be pleased with him, he thought, he was at least obeying the 'wash your hands' rule.

**

John was also washing his hands. He emerged from the bathroom and shouted to his wife, Ali, that he was about to leave for work. It was going to be a tough day, and not one he relished. He was due to help police another protest march in London, followed by a rally at the square. He hoped there wouldn't be any trouble, but you never knew. They had been lucky so far.

Not, he thought, pulling on his boots, that the trouble was likely to be with the protestors. They had his sympathy, mostly, though he wished they could find another way to voice their protest. Some of them were definitely targeting the police with their chants, and he knew from the way they looked at him, that he was lumped together with all other police under the label *'racist.'* He shook his head. With a partner of colour, and therefore at least half of his friends and in-laws non-white, he was far from a racist. But he did understand, he'd heard several of his colleagues making comments they shouldn't, even among their black work mates, some of the teasing went too far, some of the 'jokes' were offensive rather than funny, and if he was honest, he didn't always speak up, didn't always try and correct them. It was easier to keep quiet, too easy to make an enemy.

Of course, he thought, reaching into the cupboard for his bag, the issue of profiling was a less easy one to solve. The sad fact was, many muggings and knife crimes *were* committed by people of colour, and so if the force was going to stop and search the most likely culprits, then they were going to be mostly stopping young men, and potentially more black men than white. John shook his head, he couldn't see a way round that one, not in the short term. The black communities needed to realise there had to be a decrease in crime in those areas before the police could back away. It wasn't a race issue, it was a crime issue, and not one the police could solve alone.

"Bye love, I'm off."

Ali appeared in the kitchen doorway, an apron thrown over her dress, a knife in her hand. She came towards him, and he smelt onion and garlic, and when she kissed him, as she always did when he left for work, she told him to be safe, and to remember he loved her more than his work partner.

John grinned. His work partner, and his affection for her was often discussed, his wife accusing him of caring more for his work partner than he did for her, saying that one day she was going to arrive home to find her rival was living there too. *The day I get home to find Di has moved in, there's going to be trouble!* she often said. There was some truth in the accusation, John admitted, as he shut the front door behind him and walked to his car. Although he loved his wife more, undoubtedly, his work partner owned a big chunk of his heart, despite her moods and unpredictable streak.

John thought of that unpredictability as he drove to work, and it worried him. He understood, of course, Di was fairly inexperienced, and certain situations worried her more than they should. He hoped she would cope okay today, it would be tough on her, especially if the crowd got violent, if trouble started to spiral. In the past, she had been brave enough with crowds and noise, but close contact sometimes set her nerves on edge, and however much he reassured Di, he could see her nerves in the tiny spasms of her muscles, and the way she held her head. She'd always held it together, never done anything wrong, but he knew she was scared, and it bothered him, made him wonder if a situation might arise where she forgot her training, stopped obeying orders immediately.

He arrived at the stables and went to prepare the kit he'd need for the day. First he had a quick chat with the stable hands, thanked them for taking care of Diamond—or Di, as he thought of her. He was always careful to remember to thank them, because he knew it was important. Although he did his share of mucking out and cleaning tack—not much fun at the end of a tough shift—he knew they did the majority of the work. If they felt appreciated, John hoped it would translate into better care for his mount.

Then he went to see his partner. She was standing in the stall, leaning over the gate because she'd heard him arrive. He rubbed her nose, feeling her snuffle into his fingers. Diamond was the only mare in the stable, usually the force bought geldings due to their size, but Diamond was special, thought John, she stood out with her colouring and her size, her height allowing him to see over crowds, her strength able to carry all the equipment that John brought with him.

"Good girl," he murmured, as he stroked her neck. "We've got a tough job today, you make sure you trust me, and we'll be fine."

John left the horse, and went to check the hay net was ready in the transport, she could have a good feed to settle her before they arrived in the city centre.

***

In his neat semidetached house, Timothy was also checking everything was ready for the day ahead. He had finished weeding the flowerbed—the last thing on his list of preparations before he persuaded her to come home.

He glanced at the time. He would need to leave soon, otherwise he would miss her, and the chances of finding her in the city were remote. They had spoken last week, and Timothy had been patient, listening while she told him that she wanted a divorce, saying that she couldn't live as a prisoner any longer. *A prisoner!* After all that he had done for her, she felt like a prisoner.

But Timothy had heard something beyond her words, he had detected a softening of her voice when she spoke about their time together, a longing in her tone when he had made her speak about their early days, reminded her of their honeymoon, their plans. He hadn't mentioned having a baby again, because maybe that was what had frightened her away. Nor did he mention the man he had seen her with, playing along with the fallacy that she was living at her mother's house and had been there the whole time.

But she had mentioned going to London today, was planning to meet "a friend." Timothy had known, without a doubt, that this was her lover, the man who had stolen her heart. He said nothing, not wanting to acknowledge he had heard and alert her to the fact that he knew this person was significant. Instead he had moved the conversation away, asked about her mother, whether she was well. He heard the relief in her voice, knew she was hoping that the slip of information hadn't been noticed.

Unseen in his sitting room, Timothy had smiled. He would follow her, confront her and the driver he had seen, make her realise that she belonged with him. They could get past this, he was willing to forgive her. Then he would bring her home, they could forget this silliness of living in her mother's house.

Timothy looked around the house before he left. The sun shone on the windows, lighting the patch of garden, where a robin was sitting on the fence. She would like that. He glanced at the cushions, placed as diamonds on the backs of the sofa, the side-table was polished, the coasters positioned equidistant from the edge, ready for celebratory glasses of fake Champagne. In the fridge, the over-priced wine was cooling—sweet because she never lost her love of sweet wine—ready for when they returned.

He walked into the hallway. The stairs had been vacuumed. In the bathroom, her towel was washed and folded and placed on her rail next to the bath. In their bedroom, the bed was made, the duvet stretched tightly across the mattress, the pillows heaped at one end, covered with cushions, a throw placed exactly two feet from the bottom of the bed. Timothy smiled again. Yes, everything was ready.

He drove to the next town, and parked in the road near her mother's house. He thought she would walk to the station, but wanted to be cautious, just in case she decided to catch a bus. He left the car, and walked around the corner. At the end of her mother's house was a small corner shop, and Timothy decided this was a good place to wait. He could loiter near the cans of cat food while watching for her through the window.

A bell rang when he opened the door, and Timothy nodded at the masked man standing behind the Perspex-screened counter, before moving next to the shelf of cat food. Bags of pet food were stacked on the floor, their dusty aroma mingling with concentrated flavours, rising up as a porridge of slightly sour smells. Timothy wrinkled his nose and moved to the end of the shelf. He had a good view of the road, and could almost see her mother's house. He hoped he wouldn't have to wait long. Behind him he could feel the shop owner watching him, wondering why he was staring out of the window.

He finally saw her, shifting her bag onto her hip, pulling out a facemask and looking at it, as if trying to decide at which point on her journey she would wear it. He wanted to remind her that she should wear it before she contaminated her hands by touching money or a door handle, or the ticket from the machine.

But he didn't. He simply glided from the shop, hoping she wouldn't notice that wretched bell ringing, and slid across the road behind her. He would follow her, catch the same train—yes, she was heading towards the station—he would sit in a different carriage, follow her when she arrived at her destination. He would be careful, stay well back, hidden until she met her driver-lover.

Then Timothy would reveal himself, confront them, force her to realise that she belonged with *him*. Then they could return home, put all this silliness behind them.

Part Three

Chapter Twenty-Seven

I pulled the mask over my face when I reached the station, hooking the elastic behind my ears. My mother had made it for me, sewing folds of material together, lining it with white cotton, shaping it to fit my nose. The lining was a remnant from my wedding dress, and I remembered the hem that had dipped, the anticipation of the day, the hopefulness of the promises I made. I knew that my mother had tried, done her best, but the mask didn't quite fit, and slipped down when I was trying to find my credit card.

The train was almost empty, just two other people in my carriage. I saw the backs of their heads, saw they were sitting in isolated places, huddled close to windows, staring out. I sat towards the back of the carriage, and pulled my book from my bag, tracing the title with my finger: *A Tale of Two Cities by Charles Dickens*. It was a trusted friend now, the pages worn from being read so many times, and there was something comforting about it. I wasn't sure why I felt the need of comfort, I was meeting Jason and should have been full of optimism and excitement. But some premonition, some unconscious thought, was unsettling me. Perhaps it was the collision of my two worlds, living back with my family, speaking to Timothy—neither sat easy with my feelings for Jason. He belonged in a bubble of unreality, our relationship had been one of seclusion, and this attempt to 'normalise' it, to incorporate that weird time with real life, jarred.

I opened the little book at random, read a section near the middle. Charles Darnay was leaving his new life in England, travelling through a France ravaged by the revolution. He travelled through barren fields, on mired roads, past burnt houses. I stopped reading and stared out of the window. We were passing fields full of golden barley, trees in leaf, children in a playground, a field of wheat blowing in the breeze like bronzed waves on a sea. Everything was lush and plentiful, and although we hadn't had much rain lately, there was no drought, no poverty, no desolation. My world was far removed from that of Charles Darnay.

I looked down at the book, smoothing the pages with my fingers, thinking about how the story ended. The man was travelling through France, a dangerous, turbulent France, with no idea of the danger he was about to encounter. As he travelled, he began to notice the unrest, started to realise his mistake, and I understood that feeling of doom that was unfolding in the fictional character's heart. My own heart was heavy, I felt lost in indecision, the mire of my past was tainting the potential of my future. I took a breath, and told myself I was being stupid, this sense of disquiet was irrational, I was meeting Jason, and he would make everything better again. I could start to get my feelings into perspective, ignore the doubts that Timothy had sown.

My conversation with Timothy had not, I felt, been successful. After living with my family for a few days, while my mother treated me as if I was as fragile as glass and my sister behaved exactly as she usually did—with the tact of a sledgehammer—I felt strong enough to phone Timothy. Really, I should have met him, I knew that I was being a coward; I was not like the heroes in the story I had absorbed.

Timothy had been gentle, and loving, and terribly persuasive, telling me that he loved me, that we could rectify the mistakes of the past, move into the future together. As I listened to his voice, those warm feelings returned, that longing within me for him to notice me was as strong as ever, and I wanted to return. I knew it was weak, knew that I was taking the easy path and would regret it in the future, but *oh!* he was so certain, so confident that we could change things, make our marriage work. I so wanted to please him, to acquiesce to his will.

Yet even while I was drawn to him, tiny niggles reminded me of why I had left. He called me *Ten* and *Wifey*, terms of endearment that once had thrilled me. But never my name. He was persuasive, and charming, yet he neglected to ask me *why* I had left; he was still making the decisions for both of us.

I glanced again at my book. The character, Darnay, had chosen a new name for himself—just as I had chosen *Charlie* to remain anonymous, he too chose a name to keep him safe. But his own name was significant, it said who he was, identified his character, and when he returned to France he returned to the name he owned. Timothy never used my name, even as we talked, as he reminded me of the happy times in our relationship, tried to persuade me to return; he never used my real name.

"Does it matter?" I asked myself, my eyes unseeing as the view flashed past. "Does his refusal to use my name signify a refusal to see me as I am, or am I being daft, linking it to the restrictions he placed on me, the control he had over me when really, he simply liked calling me by a pet name? What is real?" I wondered, scrabbling to work it out, to find clarity before I met Jason. "Is Timothy right, have we just encountered a difficulty that can be solved, or has my love for him gone forever?"

I thought about his unfaithfulness, seeing him with that woman, hearing his laugh on phone calls, reading messages he had sent to her; I felt again that twisted knife in my gut, the tension of my muscles as I relived the devastation of my discovery.

I had decided not to confront Timothy with what I knew; not in a phone call. I needed to see his face for that conversation, wanted to gauge his reaction, know when he lied. A meeting, face-to-face, was inevitable; I needed to arrange one soon.

"It will be like going back," I thought, almost speaking to the ill-fated character in the book. "But unlike you, I will know what the future holds, I'll be dipping back into my past in a safe way. At least in our modern world, no one gets sent to the guillotine. We might have our problems, but we don't get killed."

I closed the book and stared at the view. We had left the countryside behind us, there were snatched views of allotments, a new block of flats, some industrial units huddled under railway arches. The tall buildings of the city came into focus, looming in the sky, glowing blue and silver, stark and tall, giving shape to the city, an identity. We passed the new flats wrapped around the old power station, a monument to glass and steel, some of the cubes were filled with the untidiness of humanity—a bike on a balcony, plants in tubs, washing on a rack—all contained in the austere units of glass. We rattled across the bridge, a flash of water, slowed past the lego buildings of the transport police, before edging into the station.

I pushed my book back into my bag, pulled my ticket from my pocket, and started to stand, then stopped as I remembered I should keep a safe distance from my fellow travellers, we couldn't huddle by the door, couldn't crowd together at the barriers. I waited for the train to stop, the doors to slide open, the other passengers to step onto the platform. I followed them to the barrier, feeling my mask hot on my face, wanting to secure a loose hair that was tickling my ear, knowing my hands were now potentially contaminated.

There were several police officers standing on the station, one was a dog handler, walking between the passengers, his face grim while the dog strained at the lead, tail wagging, nose busy. I left the station, and began to walk to the square, to where Jason was waiting.

There were more people now, some were carrying placards, and I noticed there were more police too. Obviously something was happening, probably another march for black rights. I realised I had again been lost inside my own head, preoccupied with the problems of my own life, and ignoring news of the wider world, and once again it was a mistake; I was not immune from its impact. I looked for signs, posters that would tell me what was happening, where the march was due to start and end, but there was no information, only tides of people swarming up the steps from the underground stations, jumping from buses, arriving on foot. As I walked along the street, obeying traffic signals, trying to avoid being near anyone, attempting to obey the two-metre rule, I realised it was impossible. I was one of a swarm, a heaving buzzing mass that was heading as a unit towards the square where Jason was waiting.

The park was sealed off, mounted police sending people along the road, not allowing banners and placards to cut through a park owned by the monarch. I stayed with the crowd, it was easier than trying to branch out and then rejoin them, impossible to avoid the tide. I tried to social distance, adjusted my steps so I didn't catch up with the group ahead of me, but people were passing on all sides, some wearing masks but the majority had uncovered faces, their expressions excited. As I approached the square, I realised my mistake in full.

The square was a heaving mass of people. I saw black faces and brown faces and white faces, all shouting slogans; bodies jostled against each other, placards were waved, sometimes bumping the people standing near. I tried to slow, thought about turning, returning to the station, phoning Jason to rearrange the meeting place. But someone pushed me from behind, I was propelled forwards, and when I tried to turn, my elbow was caught, I was spun back, jolted from the side, someone kicked my calf—I knew that to try and turn, to force my way against the stream of people, would be impossible and I might be trampled. I had no choice but to keep walking forwards, towards the square and hopefully, somewhere, Jason.

I scanned the crowd as I was half-pushed across the road, ignoring the red warning light, impossible to stop, though there seemed to be no traffic. The square was a swirl of people. There was a line of police, with linked arms, separating a multi-cultural crowd waving banners, from a line of white men waving their fists and holding banners that could only be described as hateful: racist slogans of ignorance. A few mounted police were circling the square, and I could hear more behind me, driving the crowd I was in, down towards the central mass. The chances of finding Jason were miniscule.

I stepped onto the pavement the other side of the road. A tall black man was on my right, his fist raised, his face alive, exhilaration oozing from him. Pushed against me on the other side was a young woman, her blonde hair swept back from a face red and sweaty under her face mask, her bare arm hard against my own, though she seemed oblivious. I attempted to force my way left, towards the line of police, to where the crowd was thinner. Perhaps I could make my way along the edge of the people, up to the steps, and then turn, scan the heads, hope to find Jason. I fumbled in my bag, pulled out my phone, all the time my feet moving forwards, something firm pushing against my back so I couldn't turn, couldn't stop, must march on and on, past the girls chanting in unison, past the three youths shouting abuse at the line of police, past the mother with a child in a backpack gazing at the crowd with amazed eyes and a round oval mouth. I managed to pull my phone level with my face, but someone was bumping my arm, I couldn't see the screen, there was a shove from behind as a man tripped, I was propelled forwards, my foot caught a raised kerb or foot or bag—no time to see, I staggered forwards, my phone fell from hand as I struggled to reach for support, grabbed the blonde girl next to me, who in turn reached for the woman next to her, until like so many dominoes we slid to the side, regained our balance, continued on. But my phone was lost, and there was no chance to go back for it; I was marched on.

I was pushing hard to my left, managing to squeeze in front of the blonde girl, felt her foot crushed beneath my heel, no chance to apologise, as I heaved again, still marching forwards, but leaning left, trying to force my way to where the crowd was thinner. The shouting was as relentless as the surge of people: black lives matter, equality for all, no more police brutality—all mingled together into a mash of volume, indecipherable, drowning out the racist shouts of the militant white men beyond the police cordon. The sun beat down, I struggled for air behind my mask, and could feel a bead of sweat as it left my hairline and trickled down my face—must not wipe it away, my hands might be infected, though how the air around me, recycled breath of hundreds of strangers, could possibly be filtered by one homemade mask was beyond me.

I was nearly free now, almost at the edge of the crowd, the press to move forwards was less strong, and I began to slow, to look to the side, try to assess the situation. I was no nearer the steps, but there were only a few people between me and a staggered line of police and horses. If I moved near to them, hoped they kept their ground and didn't advance, there would be space for me to stop, to possibly turn, to look for a way out of the crowd. If I could leave the square, walk away from the protest, maybe I could find a public phone, let Jason know I was leaving—or at least return home, phone him from there, explain what had happened.

While I was beginning to slow, to breath more easily, to plan my escape, there was a new sound, the high-pitched scream of terror, joined by another and another—the terrified cries of wild animals. I tried to turn towards the noise, but the mounted police were moving forwards, aiming for the noise, and the crowd was turning, moving as one, away from the sound, towards me, parting—a bubble and churning of parts turning away from the origin of the screams. Faces showing confusion as some people struggled to understand what was happening, others frightened as people fought to get away, further from the danger.

I leaned away from the moving horses, trying to avoid their smooth flanks, the wall of their muscled flesh; pressing against the bodies that trapped me, holding my ground. I smelt the sharp tang of horses, the sour breath of the man whose face was against mine, the sweat of an armpit that pushed against my nose, the strangle of my slipped mask around my neck. I could see a checked shirt, a damp teeshirt, a flash of ground, people pointing, frightened faces, the sun searing down from a blue sky. I pushed harder, against the wall of people, away from the shouting police, the moving horses.

The crowd parted, I saw Jason, his eyes bright as he noticed me, started to move towards me. My heart lifted, I took a step towards him—*what are the chances of*—then a shout, the flash of something bright, a young man, rising up behind Jason, his eyes wild, a raised knife, a scream—might be my own—people wailing, crying, the knife is stopped before the blade meets Jason's neck and the nightmare continues with a new ghost. This time it is Timothy, pummelling through the crowd, pushing Jason away, into safety. But before I can breathe, there is a new danger, one with no warning, simply the rising of hooves, the snort of anger, a new cry from the crowd:

Move! Move! Move!

A horse was bucking, black hooves against the blue sky, the flash of a rider struggling to stay mounted, more damp flesh as the crowd surged in a new direction, Jason has moved again, I cannot see him, only the damp shirts and wild arms of strangers, and then, cutting through it all, the cry I recognised, a long agonised scream—*Ten!*

Hooves rose again, another scream, a shudder from the crowd as they slam down on soft flesh and brittle bones; again they rise. Red splatters trailed the air, again they fell, mutilating, killing the body beneath them. A final rise, while the crowd screams and a rider struggles to stay mounted. They hang, those hooves, as though suspended for a frozen moment before their last murderous fall.

I pressed hard against the shoulder pushing me forwards, leaned into the arm pressing my ribs, managed to turn, to face the scream, to peer down and watch the blood seeping through the white shirt, the thudding hooves, the familiar face explode in a torrent of red that flowed from the clattering hooves and the parted crowd, the splatters that landed on jeans and shirts and arms; so much red.

The rider pulled the horse away, I was aware of it moving to the side, four hooves back on the ground, the swish of a tail as it withdrew from the crowd. I rushed to the space it had vacated, felt arms restrain me, a policeman stepped in front, his arms wide, waving the crowd back.

"He's my husband!" I yell, my agonised shout piercing the shrieks of the crowd, reached their target.

The policeman waved me past, other arms reached for me, someone was holding me, restraining me, shouting for me to wait.

"He's my husband," I repeated, choking on the words, my voice failing me now, my throat contracting as I try to push forwards, try to see what is happening. There was someone in a yellow jacket kneeling on the ground, a duplicate rushed forwards, knelt beside them. They waved at someone, a stretcher was brought, a fat holdall opened on the ground, equipment pulled out. I saw white-gloved hands that became stained with red, and the red was seeping along the ground, between the working medics, finding its way along the cracks in the pavements, and it reminds me again of the wine in the story that was spilled in the streets, and the afternoon spent drinking with Jason in a world that has ended, and I know that this is my fault; I have killed Timothy, and I know that I love him.

They make me wait. An age of standing, the sun burning my head, hands holding my forearms so I can't move, my legs shaking so that I think I might fall. Finally, they allowed me forwards, to kneel beside the limp rag of my husband, to reach out a hand and touch the red wet rag that was once his shirt, to grasp some part—an arm perhaps, and hold it for a moment, while the emotions surge inside like the crowd in the square.

"It is not Timothy," I thought, staring at the rags and the red and the strange huddled shape that could never have been a man. It is a scarecrow, I told myself, an effigy made by children, something make-believe.

But the people around me were real, and the hands that lifted me were real, and the woman in police uniform who led me away was no ghost, no fantasy of my making, but very real and solid; someone to be relied upon. They led me away, away from the crowd and their muted chants, away from the sirens that sliced through the air, away from the colours and sweat and bodies that pressed me on all sides. I was led to a quiet place, ushered into a car, given water, and a blanket to calm my trembling limbs—though I'm not cold, I wanted to say, the shivering isn't because I'm cold. But speaking was an effort I couldn't make, I had become a dumb thing, a puppet to be guided by other hands. All the while inside my head, over and over, like the press of the crowd, were the words, following each other one after the other: I killed him, my love has died, I killed him. . .

Chapter Twenty-Eight

I was collected from the house by a black car driven by a faceless man in a dark suit. For two weeks I had lived in the house, *our house,* against the advice of my mother who wanted me to stay with her, and the few friends who contacted me, some even suggesting they came and stayed with me. But I wanted to be alone. It was what I deserved.

I sat in the car, pulling my black skirt over my knees, and stared from the window with unseeing eyes. Nothing was real. My mother was waiting at the church, and Gracie, who told me I looked sad, and that she didn't like all these face masks, it was all a silly fuss.

"Yes," I nodded, knowing she was right, "it *is* all a silly fuss. Nothing matters, not really."

I glanced at my mother, and could see in her grey face the shadows of another funeral. I wondered if she would refer to it. But she simply moved to me, squeezed my arm, said that this was the worst bit and it would soon all be over. I felt tears prick my eyes.

"All be over," I thought. "It will all be over."

I stood, waiting in the doorway with my mother and my sister. There was no one else with me. Jason had wanted to come, had argued over the phone, tried to persuade me.

"But he saved me," he said, as if that gave him a right.

But I knew it would be wrong. Jason had an obligation, not a right. I thought again of that day, the sun, the crowd, the red—why did he do it? I shuddered, and felt my mother's hand on my back. Now was not the time to wonder, now was the time to clear away all my thoughts, and survive the next hour.

I nodded as a couple passed me, went into the church—they were Timothy's cousins, I had met them twice before. They weren't close. No one had been close. There were no hugs at this funeral, not even the shake of a hand, the grasp of an arm. Each of us was supposed to stay within our family bubble, convey sympathy through looks and gestures, but not touch. I wrapped my arms round myself, hugging the hurt.

The hearse arrived, flowers removed from the coffin, which was heaved out by four men who looked somehow squashed by it, their faces above the masks concentrating on the weight, attempting to look dignified. My mother spoke, taking charge, telling Gracie she needed to walk nicely and not speak. I stared at the aisle, the coffin being carried, and I couldn't move, I could not be the trigger that caused the service to begin. I felt my mother's hand on my back again, the gentlest of pushes, enough to make my feet move, one after the other, down the aisle. We followed that heavy load into the church, step after step, head bowed, aware of people staring, the organ playing the music I had chosen; I followed my husband down the aisle of the church, and I remembered my wedding, and I hear his voice again:

"No *Ten*, we won't get married in a church, I know you want to be, but that's all just a childish dream, neither of us are religious." He looks at me, and I drown in his gaze, and he laughs, that soft deep laugh of benevolence. "You're not a princess in a fairytale, my love, a registry office is more appropriate."

I smile, and agree, even though my heart is heavy, and inside I am arguing, saying that I have always dreamed of being married in a church, wearing a long white dress, walking down an aisle with my father, towards my husband.

But I know he is right, I must stop being childish, I am to be his wife, and that is all that matters. We will be together for ever, just him and me, standing as one to face the world.

But today wasn't my wedding day, and I wasn't promising to stay with Timothy forever, I was saying goodbye—and I didn't know how.

I arrived at the front of the church, taking my seat while the coffin was placed on a stand, and flowers were placed back on the lid. The church felt empty, only thirty people were allowed to attend, and they barely fill the seats in the first few rows, even with gaps between them.

A vicar, who never knew Timothy, led the service. He addressed me a few times, but I didn't look up, kept staring at my lap, my folded hands clutching a damp tissue. Then a young man who I have never met, but who worked with Timothy, stood and told stories about someone who I don't recognise, who occupied a world I was never part of. Some of the stories were funny, and there was a smattering of subdued laughter, and next to me I felt Gracie turn round, to see who was laughing when she had been told that this was a sad occasion, and she should be silent and serious. I wondered whether it would be easier, to live in Gracie's world where everything was black and white, where if something was sad, laughter should be banned; where if you loved a man you stayed with him, whatever happened.

There was a hymn, played from a speaker because singing wasn't allowed, while people shuffled in their seats and hid their faces. Only the vicar joined in, silently mouthing the words. I felt embarrassed and thought that perhaps I shouldn't have included a hymn in the service, whatever my mother advised, because none of us were religious, we didn't know any hymns.

The coffin bearers arrived, and we followed them out, into the damp afternoon, to where Timothy was to be buried. We stood on the pathway, each group separate from the next, and I felt my mother next to me, knew she was looking at my face, trying to discern whether I was coping. But nothing was real, I was dreaming this, and when it was finished, I would wake up, and be in bed, in our home, with my husband.

I stared as the coffin was lowered, and my mother whispered that I should scatter some mud on the lid, and handed me a bag of soil, and indicated when, during the sing-song recitation of the vicar, I should throw the mud.

"Now you should wash your hands," I heard Gracie say, and I glanced up, and saw people were smiling, and I wished they would leave.

The vicar finished, and moved to offer his personal condolences, before walking away. I stood, staring into the hole, waiting to wake up.

"We should go, and let the grave diggers finish," said my mother, squeezing my arm. "We can come back later, if you want to. Sometimes it's better, when everyone else has gone, to say your own goodbye, in your own time. . ."

I nodded, and let her lead me away, back to the house.

"It's odd, not being able to have a proper wake, invite people back for a drink," she was saying as we walked. "I don't know, maybe it makes it easier, means you don't have to perform for as long."

I nodded, wondering how my own performance had been, whether I matched the grieving widow that people expected.

***

I walked back to the grave in the evening. It didn't feel like evening, the day stretching long past the time when it should have been dark, and as I walked between the graves, there were even birds, still singing in the trees, insects busy in the air. I walked towards the mound of fresh soil and stood, staring at the scattered flowers, thinking that it was a waste, all that time and money making arrangements and now they would just be left to wither, unseen, forgotten.

I had changed into jeans, and I knelt down, next to the grave, and stared hard at the earth.

"Can you hear me?" I asked Timothy. "If you can, will you forgive me? I never meant for this to happen, I never stopped loving you, not really. But you made it too hard to stay, I didn't know who I was anymore, and I was too weak —I know that now—I should have said something, forced you to change. But I didn't know how, and the thought of a child. . ." I stopped, the tears flowing down my cheeks. I wiped them away with the back of my hand, forced myself on, to say what I should have said two weeks ago, when he could respond. "I couldn't let you control a child like that," I told him, "and I didn't think I would be able to protect our baby from you. I was like a prisoner, and I loved you, but it wasn't . . . it wasn't *normal* was it? Our relationship wasn't balanced, it didn't allow our love to grow, it stifled it —*you stifled it.*

"And yet, I loved you. Part of me will always love you."

There was a sound, and I jumped, suddenly realising that I wasn't alone.

The mound of earth was high, almost as high as my head while I knelt, and I realised that the person approaching from the other side probably couldn't see me. I was about to stand, to reveal my position, when something made me stop. Something about the furtive walk of the woman approaching, the way she was clutching a bunch of roses, twisting them in her hands. She was looking around as she walked, scanning the churchyard for other people, but not looking directly at the grave, which meant she didn't notice me, and continued forwards, walking and looking and twisting those flowers, her face nervous.

As she reached the grave, I stood. We were facing each other, and I stared across the mound of earth, knowing she was trapped, she couldn't turn and walk away without appearing odd—and she was not a person who would like to appear odd.

She was a tall woman—older than me, but attractive, her shoes and handbag looked expensive. She wore dark linen trousers, and a silk shirt, and her blonde hair was tied in a complicated knot at the back of her head. When I stood, she started, and I saw her eyes assessing me, searching my face, while her own cheeks flushed scarlet.

"I'm sorry, I didn't mean to disturb you," she said, and her American accent sounded out of place in the little churchyard, changing the words to something that belonged in a film, not here.

I nodded, and stared. I knew I was being rude, odd even, but I knew who she was, and I didn't care. She had no right here. In death, Timothy was fully mine, I owned him in a way denied me in life, and this woman, with her expensive clothes and film-star accent was intruding.

"I brought some flowers, for the grave," she said, as if only just noticing the roses in her hand. She moved, as if to place them on the grave.

"No," I said, shaking my head. "No."

The woman stopped, half bent, her hand outstretched ready to place the flowers, she stopped, frozen. Gradually, with her body left in that awkward pose, she lifted her head, looked at me.

I stared back.

"No," I said again.

She opened her mouth, I thought she was going to argue, to say that it wasn't my decision, Timothy belonged to neither of us now. But instead, she straightened, and withdrew her arm, clutched the roses to her chest, crushing the petals.

For a long moment, we simply stood there, staring at each other across the dirt mound, over the crushed body of my husband. I wondered what he had enjoyed in that rounded body, the made-up face, the perfect hair. I stared, hating her, making this one, futile stand, the only power I had. I examined her, looking for signs of why she was better than me, wondering what was missing in myself that my husband should seek her out.

If I had not been so *exhausted* I may have tried to hurt her. I couldn't see anything special in her appearance, there was nothing that marked her out, and the weariness inside rose up again. It all seemed so random, so pointless. They had enjoyed their illicit relationship, and I had harboured hurt and anger for so long, and now, when I looked at her, she was nothing, just a person, someone who had been available. I realised, with a great weariness of heart, that she simply was not worth my anger. It had all finished when I saw the limp remains of Timothy, when I was faced with the reality of how futile life was, how meaningless all our actions are, how fleeting our time is. As I looked at this painted woman, I knew; I didn't care.

"Sorry," she said again, and I wondered what she was apologising for. Was she sorry for spoiling my marriage, taking what wasn't hers, walking where she should never have trodden? Was she sorry *for me?* I didn't want her sympathy, nor would I be left at the grave while she walked away.

I held out my hand, forced her to pass the roses over the grave, to place them in my own hand. I snapped the stalks, petals floated down, I brushed them off. Turning, I started to walk away, to leave her, standing with the dead, while I went to join the living. I dumped the flowers in a bin designated for dog excrement, and marched away.

Chapter Twenty-Nine

It was November. The rain was splattering the windows, running in rivulets down the panes. I paused from pulling on my socks to watch it, looking out into the garden where the grass was sodden, weeds were growing in the flowerbeds, and the little ornamental tree was fighting with the wind, its long trailing branches waving like so many arms, a multi-limbed being shaking in excitement.

I smiled, feeling my own excitement as I finished dressing. The weather was wild, and soon I would need to brave it, to huddle inside my coat and walk to the bus stop, but for now, I was safe and warm in my house. In the house that Timothy had bought.

I glanced around the bedroom. It was messy now, clothes heaped on the floor in the corner, the bed unmade. Timothy wouldn't have approved, I thought, but this was me, this was how I lived. Try as I might, I *was* untidy, and without my husband to look constantly over my shoulder, dirty clothes did not always get as far as the washing hamper, the duvet did not always get pulled tightly over the mattress, and the scatter cushions tended to remain in a heap on the chair.

I walked downstairs, my hand trailing the bannister rail, my eyes looking around the house. The door to the sitting room was open, and I wondered whether Timothy would approve. There was colour in there now, purple cushions and a yellow throw were stark against the beige. Timothy liked beige and white, but when one day, a few months after the funeral, I had opened my eyes and actually *looked* at the house I was living in, I realised that I preferred colour. I liked to see cushions randomly thrown, and colours to warm my living space.

I pulled my coat from the cupboard, and turned to look again at the house, *my* house, and I realised with a rush of affection that I loved living here. Timothy had worked hard to buy this property, and he was proud of the position in the little cul-de-sac, pleased it had a patch of garden and a spare room for visitors who never came. But although I had lived here with him, it had never felt like home, never been truly mine—even in marriage I had felt like Timothy's guest. When he died, I thought at first that I might sell it, maybe buy a flat somewhere, and perhaps, in time, I would. But for now, it was my shelter, a place where I could relax and hide from the world. A place to come home to; a place that was mine.

I checked my bag for keys and purse, then pulled open the front door. A blast of wind rushed in, and I stepped out, into the storm, and clicked the door behind me before heading towards the station.

The train was on time, and I sat in the corner, watching the fields race past. I remembered my fated trip to London, when the people had marched to protest for black lives, and a disturbed young man had managed to steal three lives with his knife, and I had lost my husband.

Sometimes, during our evening phone calls, Jason and I discussed why it had happened, and why Timothy had saved Jason. It felt too significant to be random, I knew in my heart that Timothy must have somehow known that I was meeting Jason. For Timothy to be following me was understandable, I knew his character, recognised the obsessive urge that would cause him to behave like that. But to save Jason? To risk his own life for one of my friends?

I shook my head; perhaps we would never know. Possibly it was an instinctive reaction, Timothy disliked randomness, and a man wielding a knife in a crowd would have angered him, when he saw an opportunity to step in, it would be natural to act.

But I liked to think that it was more than that. I knew that in his way, Timothy loved me, as I had loved him. His was a warped love, based on the desire to own and control, but it was, I felt, love. Had he somehow known that Jason was special, and when he saw him in danger, did he decide to save him? Perhaps, I thought, it was part of his obsession, the realisation that if Jason died, Timothy would never win me back, because who can compete with a memory? The martyr always wins.

However, I preferred to believe that Timothy wanted me to be happy. In my mind, Timothy had taken the place of Carlton in the book I loved to read, and he had given his own life so that I could be happy. I would never know the truth, and this was the option I chose to believe.

My thoughts edged back to that march, the people shouting that black lives matter, the press of the crowd, and those hooves that rose, paused, fell, with sickening regularity. Fleeting memories seeped into my head, images that I backed away from in horror, and struggled to block with the security of the present.

But like an uncontrolled force those memories returned, and I realised those hooves were like the guillotine that rose, waited suspended, then fell with murderous repetition to end the lives of the people below. Unlike the scores of French nobility in the story I loved, only Timothy, my husband, was trapped beneath the inescapable blade.

The tannoy announced we were arriving at the station, and I took a breath and rose from my seat. People were standing on the platform, a conveyor-belt of painted faces peering in. A memory of another journey fluttered through my mind, another station, on another day, when I thought I might be free. I walked to the hissing doors, and jumped down to the platform, knowing that today, I understood what it meant to be free.

As I walked through the barriers, I searched for Jason, looking for the mass of dark curls; I saw him, easing away from the post he was leaning against, coming towards me. I walked to meet him, seeing only him, his familiar shape, his untidy hair, his smiling face.

We met in the middle of the concourse, and he put his arms around me, and bent his head, and kissed me, tentatively at first, as if testing for my reaction, and then firmly, warmly, holding me close. When he pulled back, I looked up, drowning in his deep blue eyes. I heard him whisper.

He simply said my name—my *real* name. I knew in that moment that this man saw me, and knew me, and that I could love him without losing myself.

I had arrived.

***

To be continued. . .

Also by Anne E. Thompson:

Hidden Faces

Counting Stars

Invisible Jane

Training Toby

*

Joanna - The Story of a Psychopath

Clara - A Good psychopath?

*

Ploughing Through Rainbows

Sowing Promises

Non-Fiction

How to Have a Brain Tumour

The Sarcastic Mother's Holiday Diary

Thank you for reading.

You can follow Anne's blog at:

anneethompson.com

Acknowledgements

Thank you for reading my novel, I hope you enjoyed it.

I must thank my beta-readers, James and Heidi, who gave honest feedback and told me what to change. They helped to correct several mistakes and offered good advice.

Thank you to the people local to Norfolk, who answered my questions about trains and timetables. Any mistakes are my own.

A special thank you to my friend, who showed me what the world looked like through the eyes of someone with autism.

As ever, thanks to my family, for their encouragement and support.

Printed in Great Britain
by Amazon